For MU

Year follows year, the tide returns again,
Day follows day, all things have second birth;
The earthquake is not satisfied at once.

William Wordsworth: *The Prelude*

27 DECEMBER, 1940

1

'This is the one,' Helena Barr said. She glanced at Ernie, her brown eyes shining, her smiling face betraying her nervousness. Through the thickness of woollen gloves, he could feel her hand gripping tightly. 13 Prospect Mount was almost in the middle of the solid row of three-storey Victorian houses leading up the steep hill away from the harbour and the railway station they had just left behind them. Helena pushed open the heavy iron gate and walked up the narrow path. The wet soil and pinched shrubs on either side had the brittle, dead, mid-winter look. They climbed the three worn stone steps halfway along, then up five more, gently depressed in the middle where generations of feet had stepped before them, to the neatly grained, varnished front door.

They waited a while in silence after Helena had pulled the bell in the wall to her right. A thin woman, with black hair cut short, but softly waved about her face, smiled with polite enquiry. She was wearing a dark blouse with tiny white spots. A clean pinafore was tied at the waist and hid most of her skirt.

'Hello, Mrs Turner? I'm Miss Barr. Helena Barr. I telephoned you about the room.' They shook hands, and Mrs Turner's gaze was directed at the young man in the dark, jaunty sailor's cap with its gold lettered HMS and the navy overcoat which covered him to his ankles. The gleaming toecaps of his boots peeped from the exaggerated width of the bell bottoms. 'This is Mr Wheatley, my fiancé.'

'How do you do.' Maggie Turner extended her arm stiffly, her face set in a carefully neutral mode. She turned slightly, gesturing them in. 'Like I said, it's just the bedroom, with a bit of a kitchen place with a sink in. Bathroom and toilet are on the landing one floor down. You share with the two rooms below.'

The hall, though gloomy on this dull, almost freezing day, looked pleasantly tidy, not over fussy, and smelt fragrantly of polish. There were none of the cabbage-water odours Helena associated with such places from her childhood experience of seaside holidays. She caught a glimpse of herself in the oval mirror of the hallstand, around which coats and scarves and men's hats were clustered. In the woollen beret, and with her scarf wrapped about her throat, she looked distressingly young. Younger even than the eighteen years she had celebrated three and a half months ago. She tried to fix an appropriately worldly, grown-up look on her face. Then they were climbing the wide staircase, with its highly polished dark wooden banister. There was a right turn to an equally wide landing on the first floor, then a short flight to a smaller landing. Mrs Turner nodded. 'That's the bathroom, and toilet next to it.' The final flight was narrower, and led to the top of the house. 'Used to be part of the attic,' Maggie Turner said, a little out of breath. She snapped on a light switch, to show a tiny room, scarcely bigger than a linen cupboard, but containing a deep enamel sink and enamel cooker.

She opened the door at right angles to it. 'This is the main room.' It was surprisingly large, with two dormer windows. Clean lace curtains stretched around their three sides, the panes of glass criss-crossed with the pale anti-blast tape. The heavy blackout curtains hung almost to the floor. 'You have to be careful with the blackout. We've had a warning already. I don't suppose you're bothered that much in – it's Kilbeck you're from, you said?'

'That's right. It's not far. But with the war and everything – I'll be working at the hospital here, so it's handier for me to be in Whitby. I can always get home when I'm off.' She blushed. Why was she sounding so apologetic? Ernie was looking ill at ease, too, red-faced and grinning like mad. 'It's lovely,' she went on, with genuine enthusiasm. She moved to one of the windows and stared into the unblinking eye of a seagull perched on a neighbouring, buff-coloured chimney pot. The shrill squeals of countless of his companions came faintly through the tightly closed windows. 'Look, Ernie! You can see right down to the harbour. See! You can see the masts of the fishing boats sticking up.'

'Oh, aye,' Mrs Turner said, with a faintly ironic amusement. 'You get a fair old view from up here. When it's not all hidden by the mist.'

Helena turned round to gaze at the interior. Beside the other window stood a scarred but serviceable dining-table and four chairs. On the wall opposite the door was the tiled fireplace, with its small, high grate and black canopy below the narrow mantelpiece. A filled coal bucket stood in the tiled hearth, in front of which were two veteran armchairs. A great deal of the remaining space was taken up by a brass-knobbed, seemingly vast double bed. Helena's cheeks grew red once more as her eyes were drawn to it. 'I think it'll suit me down to the ground. Four weeks' advance, you said?'

Maggie Turner nodded. 'It's not really much good for entertaining,' she said evenly.

Angrily, Helena felt herself positively glowing with embarrassment. 'Oh, don't worry. I'll not be doing any of that. P'raps my family might call in now and then.'

'Your father's a headmaster, I think? Are you from a big family, Miss Barr?'

'Please. Call me Helena. Miss Barr makes me feel like some ancient spinster. I'm the eldest. I've got a sister, Elspeth, fifteen, and a brother, Kit, who's coming up twelve. He's a monster.' They laughed. 'I had another brother, Wilfrid. But he died when he was five. Nearly ten years ago now.'

'I *am* sorry.' There was the faintest hint of reserve in the attractive voice before Maggie Turner continued, 'I had a similar loss myself. About the same time. 1931, it was. But they were just babies. Twins. Both girls. Ginny died after only a week. There was something wrong with her mouth. Malformed. She couldn't take food, poor bairn. And Valerie had something wrong with her heart. She went after three months.' Helena murmured her awkward condolence, and Maggie Turner nodded. 'It must have been far worse for your mam. Five years old. That's awful.'

'Yes.' Helena hesitated. 'Have you any other family, Mrs Turner?'

The landlady smiled, the warmth lighting her face, and Helena was startled by the realization how beautiful she was. 'My eldest, Thomas. He's twenty-three. He's in the army. Out in Egypt somewhere. And there's Vicky. She's thirteen. You'll see and hear far too much of her, I'm sure. Alf, my husband's away a lot. He's working through at Middlesborough just now. Gets home when he can. But you'll find no one'll bother you much. You can always come down for a cuppa if you've time. I'm glad of the company.'

She turned to Ernie, who had been standing somewhat awkwardly during the exchange. 'And whereabouts are you from, Mr – er....'

'Ernie Wheatley,' he supplied, still grinning. 'Ah'm from up t'coast. Kingstaith. Me dad fishes out o' there. Most of me folks've been fishermen.'

Helena could tell how embarrassed he was by the broadening of the local accent. 'Ernie joined up in April,' she said proudly. 'He's on a battle cruiser. HMS *Hood*. Up in Scotland.'

'Now now, Helen! Careless talk, and all that, eh?' The three of them laughed once more. 'Yes, ah'm just on a few days' leave. Half of us drew Christmas, the other half New Year. Ah'm off back tomorrow.'

'Ernie can drop off some things for me. I can see him off from the station. I'll move in properly next Monday, if that's all right?'

The landlady nodded. 'This blessed war,' she muttered softly. She gave that warm smile again. 'You two see what you think. Get the real feel of the place. Then pop down and have a cup of tea before you go. In the kitchen. At the end of the passage.'

When she had gone, Helena hurried over to him, clasped his hands in both hers. 'I like her. And I like this place, too. You'll be able to picture me here, won't you? I'll soon have it all cosy. I wish I could see your ship. Where you live.'

He pulled a comic face. 'You wouldn't! There's thirty of us in a mess no bigger than this.' He had slipped off the greatcoat, and adjusted the complex combination of blue collar, white lanyard and black silk scarf, bound by the cut-away tapes of the tight jumper.

He tossed the round cap on the bed and went to sit on it. He bounced up and down vigorously. 'By 'eck, lass. Feels good. How about trying it out, eh?'

Her face coloured up. 'Now stop that, Ernie!' Her tone was tinged with genuine upset, though she moved to sit beside him. She, too, had slipped off her coat, with its tailored waist. Beneath it, she wore a heavy knitted pepper and salt cardigan, with big square buttons, and a thick tweed skirt over grey lisle stockings and ankle boots. She took his rough hand, wove her fingers about his, and lifted it to her lips. She kissed it lightly. Her brown eyes were solemn on him. 'You *do* love me, don't you?'

'You know I do,' he answered, almost brusquely, and pulled his hand free, before he seized her by her shoulders, pushed her down on the coverlet, leaning over her. His mouth dipped slowly, then fixed on hers, which, after a fractional hesitance, opened to return the long passion of the kiss. She was gulping for breath, could feel her breasts straining against her clothing, the weight of him pressing her, his leg against hers. 'Don't Ernie!' she whispered pleadingly.

At once, he swung himself off her; the bed creaked as he stood. 'Sorry,' he muttered. 'But I want you. Ah'm off tomorrow,' he cried.

As if I didn't know, she thought, and all at once was sick with hollow fear and uncertainty, both at what she had done, and the blankness of the future facing them.

2

'You think a lot of yourself, don't you?' Elspeth's brown ringlets tossed in what was meant to portray disdain. Twin spots of red stood out like clown's make-up on her thirteen-year-old cheeks.

'Ah've got a right to, haven't ah?' the speaker grinned. His short brown hair was tousled, his face sweating and red with the exertions of the game. He was still wearing the claret and black-quartered football shirt, and beneath the black shorts, his knees were covered in mud. The players' studs tap-tapped on the wooden floor, depositing their little curls of mud as they jostled and crowded round the trestle table, with the steaming kettles and mounds of sandwiches.

'Yer should've tekken yer boots off afore ye come in!' Mrs Wetherall, who was responsible for cleaning out the village hall, wailed.

'By gow, yer eyes'd be waterin' then, missus!' the younger man who had been joshing with Elspeth said. He looked at Helena, who was hurriedly doling out the cups of tea. 'Six sugars for me, love!' he grinned. She looked up, and blushed at the direct admiration she saw in the bold stare. She became even more flustered.

'You'll be forgetting what sugar tastes like if we have to go to war, young man.' Joseph Barr was still wearing the thick Guernsey sweater he had donned to referee the match, which the home side had just lost by three goals to one. Which was no doubt why these youngsters from the coastal village of Kingstaith were so cocky.

'Nay, mister. That Hitler feller won't tek us on. He's got more sense.'

Another one, thought Joseph irritably, then stifled his annoyance. It was no good going on about it to this lot. 'Just t'schoolmaister off on 'is 'igh 'orse agin.' That's how they'd see it. He had heard on the wireless only yesterday about the British and French guarantee to Poland after Germany's dismemberment of Czechoslovakia, once again apparently without a shot being fired. Where did they think he was going to stop, Chamberlain and the other politicians? He was out for revenge for the last lot, and he was going to have it. Then he forgot the portentious world affairs as he saw the looks the young man was giving to Helena, who seemed to be enjoying them in spite of her blushes. Worry and pride intermingled. At sixteen, she was far too pretty for her own good. 'Better put some more water on, Helen,' he said loudly.

The young man sought her out when she managed to get from behind the tables. 'Ah'm Ernie Wheatley,' he said directly. 'The ref's your da, is he? Ah'd better not say owt then, eh? He's schoolmaster an' all, isn't 'e?'

'You know all about us, I see,' she said, cursing this seemingly permanent affliction of blushing which had struck her.

'I could see he were your dad, right away. You talk just like him, all posh.' She noted with surprise how he had moderated his own accent considerably.

'Oh, I'm sorry,' she quipped, in tones of mock offence. 'I can't help how I talk, now, can I?'

'I think it's smashin'. I could listen to yer all day, straight up.'

Her face burning, she answered, a little breathlessly, 'There's no need to be sarky.'

'Eh, lass! Ah'm not kiddin'. Yer sound as nice as yer look, an' that's sayin' summat an' all!' She looked at him shyly, saw the sincerity in his expression, and glanced down at her plate. There was nothing she could think of to say. And, for a second, he, too, seemed to have run out of repartee.

'Come on, our kid! Stop jawin'. Let's be off.'

'Who's that?' she asked, glancing towards the speaker, who was both broader and taller than the youth who so plainly admired her.

'That's me big brother. Reg. And that's another, the goalie. Our Rupert. Ah'm the youngest. Just a little un.' He was beaming again.

'Goodness! Your family makes up half the team.'

'What about you? The young un there's yer sister, right?'

'Yes. That's Elspeth. The pain in the neck. I'm the eldest. There's one more. My brother, Kit. He's only nine.'

The bulky individual named as Reg came over, nodded perfunctorily at Helena. ''Ow do. Come on, Ern. We wanna get back. Ah'm off out tonight.'

All at once, she sensed that he was reluctant to go. 'Might see you around?' he said tentatively, his cocky manner gone. His team mates were filing out into the chilly late afternoon. The coach's motor was roaring. She nodded, at a loss, startled to feel her own sense of regret. Then he was gone, with the others. She heard the roar of the departing bus, the grind of gears, as it prepared for the steep pull up the long hill to the moor road that led back to the coast nine miles away.

'Fancies you, doesn't he?' Elspeth teased, and was rewarded by Helena's guilty and swift denial.

'Don't talk daft! Start collecting those crocks. We'll be here all night.'

Two weeks later, when the church youth club organized a bicycle ride across to Kingstaith, Helena was quick to volunteer her name. They wheeled their bikes down the steep hill to the cobbled High Street which led to the small harbour. The red-tiled cottages clung precariously to the foot of the cliff, intersected by narrow alleyways which were gently stepped. After the group had leaned their bicycles against the sea wall, Helena made an excuse to shake off her friends. 'I'll just have a wander round,' she said casually. 'See you back outside the pub.'

Most of the cobles were moored in the mouth of the beck, at the bottom of the steep gorge which ran inland. She could see groups of fishermen working on them, or lounging outside the lifeboat house. A few were mending the lobster pots on the small stone quay. The tide was out, and the stream of water was scarcely more than a trickle. The brightly coloured boats, painted red or blue, with the names fancifully scrolled in black on a white background, were tilted at angles, resting on the sand and banks of shingle. The seaweed, salty tang was strong in her nostrils.

She crossed the narrow bridge over the beck, sauntered slowly, peering at the knot of working men. Most were in the dark jerseys, and oilskin trousers, with grease-stained caps pulled on their heads at an angle. With a sharp stab of disappointment, she became aware that the figure she was seeking was nowhere to be seen. They squinted up at her, grinning and nodding, one or two giving her good day. Then she saw a bulky figure rise from one of the cobles, where he had been working on the engine, and she recognized the shape of the brother, the tanned features, the dark hair.

Reg Wheatley looked up at the slim girl standing high above him. She was not much more than a silhouette against the April light. 'Excuse me,' she said, her voice piping as she called down. 'Is your brother ... he said he might ... I met him at the match. In Kilbeck.'

Reg grunted. 'Oh, aye.' This was just a schoolkid. 'That'll be our Ernie. Lazy little so- blighter's still at 'ome. Supposed ter be sortin' out t' pots fer us.' He nodded back to the side of the beck she had just crossed from. 'Along Sisters' Yard. Past Chapel Garth and fust right. The blue door at the end. Ye'll prob'ly see 'im in t' yard. All right?'

'Yes. Thank you.' Cheeks hot, Helena turned about and marched quickly away. She couldn't go looking for him in his house! What if his mother – the rest of the family – were there? What would they think of her? But she saw the cottage by Chapel Garth, and the alley sloping slightly upwards, to the right. Heart beating, upbraiding herself for her foolishness, she made her way between the cottages. There was the one at the end with the blue door. There was a low whitewashed wall around the small enclosure of the yard, which was piled untidily with the curved mesh of the wood-framed lobster pots. And no sign of anyone working on them.

She stood irresolutely, arguing with herself. Just go up and knock at the door! Don't be daft! Just say, 'Excuse me, is Ernie in, please? He asked me to call....' Forward hussy! How could she? She was about to turn away, then started as, suddenly, he was there, out of the door, in shirtsleeves and no collar, his face red, hair still tousled. He saw her at once, stared, then peered incredulously before his face was split by a beaming grin.

'You said we'd meet again,' she said helplessly, suddenly feeling ridiculously close to tears, and not knowing why.

3

They met more or less secretly at first. She used to cycle to the coast but not down to the village. She left her bike at the little station, along with all the others parked there by the folks who came to walk the cliffs at the weekends. He met her at Bank Top, and they would go off walking themselves, along the narrow margins at the seaward edge of the sloping cornfields, or the cropped turf of the pastures where sheep strayed. Generally, they liked to head south, to the next cove at Port Hilda. They would pick their way down the side of the 200 foot cliff, following the bramble clutching animal tracks that zigzagged down, the hacked-out steps that made the final descent past the gaping blackness of the arched tunnel, to the blackened, charred timbers, like jagged stumps, of the old jetty destroyed by fire several years previously.

Port Hilda had been what its name implied in the latter half of the last century, when ships came to load the iron ore which came in tubs through the tunnel in the cliff, from the mine more than a mile inland. At one time, the whole area was dotted with iron mines, all working furiously to supply the voracious appetites of the industries of Teesside and the Tyne. Now, like this one, they were nearly all done, though there were still the big iron and steel works further north, like Skinningrove, where the beck ran bright orange to the sea, and where Ernie periodically threatened to go seeking work when he got fed up with the fishing and his father's bullying ways.

They talked almost incessantly, got to know each other's backgrounds well, though they still kept their friendship a secret from their families. One day, in the middle of the week, to her hot-faced, burning chagrin, Ernie was waiting at the station at Whitby, leaning against the wall, grinning, when she came along with her cronies, the senior élite of Whitby Grammar, in her gym-slip and ribboned summer straw hat, her prefect's sash about her middle, her black-stockinged legs much in evidence. She gaped at him speechlessly for a while, and the others moved on, pushing and giggling all too audibly.

They had their first quarrel. 'Ashamed of me, are ye?' he asked fiercely, and she knew he had been waiting, wanting, to say it.

'No, of course not!' she returned angrily, wondering if it were true. 'You just – I wasn't expecting to see you. The others – there's girls from Kilbeck there.'

'Wouldn't want yer fam'ly ter find out, would yer?' he sneered. Her eyes stung; she felt a lump in her chest, as, miserably, she recognized the justice of his accusation.

They walked in silence past the harbour, and the bobbing masts of the smaller craft in its inner reaches, then over the swing bridge to Old Town. They were halfway along Church Street, before he spoke. Impatiently, he caught hold of her hand. 'Sorry,' he offered gruffly. 'Ah just wanted ter see yer, that's all. Ah was in Whitby, and thought it was a good idea.'

'I'll get into trouble if anyone sees me.' She nodded at their linked hands, did not try to release his hold. 'In my uniform.'

'Oh.' Chastened, he let go of her.

She grinned at him, her best, wrinkle-nosed special. 'I feel a right fool in this get up. I'd've died before I let you see me in this. This is my last term. I'm leaving in July.'

'Aye, there'll be all sorts happening, for sure,' he mused, with uncharacteristic sobriety. 'Ah think yer dad's right, yer know. What 'e says.' She had passed on her father's gloomy prognostications of future events. ''Itler's not gonner stop, is 'e? Not till somebody stands up to 'im, like.' He grinned. 'Ah'll be off like a shot. Ter the navy, me. They not gettin' me trampin' about all over t' place in army boots. What's wrong, love?' He stopped, gazing at the serious expression on her face, as though he had hurt her. 'Nay, don't fret yersel'. Come on. Let's go up Abbey steps, blow cobwebs away.'

They had been going out together for a considerable time before they kissed properly. One Saturday they planned to go swimming. She had brought a towel, along with the sandwiches and drinks, in her haversack. 'The tide'll be right,' he said. 'We can walk along bottom.' They picked their way over the rocks, round the point, to Port Hilda, though they stayed at a spot north of the old harbour, where ramblers were not likely to penetrate. 'Yer can change over there, behind the rocks. Ah'll not look,' he added gallantly.

'You can look all you want,' she said boldly. She unfastened the grey, divided skirt, let it fall around her white-socked ankles, then peeled her jumper over her dark head. She was wearing her black woollen bathing costume underneath. Still, she blushed and giggled, acutely conscious of its clinging contours. She plucked at its tight crotch instinctively, then sat and tugged off shoes and socks. 'Come on, big baby! Scared to get wet, eh?'

It was when they came out and ran, spluttering and laughing, up the pebbly sand to their clothes. Her teeth were chattering. Drops of water clung to her face and arms. She pulled off the white rubber bathing cap, shook her head violently. He placed her towel over her shoulders and began to massage her. 'That's right. Rub me.' She shivered, laughing, her mouth open, and then, suddenly, he was kissing her, his mouth over hers, trapping her. She felt his tongue invade her, and she couldn't cry out or stop him. Then she didn't want to; her arms went fiercely round him, and the towel fell to the gritty sand.

Their cold, hard bodies, almost naked, pressed together in an ecstasy of physical hunger for each other. His weight was on her, new, and hard and crushing, threatening, yet she wanted it, too. She felt her shoulder strap pulled down, then her breast was out, bared, and his fingers touched her rubbery hard little nipple, and his face was suddenly burningly hot on the softness of the white flesh, which she pressed sacrificially into him. She was all melting need, wanted him everywhere.

She was sobbing when, finally, they broke. He rolled off her, turning away from her in agony, hiding the straining swell of his trunks, while she hastily flipped the costume back over her breast. 'Sorry. Ah'm sorry,' he groaned. He scrambled up, stood massively over her, staring out to sea. 'Ah cannot help it, lass. Yer that lovely, yer really are.'

She slowly got up. She felt strange, weak and trembling, oddly different inside. He put her arms round his shoulders. He felt warm, beating, alive, and she laid her cheek on his sweet skin. 'So are you,' she whispered.

4

He was the first to take her home. She was more scared of the women than the men. Billy, his father, grunted at her, his head wreathed in clouds of pungent smoke from his pipe, then virtually ignored her. The eldest of the brothers, Clifford, was away at sea, in the Merchant Navy. Reg, at twenty-seven, married with two children, lived only a few cottage doors away, and Rupert, two years his junior, still lived at home, sharing a room with Ernie. The menfolk, all big, made the dim place seem even tinier. The brothers' rough, taunting humour was innocent enough, and Helena didn't mind their teasing. 'So! This is your lass, then, Ernest? Yer wanna watch 'im, love.'

But Reg's wife, May, was watchful, her expression one of thinly veiled hostility. Ernie's mother was cautious, ill at ease with her, and Helena felt miserably uncomfortable while she sipped tea from the best cups and nibbled at a biscuit. All the men except Ernie were puffing away, and the air was a tobacco fug which added to her discomfort. 'Yer da's a teacher, then?' May probed. 'Yer still at school? 'Ow old are yer? Seventeen in September? Fancy that!' She laughed spitefully. 'By 'eck, Mam, 'ear that? Ah'd bin workin' near three year when ah was seventeen.'

Ernie got her out as quickly as he could. 'They're not that bad once yer get to know them,' he said defensively.

'They're nice,' she lied, blushing.

They walked along by the railway line, after they had climbed up out of the lower seaward end of the village, then veered off to the clifftop path which was one of their favourite haunts. They passed the coastguard hut, and continued until they could just see the end of the jetty at Port Hilda. They settled on the grassy lip of the cliff edge. The sun beat down, the breeze, from the land, was gentle. The sea was an unruffled blue, fading to a haze at the horizon. Gulls wheeled, on a level with their eyes, while, behind them, larks bubbled in their incessant bliss.

Helena chewed a dry grass stalk. 'You can't believe in all the troubles on a day like this,' she murmured, savouring the sun's enveloping touch on her bare limbs, and through her thin clothing. She had worn her prettiest summer frock, in honour of the occasion, and her best silk stockings, too. She would have liked to slip them off. The fashionable shoes had rubbed her heels painfully. They were not meant for walking, not over this ground.

'Aye. There's gonner be a war all right,' Ernie declared. Even he had taken to reading the papers recently. 'That Eye-talian feller's gettin' in on it an' all. This Pact o' Steel carry on. We shall 'ave ter tek 'em on soon.' He slipped an arm round her slender shoulders, drew her towards him, nuzzling his forehead against her cheek. 'Best make the most of it, pet.'

They kissed, leaned back until they were lying together, the passion building inexorably, until she managed to break free, moving his hand off her silk-clad thigh. The dress had been pushed up until the rolled top around the garter almost showed. 'Please, Ernie!' she panted, clinging tightly to his hand, her eyes huge and frightened.

She saw the tight clench of his jaw, the redness of his neck as he sat up, looked away. 'Ah feel—' He shook his head desperately, turned to her, his eyes blazing with intensity. 'I can't tell yer 'ow I feel for yer, lass. Ah reckon – ah love yer!'

'I love you, too.' She was scared as soon as she said it. Both of them sounded reluctant to have to admit it. Helena was tormented with uncertainty, doubt. She had such powerful feelings about him. New, frightening emotions, felt with her body as well as her mind. She was deeply shocked by the depth of her newly awakened sexual desire, longed to tell him she was fighting against that desire as much as the passion she could feel in him when he held her. But she was too shy.

She left school that July, was offered a job in the Whitby office of Surtees and Johnson, the solicitors. 'I'm sure you'll get a good School Cert, Helena,' Philip Surtees, the younger partner smiled. 'I'm sure you take after your dad, anyway. Brainy family, yours.' There was something in the way his middle-aged eye swept approvingly over her that embarrassed and shamefully pleased her, but she'd got the job, and that was the main thing.

Her father tried to be pleased for her, though he had wanted her to stay on for Higher and go to college. One thing she was quite sure of, though: she did not want to be a school ma'am. She was due to start on 11 September. 'I'd better make the most of the next four weeks,' she told Ernie excitedly.

'A workin' girl, eh?' he teased her fondly. 'An' a secretary an' all. Yer'll not want ter bother wi' a common ould fisherman now then!'

She punched him vigorously on his arm. 'Stoppit! Anyway, I'm an office junior. Not quite a secretary yet awhile.'

The Sunday morning of the week before she was due to start work, St John's, Kilbeck, was practically empty, and she knew why. She and Elspeth were the only members of the family to attend. When they came out, they could see the knots of people gathered on the green that led down to the river, outside the Wheatsheaf Inn. 'It's happened,' Elspeth said. 'We're at war.'

5

On the surface, life in Kilbeck seemed little affected by the great event. The bombers people had predicted would come flocking over to bomb the towns out of existence failed to materialize. Joseph Barr was warned to be ready to receive an influx of evacuees from the towns of Teesside and from Newcastle, but they, too, failed to materialize, much to his relief. Helena started her new job with a great deal of enthusiasm, three days after her seventeenth birthday. She, at any rate, was determined things were going to be different. She was grown up now, no longer a child.

'I want you to meet someone,' she said bravely, though her stomach was churning. Her parents waited, tight lipped. 'A young man. I've known him for quite a while. He's – very nice.'

'I see.' Lizzy, her mother, breathed deeply. 'I had an idea you were off with somebody. All these bicycle rides. Who is he then? Do we know him? A Kilbeck lad, is he?'

'No. He's from Kingstaith. He's a fisherman.'

They took it as badly as she feared they would. She brought him for the ordeal of Sunday tea, her heart bleeding for him as she watched him, face as red as a beacon, totally foreign to her in a dark, funereal suit, brilliantly polished, squeaking black boots, and a tie and starched collar that looked as if it were strangling him. They were freezingly polite to him, that's what made it so bad, with their devastating questions about his family, and talk of 'prospects'. Elspeth tried to make up a bit for the frigid atmosphere, but her attempts at humour failed, died like a wilting flower in the desert of the Sunday drawing-room.

'I'm sorry,' she said simply, gulping down the threatened tears, when they finally escaped.

He caught her hand, held on to it tightly. 'Don't fret, lass.' He grinned at her, and she felt the tears spring to her eyes and thought suddenly, Yes, I *do* love him. 'Mebbe we can get yer da and my old man ter go out fer a drink together some time.'

'Oh, Ernie!' She started to laugh unsteadily at the notion, and then the tears came, splashing down her cheeks, and he grabbed her to him, and kissed her hard, hurting her mouth, and she was exultant.

'Stuff 'em, both lots! The'll come round. An if they don't, then too bad, eh, kid?'

They didn't, and life became fraught with tensions and difficulties for Helena at home. Their relentless pressure, however, made her all the more determined not to give way, and Ernie came to mean more and more to her as they moved through the first months of the war. He was increasingly fretful and restless, she could see, especially when a really savage winter set in, with bouts of enforced idleness when the boats couldn't fish, and the iron grip of snow, frost, and ice kept them apart for long periods.

The railways generally remained open, so they were able to meet in Whitby, Ernie travelling in on the coast line from Kingstaith, while Helena came in on the line which came down from Middlesborough through the dales. Usually, he would come in on a Saturday morning and be waiting at lunchtime outside the office. They would sit at a corner table in the Empire café, whose windows were steamy and dripping with a crowded, cosy fug, their knees bumping, hands touching over the tea stains, eyes locked into each other avidly.

One March day when there should have been signs of spring, but the countryside was still locked in the damp chill of winter, she could see at once that something was wrong. His eyes couldn't meet hers, he was uneasy, and she was shocked at the engulfing pain which spread through her so that she felt physically sick. He wants to finish it, she thought, utterly desolate.

'I'm gonner join up,' he told her, almost timidly. 'I'll be gettin' me call up any day now in any case. I want to get in the navy. I'm goin' into the recruitin' office on Monday.'

'I thought fishing was one of those – what do they call them? – reserved occupations. That's what Dad was saying.'

'Not the inshore, the cobles. Any road, there's that many rules an' regulations, you can't 'ardly mek a livin' any more. I've got to go, Helen, love.'

At first, she had felt such immediate relief, then the misery came flooding back at the thought that she would be losing him after all.

But he was right, he would be conscripted in any event. And he would be better off in the navy. Certainly safer than being in the army. She had to be proud of him. 'I can't bear to think of you going away,' she murmured, her eyes filling. 'I'll miss you so much.'

She had vowed not to cry when they said goodbye at Whitby station, on a chilly April morning. She had made an excuse to get out of the office for an hour, was waiting when the two-carriage train from up the coast chuffed in. They had an endless half-hour to wait for the train to Middlesborough, and sat in the station buffet, staring at each other miserably, while she lashed herself for not being brave and cheerful, sparkling with resolute wit. They were both secretly relieved when it pulled in to the buffers.

'Write as soon as you know where you are. I mean, what your address is, won't you?'

He nodded. 'Yer'll not have to mind me spellin', lass. Don't let yer old man see it, fer God's sake.'

She smiled, and two big teardrops formed, clung to her curling lashes, then rolled down her cheeks. 'Don't cry, love,' he begged.

'I'm not,' she answered, the tears streaming now. He leaned out of the door, and lifted her off the cold floor, hugging her, kissing her cold lips desperately.

'Ah love you.'

'Love you.'

Life became a routine of work, rides home on the train whose service grew more erratic as wartime exigencies took bite, hurrying up the bank to home, glancing at the mantelshelf to see if there was a blue envelope there for her. She wouldn't open it in front of them, sat through tea dying to escape upstairs to the room she had to share with Elspeth, but who was mercifully absent while Helena lay on her bed, aching with her love for him, devouring every stilted line. Elspeth used the drawing-room for homework, so Helena could still be alone as she lay on her stomach, and wrote her heart on to the thin sheets of paper. She wrote something every night, posted off two fat letters a week, without fail.

As they moved into summer, the war sprang to evil life. The first disaster was the Norwegian campaign. The battle of Narvik, only days after Ernie went off to his basic training, brought the navy spectacularly into the headlines. Captain Warburton-Lee and HMS *Hardy*. Hero and heroine. But the hero was dead, and Helena fearfully revised her assessment of the relative safety of the senior service. Her 'Take care of yourself, darling', with which she ended every missive took on an added significance.

Then came the greater disaster of Dunkirk, when, for a briefly hectic time, the war really did come close to everyone, and people waited in trepidation for the church bells which would herald the invasion. It didn't happen. Instead, still uncomfortably close, at least for those living further south, the Battle of Britain was fought in the summer skies, and won, though many did not realize it at the time.

The end of his training coincided with her eighteenth birthday, on September 8th. He had a whole week's leave before he travelled back to barracks to be drafted to a ship. 'Or a stone frigate,' he told her cheerfully, grinning at her blank look. 'A shore establishment,' he explained patiently. But, being in the Seaman branch, and specialized in gunnery, there was little chance of that. However, he kept that knowledge to himself.

Summer continued through that September week, so that they were able to indulge in all their favourite walks again. They revelled in the nostalgia like an old married couple. Remember the first time.... But time was there, hovering insistently. On the Sunday, the day before he was to return to the navy, they sat in their favoured spot on the cliff, above Port Hilda. The army had already blown up what was left of the old harbour as a defence precaution. 'Imagine Jerry landing here,' Ernie chuckled. 'That'd cause a few pints to tremble down at the Mucky Duck.'

He took her in his arms, and they held each other, sweetly tormented by the kisses, the feel of their eager bodies in contact. Helena was wearing a frock again. This time, there were no stockings, just her smooth, exciting skin, and she didn't, couldn't, push his hand off her leg, not even when it crept burningly up to the roundness of her thigh, not even when it swept up to the lace and silk of her best underwear, and his fingers pressed between her legs, and touched for the first time the centre of her need for him, and caressed her until she wept, and grew wet for him, and his fingers were inside the wet silk, touching her, the springy coils, the slippery fold of her sex, and she shook and shook, and cried and ached for the more she was terrified of, until suddenly, desolately, he stopped, groaned and rolled away from her, on the edge of tears himself, with longing and love.

'Someone might come,' she whispered, finally, feeling the clinging wetness, feeling strangely hollow, and defeated. 'I wish – there was somewhere we could go.'

They walked back towards Kingstaith, without speaking, until she stopped before they reached the first of the allotments at Bank Top, and pulled him to her. 'You know I've never – you know you'll be the first? The only one?'

'Course ah do, lass.' He held her gently.

From autumn into winter, with only the long letters to try to satisfy their need, only now she had to write to 'Mess 35, HMS *Hood*, c/o GPO, London', even though he was based up in the wild Orkneys, at Scapa Flow. When the letter came telling her that he would be coming home on 23 December, until the 28th, she couldn't contain her happiness. She had to tell someone.

'It's not healthy, your – obsession with that lad. You've got to get out with young people. Meet somebody more—'

'Suitable?' she cried at her father, her eyes flashing. 'You'd better get used to him, 'cos we're going to be married! I love him!' She thought for a second her father was actually going to hit her, for the first time in more than ten years.

'Don't be ridiculous! You're just a bairn, still.'

That was when she decided definitely she would leave home. They were starting to conscript girls. She was eighteen now. Not a bairn. She fixed up a job as ward assistant at the hospital in Whitby, to start in the new year, looked around for some digs. 'Let her go,' Joseph told his frantic wife. 'Let her see what it's like being on her own. Might bring her to her senses.'

She phoned Mrs Turner the day before Ernie was due home, arranging to come and look at the room the day after the holiday, on the 27th. She was waiting for him at Whitby, sobbed happily in his arms, smothered on his chest.

She suffered guiltily through the interminable 'festivity' of Christmas Day. The atmosphere was electrically charged, everyone waiting for the spark to set off the explosion. Her parents struggled to ignore her, concentrating their jolliness on her sister and brother, bravely battling on. They sat like stiff-faced martyrs when she announced that she was going out in the afternoon. 'I'm going over to Ernie's folks for tea,' she declared vindictively.

There were no trains or buses, and a sleety shower caught her on the top of the moors, but she was warmly clothed, with sou'wester and voluminous cape over all. She felt daring and brave, racing along the deserted, shining road in the louring clouds. He was waiting at the top of the hill for her. The Wheatleys' cottage was crammed to overflowing, the menfolk red-faced, sweating with ale and spirits, the women, in unaccustomed finery, spotlessly clean pinnies, hair crimped and curled into iron neatness.

'We're off out,' Ernie said, much later. It was pitch black outside, the rain rattling down. But nobody noticed, apart from Reg, who winked broadly. Ernie hurried Helena along the wind-blown alley, an arm round her shoulders. 'Come on!'

'Where are we—' He led her up another narrow alley, stopped at a door, fumbled, and opened it. 'Our Reg's,' he said, pulling her inside. 'He said we could use it. They'll be stoppin' at ours till dawn, ah reckon.'

The fire had been banked high with sea coal, and looked almost dead, but the small room was warm. 'Come here, lass,' he said, huskily, and she went to him. He folded her under him, on the clippie mat in front of the fireside. Soon, their blood was throbbing with the long kisses and the touch of their hands on bodies, on warm, vibrant flesh. His hands slid over the smooth silk of her slip under the thick jumper, felt the curves of her breasts, and she groped for him, tugging, fighting the shirt out of the broad leather belt, then sliding and clutching rapturously in her turn at his wonderfully smooth skin.

His hands were moving now, under her thick skirt, the thick black woollen stockings, tracing the contour of her leg, right up to the sudden cool of bare skin over the roll of her stocking top, scrabbling into the tight legs of her winter knickers, fingers remorselessly pushing, exploring, over the cap of her pubis, blindly seeking, locating the damp divide of the vulva. 'Come upstairs.'

She was shaking violently, her teeth chattering. The bedroom was cold, smelt intimately of its regular owners, but she was past caring or the power to stop. He was throwing off his clothes, naked before she had started to undress, and she stared at him, weak at the sight of his lean, hard strength, the demanding masculinity that drew her helplessly, the long, potent rise of him. Then he was pulling back the blankets, calling for her, and she frantically kicked off shoes, shrugged down the skirt, then the knickers.

'Cheat!' he growled, pulling her in against his nakedness, for she was still in her slip, stockings, and brassiere. She felt his penis thrusting in her belly, touched it with real fear, but knowing she wanted him to take her. He pulled her slip up, thrust it over her hips, turning her, parting her legs, drawing her up, his fingers parting her, opening her to him, and she tried not to tense, not to cry out, but she had to, the pain was burning, he was hurting her, and she cried again at his plunging thrusts, feeling him literally tearing into her, wondering why she couldn't stop it hurting so much. Then she shivered at the rush and urge of his discharge, and they were clinging and crying and she felt tears on his cheeks, and was swamped by the immensity of her love and her gladness that she was his.

6

In the back parlour at the end of the long passage at 13 Prospect Mount, Maggie Turner sat with the final cup of tea. The decorations hung in festoons from the lampshade, looping away to the corners of the room. More were draped over the pictures, and along the top of the mirror over the high mantelshelf, which was packed with cards. Her thoughts, as so often, were far, far away, visualizing an Arabian Nights' setting, of moonlit dunes, star-spangled vastness of sky. Too many films like *The Sheikh*, she mocked at herself. She was sure the reality would be dustily, parchedly different. She prayed for Tommy's safety, hoped he had

had a good Christmas, nursed the ache of her worry for her son like a pain under the ribs.

'That young lady, Miss Barr, came to see the room,' she said to Vicky, who had just come in from a party. She looked at the solid thirteen-year-old. She looked too robust for that frilly party dress, her bare arms, red at the elbows, swelled out of the dainty, puffed sleeves. Her cheerful, plain face was so like her father's it made Maggie smile. 'She seems very nice. She had a young man with her. A sailor.'

Unbidden, the old pain caught her, startling her with its sharpness, and she felt her throat tighten. 'Will Dad be back at the weekend?' Vicky asked, flinging herself down in his armchair, crossing her solid legs. The ankle socks looked very white against the patent black shininess of her shoes.

'I don't think so. Not after he had Christmas off. They're having to work round the clock now, you know.'

'I know. This bloomin' war. I hate it!' She giggled, and Maggie thought lovingly she was still very much a child, after all. 'Mavis Thompson nearly brained herself on a lamp post. You can't see a thing, specially with them daft torches.'

'Those,' Maggie corrected automatically, almost blushed as she saw her daughter's grin.

'Oh, I'm ever so sorry, your ladyship,' Vicky teased. Yes, just like her dad. He was always making fun of the way Maggie spoke. 'More tea, Vicar?' he would mimic, in a shrill, exaggeratedly aristocratic drawl, his little finger crooked to the side. She felt the warmth of her affection for Alf. He was a good man. She loved him, she really did, for his kindness. She thought again of his nobility, taking her on, with little Tommy, and all her shady past. Even without that, he was noble. A widow with a seven-year-old child, and a slowly disintegrating boarding-house. No great catch.

She remembered his homely face, creased with attention and embarrassment, when she had weepingly told him the truth, forcing the pain of it all out in words. He had held her then, gently, his voice gruff with the effort of expressing his emotion. 'Meks no difference to me, what's happened in the past, love. I'm sorry you had to go through it all, that's all. I want to be with you. Look after you. I want you for my wife.'

A good man, truly good. She glanced at the comfortable room, transformed by the decorations, the glittering tree. Christmas was always a sentimental time, a time for remembering. Vividly, the picture of that young sailor on the doorstep came to her mind again. She shivered. Yes, a time for memories, for ghosts to make their presence gently felt.

1 AUGUST, 1910

1

' 'Appy birthday, Miss Alice!' Alice tossed back the long black plaits of her hair over her shoulders, grinned back at the speaker, puffing out her red cheeks. Tommy Cousins was red, too, not just with exertion.

'Can you help me find the ball, Tommy?' she asked, moving carefully down the long rows of vegetables. 'We've lost so many we'll have none left soon.'

He glanced across to the smooth lawn of the tennis court, where four childish figures were playing. Others were sprawled on the gentle slope of the grass bank above, neatly punctuated by the sets of three shallow stone steps at each end. 'Yer could do wi' some help,' he said.

Alice Margaret Guthrie laughed again. 'It's *my* party. I have to do all the skivvying.' They were moving between the tall cabbages, searching under the broad leaves. 'I've caught you up, Tommy. I'm twelve, too, now.'

'Nay. Yer'll nivver catch me up, Miss Alice. Ah'll allus be fower month older.'

She turned, poked her tongue out at him, her brown eyes sparkling with humour. 'Have you seen what Mama and Pa bought me?' she asked excitedly. She nodded up towards the paddock, on the landward side of the tennis court, where the new pony was grazing. 'She's absolutely gorgeous! You'll have to help me think of a name for her. We'll take her for a ride along Dalton's Meadow when she's used to us, eh?'

He nodded. ' 'Ere it is.' He picked up the ball, drew back his arm, and sent it curving high into the air, showing off.

'Thanks, Tommy. I'll see you later, yes?' He watched her pick up her blue skirts, saw her thin, black ankles as she skipped quickly back through the plants.

'Ruddy idlin', as usual.' Sam Gough, the gardener, frowned at him, and Tommy reached guiltily for his fork. 'Yer not one o' the gentry, tha knows, ter stand gossipin' all day. Gerron wi' it, yer lazy little tyke!' As the short, stocky individual made his way back towards the long greenhouses, Tommy favoured him with a malignant glance and some very uncharitable thoughts. He bent to the dry, crumbly soil again, turning it gently, to clear the weeds between the uniform banks about the vegetables.

He worked steadily, the cries of Alice's guests drifting clearly across to him. True, he was not of the gentry all right. An uncharacteristic but keen envy suddenly seized him. He straightened and glanced about him. Straight ahead, over the already goldening, waving plumes of wheat, the sea was a deep, picture-book blue, the hills on the left of the horizon shimmeringly indistinct in the summer heat haze. Beyond the cornfield stood a row of cottages which were perched on the clifftop. Nothing could be seen of the long jetty, the high, wooden gantry along which the wagons of ore came rumbling out of the tunnel in the cliff, to tip their loads into the boats moored alongside. His dad would be down there now. He had the late Saturday shift today.

To his left was the flat tennis court and at the far side he could see the trimmed rows of the fruit trees in the orchard. There were a lot of new ones this year. He had helped Old Gough stake some of them. Even the master, Mr Guthrie, had fussed about, rattling off the fancy names as he supervised them. Behind him, Tommy could see the two long glasshouses, then the honeysuckle-clad brick wall beyond which was the yard, and the house itself.

Port Hilda Hall didn't live up to its grand name. The most noticeable feature was its tall chimneys. You could see them finger pointing at the sky from miles away, fixed with iron stays like ships' masts to the steep slope of the roof. The house itself was low and seemed to sprawl sideways. Its grey stone blocks squatted solidly at the top of the low hill it occupied. It was only two storeys, the windows of the bedrooms jutting out of the steeply sloping slates, dormer style, pretty enough with their white, decorative woodwork, but adding to the impression of untidy angularity. His da had said it had to be built like that. 'Winds we get round 'ere 'ud blow t'bugger away if it were any 'igher.'

It was certainly a big, rambling place inside, and the gardens surrounding it were extensive enough. He should know. He helped to look after them at weekends and after school, and he would no doubt be starting full time next year. Gough had already said that he would be taken on if he proved himself, and the master and the family liked him well enough.

All at once, the unaccustomed feeling of discontent and unfairness assailed him. Alice was such a pretty thing, and not daft like most girls. Guiltily, he told himself she was Miss Alice, but then truculent defiance seized him. Why should she be? She didn't bother when they were alone together. They were just mates; she grabbed his hand when they were scrambling on the cliff, pushed and shoved him when they chased and wrestled on the beach. Angrily, he jabbed the fork savagely into the earth. He thought of the imposing, high iron gates on their carved pillars, the great sweep of pebbled drive, perfectly circled round the lawn and the fragrantly profuse rose bed at its centre, the sneering stone lions at the foot of the wide steps leading up to the front door of the hall, the colours of the stained-glass porch, opening to the splendour of the entrance hall with its high, solemnly ticking clock, the horned heads staring unseeingly out from the walls, the powder horns, the great, gilt portraits, the big stone fireplace, on and on to the start of the wide stairs, before its short flight branched to left and right.

You could fit the whole of their cottage easily into that hall, Tommy reckoned. Mine Row. Over thirty of them, one long terrace. Front room, kitchen, scullery, yard. Two bedrooms and a cupboard-sized room tucked away at the end. Yards like sheep pens, then across the narrow dirt alleyway the closets, like pigeon cotes, and beyond them the long ribbons of gardens. If he looked over to his right, past the leafy chestnuts that marked the boundary of the hall's gardens, he could see the long row of identical chimneys, like jagged little teeth against the wash of blue.

A shout went up. The latest game had come to a halt. He saw Alice's thin figure in the white blouse, darker skirt. Evie, the lady's maid she was called, was bringing out fresh drinks, putting them down on the card table which had been set up by the steps. The children clustered round, laughing, calling out. I'll not work here, Tommy thought, with sudden hard resolution, though he enjoyed gardening, had looked forward to it. I'll get Da to try and fix me up at the mine, or down on the jetty. He didn't want to see Miss Alice like this, every day. They were miles apart. I'll still be working for her da, though, he reflected bitterly. Guthrie and Powers. He owned the iron mine, held sway over the lives of all the people of Port Hilda. The rich man in his castle, the poor man at his gate.

2

'What's wrong wi' you? Yer look as if ye've lost a tanner an' found a ha'penny. Sit yersel' down and get yer tea.' Ginny Cousins looked at her youngest son from her place at the head of the table, where she was pouring from the large teapot. She finished filling the tin mugs, then put it back on the small, round metal grill which was swung out from the range The blackleaded metal gleamed, the knob shone silver, for all had been done the previous day, as always. Friday was blackleading day. Now, the fire glowed in the high grate, despite the heat of the day. The oven had been used for the meal, pans of water stood on the flat top next to the banked fire, which was rarely out for long, dependent as they were on it for all their needs.

Tommy, fresh from the scullery where he had been washing his hands and face in cold water at the pump, frowned, but stayed silent as he squeezed into his place. Youngest of her seven, and moodiest, Ginny thought, serving out the beef and potato pie in large slabs. She was glad all that side of things was over, feeling a pang of regret for her large, almost shapeless body which even her corset could hardly hold in check. Not that she bothered wearing it most of the time, for she rarely went anywhere that warranted it these days. Not even down to the village, to the Mucky Duck any more, much to her husband Will's relief, she was sure. He had never enjoyed the Friday or Saturday night ritual of having to sit in the best room for the first pint, before he could escape to his cronies in his customary retreat of the public bar, leaving her to the salacious scandal worried over joyfully by the other wives.

She was glad, too, that she had broken the habit. She was a little saddened to acknowledge that she preferred it when he was out of the house nowadays, either down at the port, or off to the pub. After twenty-seven years of marriage, they had little to say to each other that mattered. She looked round the table.

Bert, her eldest, was long gone. He'd been married three years, had a miner's cottage over at Liverton where he worked. He and Julia had presented them with their first grandchild, Ellis, nearly two years ago, and Julia was well on with her second, due in December, a Christmas baby. Mary, only fourteen months younger than Bert, was in service at Whitby, and courting strongly, too. Ginny hoped she'd have the sense, and the strength, to hold out a bit longer before she decided to wed. Already, she'd noticed the difference in her, her neatness, her manners, even the way she spoke. Wilf poked fun at her 'la-di-da ways', but Ginny was pleased. She was in a good household, and learning fast. You couldn't beat domestic service for bringing you on, if you'd a mind. Still, at twenty-four, no doubt Mary would soon start feeling she was an old maid.

Only three left round the family table now. Louise, her brown hair tumbling its rich waves all about her face and shoulders, was munching away, and gabbing at the same time, red cheeks pouched. She could certainly do with some lessons in etiquette. That job she had at the fish sheds down the road at Kingstaith was turning her into a right hoyden, not that she had far to go in the first place. Big made and big mouthed, she'd always been loud and aggressively cocksure of herself. More like a lad than a lass. Ginny had thought she'd grow out of it, but at nineteen she showed no sign of quietening down. The reverse, in fact. Mind, the lads seemed to like her. She was always going on about some boy, was out every spare minute. She'd be wed before Mary, probably. Probably have to, the madam.

Dora was different. The nearest to Tommy, in looks as well as temperament, and, at fifteen, only three years older. Her black hair framed delicate features so different from Louise's robust looks. She had started working up at the hall – 't'big 'ouse', as the village called it – just a kitchen maid at the minute, but with prospects of moving up. And she would, too. She was diligent and bright, and wanted to get on. She might even end up like Evie Swain, who was Mrs Guthrie's lady's-maid and lived in, over the stables, with Mr Jobling, the butler, and that housekeeper-cook woman, Mrs Jackson.

There should have been two more, Ginny thought, as always suffering that little stab of sadness, remembering the hurt of losing children. Little William, born between Mary and Louise, who did not last more than three months. He would have been twenty-two this year, a young man. Then a year and a half after Louise, another girl, the poor mite dying within hours, after nearly killing Ginny with the diffculty of the birth. No more, the doctor had said, but easier said than done, however much Will swore, with tearful, drunken penitence. There'd been Dora and then Tommy since then.

Tommy had been a hard one as well. It had taken her months to get over it. She had managed to keep Will from her until she hoped they had simply fallen out of the habit, but, after several violent, drunken scenes, she knew that he at least hadn't. She still blushed when she thought of the desperate alternatives she had offered and endured in the privacy of the bedroom. As he made fewer and fewer demands on her sexually, she began to wonder if he was finding relief elsewhere, and was deeply shocked to discover that she half hoped he was. Now, it was an extremely rare occurrence, as much by his choice as hers, and, though perfectly safe, left her only sore and deeply thankful at its brevity. She could hardly remember the times when she had enjoyed it.

'Come on, misery guts,' she exhorted Tommy now. 'Cheer up.'

Dora sniggered. 'I know what's wrong. It's Alice Guthrie's party today and he wasn't invited.'

'You shut yer face!' he exclaimed so fiercely that his mother and Dora stared at him in some surprise. He felt himself reddening. His eyes stung, and all at once, appallingly, he felt he was near to blubbering. He lowered his face to the steaming, fragrant pie.

'She's twelve an' all now, isn't she?' his mother was saying, unaware of the storm of emotion boiling in his chest. 'She'll 'ave ter stop 'er gallivantin' off with you and the other village lads, our Tom. 'T'isn't right. She's a young lady now.'

3

Alice wiped her hands on her pinafore and paused outside the dining-room. Richard Jobling appeared from the passageway to the left of the staircase on his way from the kitchen. 'Am I late?' Alice grimaced. He nodded and gave her his pained expression. He was dressed, immaculately as usual, in pinstriped trousers and swallow-tailed coat, and he pushed open the door with a flourish, ushering her in before him. She saw the capped and aproned figures of Evie and Hannah, their white cuffs pushed up on their forearms, standing over by the laden sideboard, ready to serve.

'Ah. You've decided to grace us with your presence, miss!' her father said, from the head of the long table. Alexander Guthrie was an imposing figure. His glossy, still dark hair, only slightly tinged with grey at the temples, was parted ruler straight down the middle. His walrus moustache sprouted in disciplined abundance over his upper lips. The wing collar was dazzlingly white, the dark tie centred with a discreetly jewelled pin exactly over the V of the waistcoat. A fresh bloom from the climber that grew at the side of the porch was fixed in his buttonhole. His brows were knitted now in irritation.

Alice blushed slightly as she slipped into her seat. Her fingers gripped the green velvet of the chair cover under the heavy cloth. 'Sorry,' she murmured. 'I just went to have a look at the pony. See that she was all right.'

'You don't feel Mr Reece can be trusted to look after her?' her father asked in his coldly sarcastic tone. Jack Reece was the head groomsman, and took care of all the horses, with two assistants.

'I couldn't wait – I just wanted to see her,' Alice muttered, lowering her head.

'You could have waited until after breakfast, Alice,' her mother chided in those long-suffering tones that made Alice cringe. 'We wondered where on earth you were.'

Did she ever disagree with father? Alice wondered, in secret mutiny. How could she bear it, his insufferable correctness, his implacable authority? She tried to imagine what it must be like, being married twenty years. Seeing to the household accounts, planning meals with Mrs Jackson, the cook/housekeeper. Tending the flower beds, visiting friends in the carriage or the dog cart. Having babies! One every two years, like clockwork.

Alice mentally reviewed the siblings, all in their strict ranks at the table. Alexander Junior, at his father's right hand, opposite his mother. Twenty years old, already in attendance at the mine, a grown man and still scared of Papa. Next to him, Herbert, the second son, eighteen, and lucky enough to be escaping to college in two months. At least he wasn't as stuffy as Alex, who was a pale copy of father.

Opposite Herbert, Olga, sixteen, developing into something of a beauty, Alice reluctantly conceded, noting the black hair piled elegantly high, the dark eyes and fine features, the enviably rounded bosom in the white blouse. Father had grumblingly decided that some time next year she should be sent to France, to a finishing school. Then no doubt out on the marriage market where she, too, would become a model wife and good little mother.

There had been another boy after Olga. Caleb, who had died when he was still a baby. Then something must have gone wrong with the system. She glanced along to her right, where little George was squirming while Hannah tried to feed him. Normally, he took his meals safely tucked away in the nursery, but on Sunday Papa insisted on the grand assembly of all the tribe. George was only five, which meant a gap of seven years between her own birth and his. What could have happened? Alice's knowledge about reproduction was sketchy to say the least, and she grew a little uncomfortable at pursuing such matters even in her thoughts. But they must be pursued. And there were other questions she must soon learn the answers to. But who would tutor her? She could not for the life of her imagine broaching such a delicate subject with her mother. And as for Olga – if she knew, she would take special delight in keeping her ignorant. 'You're such a child!' was just about her favourite phrase these days.

Suddenly, entirely unbidden, came the thought of Tommy, of his thin, grinning form waving at her in the garden. He was such a brick. She thought of the children who had attended her party yesterday, and dismissed them out of hand. There was no one she would rather be with than Tommy. They got on so well together; she could talk to him far more easily than anybody round this table. And there was none of that boy and girl nonsense, either. They were pals, simply that. She hoped he would be up at the house this afternoon. She could sneak away, they both could, with the pony, walk her down to Dalton's Meadow, put a saddle on her, see how she reacted.

She sneaked two apples off the dish as she left after the meal, and slipped into the kitchen, then out past the butler's pantry to the door leading to the cobbled yard where the stables were. She saw Dora, Tommy's older sister, emptying a bucket in the yard. She was fifteen, only a year younger than Olga. She had a grey overall on, and a piece of sacking tied round her waist. She was working in the kitchen, and Alice guessed it must be a dreary and unpleasant task, washing all the pots and pans, polishing, helping to light fires in the early mornings, helping Mrs Jackson prepare the meals. But she was always cheerful, and when she smiled she looked just like her brother.

'Hello, Dora. Is Tommy working today?'

'I 'spec' so, miss. After dinner, prob'ly. 'E likes ter get as many hours as 'e can in.'

'I'd like him to give me a hand with the new pony. She's marvellous.' Alice went across to the stables, whose doors were open. The open carriage was already standing in the yard, Jack Reece supervising the washing down and polishing with cloths. He nodded at Alice.

'Back agin, are ye? Ah'll take 'er out t'paddock as soon as we finish 'ere. Got ter git ready fer church, Miss Alice.'

She smiled, held up the apples. 'I'll just pop in and give her these,' she wheedled. 'Then I've got to scoot off and get ready myself.'

An hour later the carriage was out the front, Jobling ceremoniously holding the door while the family descended the steps and boarded. Mama sat in the middle of the bench seat, Papa on her left, Alex Junior on her right. Herbert sat opposite his mother, with Alice and Olga at his sides. Alice knew that both the boys were anxious for father to get a motor car. There were two at the mine, along with a fleet of motor lorries which were replacing the horse-drawn wagons, but though he would use them for business, so far he refused to house one on home ground.

Alice had her back to the smartly turned out pair pulling them along, and Joe, above her, decked out in his finery. She studied her mother, under the layered elaborateness of the wide hat, the little veil half down. The lace ruffles were high at her throat, her bosom swelled impressively even under the light over gown. Alice shuddered as she thought of having always to wear the fearsome whalebone corsets, all the starched and lace-trimmed underwear she had seen in her mother's bedroom. Father had his own little dressing-room next to it. She wasn't sure what men wore underneath their shirts and trousers, but she was gloomily sure it wouldn't be anything like as irksome as the female's lot.

Mother was waving now and then, regally, like the new queen herself. It was only three months since the old king had died. Black drapes on the carriage, all over the house, and everyone shaking their heads as if something dire was about to happen. But King George had taken over, and his pretty wife, and nothing much seemed to have changed.

They went slowly down the hill, Joe pulling back on the horses, calling out to them, past the Black Swan, which everyone called the Mucky Duck. The church stood on the rise at the end of the High Street, the high brick wall holding in the sloping green churchyard. Some chapel folk were walking along towards the low building further along the main street of the village. As the carriage halted and Joe leapt down leaving a boy to hold the horses while he held open the door and dropped the steps, Alice noticed Tommy with his mother. They were staunch Wesleyans, and he often joshed her about the toffee-nosed Anglicans. She called out, grinning and waving.

'Alice! For goodness' sake, girl! Show a bit of decorum, can't you? You don't go hailing garden boys as though they're your long lost chums.' Her father clicked his teeth in anger, stalking off, his wife's arm firmly captured. Alice glowed red, her eyes misted, and she was ashamed of the hot wave of revulsion she felt rise like bile within her.

4

Everyone thought summer had come to an end with the equinoctial gales. Alice lay in bed one early September morning, listening to the roar of the wind about the chimneys. The windows rattled, slates lifted, and she snuggled down with a sense of luxury in the warm burrow of the bedclothes. She wriggled closer to Olga's curved back, fitted herself to it, slipped her arm round the hollow of the waist, rubbed her feet against the round heels, like a cat. Her sister moaned, twisting, reluctant to surface from her sleep, and flounced away to the very edge of the bed.

The nursery had to double as a schoolroom, and, with George safely out of the way, Alice and Olga were sequestered with poor Mr Swales, a young man who came five mornings a week to tutor them. He was undoubtedly brainy, but not very good as a teacher, Alice thought, though neither of his pupils helped to make his task any easier. Of course, he was trying to do two different jobs at once, for Olga was, supposedly, far in advance of Alice. But she had absolutely no interest in what Mr Swales had to offer, and treated him abominably, arguing, mocking him, until her younger sister felt embarrassed for him at times. Still, she supposed Papa paid him well for his suffering.

She had hoped her father would agree to her going to the private school in Whitby. Some of the girls she knew from the area even travelled in on the train each day, and had a fine old time larking about with the boys who attended the grammar school. But her father would have none of that. She had had a part-time governess, Mrs Roderick, a relative of the St Hilda's vicar, until last year, while the unfortunate tutor of that time, another impecunious graduate, had to cope with Olga alone.

She looked at the driving grey clouds from the nursery windows. She could hardly see the cottages at the clifftop. Beyond them was a pale blank where the sea should be. She tried to stop herself from glancing towards the wall clock every five minutes as the morning crept on with agonizing slowness.

That afternoon, she went over to the orchard to help them gather up the windfalls, and Tommy came while they were still busy. He was in his high-necked jersey, and knee britches with the thick grey stockings, which made his legs look thin in the solid boots. 'You're lucky,' she grumbled, as they stooped together in the wet grass under the creaking branches. She kicked irritably at the soaking hem of her skirt under the shorter coat, and pushed a flying lock of hair from her face. 'I wish I could wear trousers. And have my hair cropped short.'

'And a right sight you'd look an' all!' She gave him a shove as he bent to pick up one of the green apples, and he fell, turned and grabbed at her, and they both howled with laughter.

'Pack it in, you two young uns!' Old Gough shouted automatically, and they grinned all the more, pulling conspiratorial faces at one another.

'Can you get away after tea?' Alice asked, her eyes winningly on him. 'We could go down on the beach after I've exercised Kitty.'

'Daft name for a hoss!' he teased, but he nodded at once.

She went out through the wide gate of the stable yard when she had finished grooming Kitty, and along the track, past the front gates of the hall, to the road that led down the hill to the village proper. At the end of the lane stretched Mine Row, the terrace of cottages that had been built for the mine workers more than fifty years ago. She ignored the front doors and the scoured doorsteps which were hardly ever used, and went along the dirt and cinder track leading to the small backyards. Several people smiled and nodded respectfully at her, and she returned their greetings sunnily.

Lou, Tommy's grown-up sister, was coming out of one of the closets opposite the back doors. She had a sackcloth pinny round her waist, and Alice could see the top half of a carelessly buttoned overall over her blouse. Her sleeves were turned back above her elbows, her dark hair untidily pinned up, with long, stray streamers curling about her head and neck. In one hand she was carrying an ash bucket with a small shovel fitted inside it.

''Ey up, Miss Alice! What you doin' round 'ere?'

'Hello, Lou. Is Tommy in? He said we'd go down to the beach this—'

'Tommy!' Lou roared, shoving open the paint-flaked, dark-brown door of the yard. Alice saw the tin bath hanging on its nail on the brickwork of the back wall of the cottage. 'Yer lady friend's 'ere for ye!' She turned, winked at the blushing Alice with a broad grin. 'You two walkin' out, are ye?' she teased, and Alice's colour intensified.

Tommy looked flustered, too, when he appeared hastily and said brusquely, 'Come on.' Louise's light mocking chuckle followed them. 'Yer shouldn't come callin' round to ours,' he muttered, moving hurriedly along the remainder of the row, down the gentle slope towards the cliff and the sea.

Alice felt a sudden anger. 'Why ever not?' He threw her a sullen look, made no answer.

They skirted the curve of the broad road which led down past Far Row, the smaller row of cottages which housed the accountant and store keeper for the mine, and then dropped down to the harbour and the workings. Instead, they took a narrow footpath off to the left, picked their way along the stubbled edge of the recently harvested cornfield. To their right, the land fell steeply away, the scrub-covered slope dropping to a long but narrow, uneven level of pasture which ran like a step in the cliff for about a hundred yards. This was Dalton's Meadow, named after the family who had held the farm tenancy for four generations and more.

They stayed on the upper path, and presently the cliff dropped in vertical, craggy magnificence 250 feet to the tumbled rock and dark shingle which showed now that the tide had receded. The curve of the port's breakwater, and the spidery network of the gantry, were behind them before they started to pick their way down the precarious, tiny track twisting its way down the steepness towards the beach far below.

'Tommy!' she squealed, in delicious terror, as she inevitably did, skittering down over the tufts of grass, her skirt flying, to crash into him, clutching and tumbling against him while he grabbed her waist to steady her, and she clung laughing, her head against his, her arms over his shoulders, while she got her breath.

'One o' these days yer'll knock us both clean ower!' he grumbled, and she loved the easy familiarity of his tone. Another five minutes and they were running about the soft shale of the beach, and picking their way between the giant slabs of rock. 'One day this 'ole lot'll come down,' Tommy informed her wisely. 'The 'all 'll be right on the edge of the cliff soon.'

'Mr Swales says it's about twenty feet a century,' she declared primly. 'At that rate, it'll take about six thousand years before we need to start worrying.' He turned, poked out his tongue, and bent to stare into one of the rock pools. 'We can get round the nab to Kingstaith before the tide comes in,' she went on. 'And walk back along the clifftop.'

They sat and he pulled off his boots and thick stockings, turning the tight bottoms of his britches up over his bony knees. The knees of the britches themselves were serviceably patched with cloth a shade darker than the brown of the rest of the material.

Alice followed suit, unlacing her own stout boots, then pushing up the gathered flounces of the hem of her white drawers to release the thick, black woollen stockings, peeling them off. She stuffed them into her boots, and, like him, tied the laces together and slung them round her neck. Finally, she stooped, and gathering up the wide, already water-stained hem of her skirt, and her petticoat, tucked and folded them under so that her limbs were free and her white drawers were on unselfconscious display. She invariably did this when they were messing about among the rocks, and Tommy was taken by surprise by the wave of uncomfortableness which assailed him.

He walked ahead, picking his way, investigating the more interesting of the mysterious frond-waving pools, gradually leading the way round the jutting arm of the cliff known as Nab Point, which separated the shallow wyke leading to Kingstaith from Port Hilda. As always, they kept a sharp eye out for exceptional fossils, for this part of the coast was an excellent area. Alice already had an impressive collection. 'Hey!' Tommy cried, swooping at the base of a flat boulder, and plucking up a jagged piece of stone. 'Look at this!' he said proudly, holding out his find.

She came close, bent her dark head to peer at it. 'Hm, good,' she said coolly. 'An ammonite. See those whorls? Dactyl something or other they're called. Mr Swales says they're common all along the Yorkshire coast.'

She gaped as he swung violently round and hurled it as far as he could out into the water. 'Aye!' he yelled, his face red, suffused with his anger. His accent was as thick as he could make it, belabouring her with it. 'Tha knaas ivverythin', tha does!'

The stretch of narrow shoreline between Port Hilda and the fishing village of Kingstaith was not greatly frequented, for access down to it from the cliff was not easy, and for a large part of the time it was covered by the tide. Many an unwary walker had had to struggle up beyond the advancing waves, and risk the real dangers of a rock skittering climb up the crumbling cliff face, or cling miserably to the precarious lower slopes and spend agonizingly long, spume-splashed hours waiting for the tide to go out again. If they were lucky enough to be seen and reported back to Kingstaith, the lifeboat would come out and pick them up, unless, as often happened, the sea was too rough for them to get close enough to at least get a man ashore with a line.

Tommy had gone trudging ahead leaving Alice shocked and dismayed at his outburst. She blinked after him, her eyes stinging, with that strange, physical, sick feeling in her stomach. Everyone, everything, seemed disturbingly different these days. He was thus the first to come across the startling sight of a gang of palely naked figures, clustered round, or perched upon, a huge, flat boulder, well up the slope of the beach, under the lee of the towering cliff. They had, even more oddly, been making scarcely any noise.

Tommy had time to observe that they were all boys, most of them about his age, some a little younger. As soon as they saw him, they began to call out in raucous challenge, and Tommy tensed for flight. Then he recognized one of them, the tallest. His sandy, cropped hair was marked by a recent ringworm scar, the small disc standing out whitely even on his light-coloured head. He was Geordie Bruce, one of the Kingstaith lads. One or two of the other faces began to look more familiar, and Tommy guessed they were all from the village.

He was not shocked at their nakedness. He himself had swum in the buff many a time. He had seen boys regularly swimming in the harbour thus, diving off the breakwaters. And in Whitby harbour, too, during the summer. But it was strange to find them here, in this deserted spot, for it was no good for swimming, in fact, downright dangerous, with the slope of beach and the pull of the tide. And certainly not the season for it, though the weather was quite mild after the storms, and under the cliff they were out of the breeze.

Still, their white and red bodies looked cold, some of them were visibly shivering, and they now started to complain with jovial loudness, shoving at one another. Their genitals, the little spouts of their penises under the still hairless bellies, had that shrivelled, raw, almost purple look. It was the sight of these that belatedly made Tommy swing round to cry out an instinctive warning, but Alice, her skirts ballooned about her hips, her white drawers emphasizing her skinny legs, boots still looped round her neck, came pattering up, to stand gawping open-mouthed at the spectacle.

'Oh!' she exclaimed inadequately. The boys clamped their cupped hands over their privates, and leaned jostlingly together on the stone's broad surface, legs crossed, hips bumping.

''Ey up! Tell yer girlfriend ter bugger off.' One or two of them broke from the group and ran hobblingly up the stony beach, their tight little buttocks flashing, so that Alice thought dazedly how beautiful they looked.

'Don't be silly!' a deep voice boomed. 'You've nothing to be ashamed of. You look a darned sight prettier than her with her silly knickers showing!'

Alice gasped again. Both she and Tommy stared at an imposingly large figure whom they had not initially noticed. It was female, they realized, from the hint of large, curved bosom under the loose grey smock. The rest of the dress was strangely androgynous. A large, extremely floppy black tam was pulled over the head and tilted sharply to one side. There seemed to be some sort of high-necked jersey under the smock, which ended at mid thigh, and from under the flapping ends emerged a pair of thick cord britches, tucked into a turned-down pair of thick, ribbed, worsted stockings, over broad, sturdy, laced shoes.

She was working at an easel set up on a cleared, flat patch right under the cliff, and Tom deduced she was one of the weird group which had only recently descended on Kingstaith, and swiftly become the subject of much local, delightedly scandalized gossip; men and women, all gentry, who had rented some of the delapidated cottages right down by the harbour, and went round painting everything, and everybody they could persuade with shillings to pose for them, and spent their nights drinking and carousing and doing far worse things to people they were not even married to. So the gossip ran, anyway.

'Gerrin' a good eyeful are ye, lass?' Alice turned away, her face burning. Belatedly, she scrabbled and shook out her skirt and petticoat, letting them fall into place, keeping her back towards the boys, who now broke up and scampered to the pile of clothing at the foot of the brown cliff.

'That's one of old Guthrie's lasses, i'n it?' a voice hissed.

'So what? She got no right ter come gawpin' at us.'

Someone else sniggered, they pushed one another, staggering as they pulled on ragged clothes. 'Bet she's seen nowt like it, eh?'

Diplomatically, the uncomfortable Tommy exchanged wary greetings with Geordie. He responded condescendingly. ''Oway, lads. Off back. We'll tek yer gear back wi' us, Rosie, if yer like. Drop it off at the cottage for ye.'

'Right. Thank you, lads. You were turning a bit blue, anyway. I may want some of you to pose tomorrow, if we get a fine day. All right?' Quickly, she packed away a large box of paints and brushes, stowed the palette in with them, folded up the wooden easel. She rolled up the thick paper which had been resting on it, and slipped it inside a cylindrical leather tube. 'There we are.'

Several of them took up her things, grinned, waved casual hands. 'Bye, Rosie. See yer.'

Alice and Tommy were privately shocked at this first name familiarity. They could not guess the age of this individual, though her large, fleshy, open face looked quite young still. Certainly nowhere near their parents' ages. And, despite her eccentric dress, she was well spoken, her deep attractive tones those of a lady. She seemed to have recovered her good humour entirely after her brief irritation at the abrupt interruption.

'I normally just sketch outdoors if I'm doing people, but I was having bother with the light. The effect of it on their skins, bless 'em. Thought I'd have a go at getting it. Bit ambitious, really. Oh, sorry! And sorry if I sounded a bit tetchy just now. My name's Rose Dwyer. Rosie, they call me. As you heard.' She held out her hand, for all the world as if they were grown ups, and, embarrassed, they shook it. It was large, and red, and felt capably strong. They muttered their names.

'You're still at school. What do your folks do?'

'I don't go to school,' Alice offered, as all three began to move along the beach in the direction of the jumble of rocks over which they would have to scramble to reach the fishing village and its harbour. 'I have a tutor comes in. My father owns the mine back at Port Hilda. Tommy's father works on the jetty.'

Rose Dwyer's eyebrows rose slightly, but she said nothing. 'You two are chums, are you?'

Alice nodded. 'Yes, we are.' She waited. Tommy said nothing. He looked away, out towards the sea, where the line of mist was already gathering on the horizon. Again, Alice had that sickly, disturbed sensation.

'You're a handsome couple,' Rose Dwyer puffed, climbing, with some groaning difficulty, over the first of the tumbled rocks. 'I'd love to paint you some time. The pair of you. Would you let me? I'd pay you, of course.'

'You mean—' Alice stopped, her cheeks grew hot.

Rose chuckled, reaching out, and playfully ruffled the tangled dark hair. 'Well,' she conceded, with pretended reluctance, 'you could keep your clothes on if you insisted.'

Alice giggled. 'We'd like that, wouldn't we, Tommy?'

'Come on. We'd better get goin',' he said, baldly.

'I'm at Gutter's End. Just behind the pub. Salmon Cottage. Pop in any time. I love visitors, especially youngsters. Even if you don't want me to make you immortal,' she laughed.

On the way back, this time following the path along the top of the cliff, Tommy trudged ahead, silent once more, until Alice suddenly reached forward, grabbed at his arm, pulling him round so that he stumbled, was forced to stop.

'Pack it in!' he shouted, and again she saw that blaze in his eyes, the eyes she loved because they were so large, so gentle always.

'What's wrong?' she asked. He saw her lips quiver, the lower one curled. They looked thin and very dark. Her eyes were huge, and swimming with sudden tears. All at once, she thought of those white, slim bodies, those tiny curls of their sex, the flat, tight buttocks, and shivered at the memory of their grace. Her throat closed, she swallowed hard. Her voice, when it came, was a scratchy whisper. 'You said I know everything, Tommy. I don't know anything. Not a thing.'

His fingers dug into the softness of her upper arms painfully as he pulled her close. He kissed her, hard, his lips on hers, pressing, staying there, until she felt the pain of her teeth mashing against the wet softness.

25 APRIL, 1941

1

'There's no doubt, Maggie. I got the results of the test yesterday. I've been going mad with worry.'

'Oh, you poor bairn! Come here!' Maggie Turner's arms were held out, and Helena moved forward, on to her knees on the worn rug, practically flung herself into the embrace, resting her head gratefully on Maggie's breast. The tears came then, in great, rushing gouts, the sobs shaking her, while she clung on, and Maggie rocked her gently, soothing her with the murmured, 'There there, there there,' until Helena was comforted like a child by the tenderness.

It was only later that Helena was able to appreciate the vital warmth of this gesture, her need for the flow of immediate love, unchecked, with no trace of condemnation, or chiding, or even doubt. Just a spontaneous giving of the care and affection she was so in need of at such a frightening, lonely time. Of course, she already knew, and valued, Maggie's close friendship, which had been offered and returned so quickly in the brief four months they had known each other.

The fearful uncertainty of the times had helped. When the wailing sirens had become a regular nightmare, not long after she had moved into Prospect Mount, Maggie was always there, at the foot of those uppermost stairs, torch waving, to make sure she was up and ready to join them down in the damp chill of the cellar. Usually, there was only Maggie and Vicky and Helena, and either

Mr Johnson or Mr Moody, the lodgers from the floor below Helena, one or the other of whom was generally on duty fire watching. Every so often, Alf might be home, though he spent the vast majority of the time at one of the Royal Ordnance factories further north, or across in Leeds. 'Might as well have joined up,' Maggie grumbled resignedly, on more than one occasion.

The bombers came over the north-east coast, and the alarmingly martial sounds they frequently heard were the AA guns of the coastal defences, for the bombers saved their lethal loads for more choice targets further inland. But it didn't stop the sirens shrieking, and keeping them up for long night hours, nor the worry that one night a plane might decide to unload its bombs on them for a change.

Maggie kept a supply of hot-water bottles and extra blankets ready to pick up before they descended the steep wooden stairs. There was a camp bed, and two narrow, webbed bunk beds against one wall. Vicky climbed into the top one, the bottom one was for Helena, but generally the two women couldn't sleep, and spent the long hours sitting huddled under blankets in companionable snugness, whispering, heads together. Maggie was a good and interested listener, and Helena found she was almost looking forward to these whispered confessions in the cold night.

She was soon talking close to her heart, of the happiness, and the sorrow, of her deep love for the young sailor Maggie had briefly met. 'I know I'm only eighteen, but I know how I feel, and I know we're not going to change, either of us.' Unconsciously, she was clinging tightly to Maggie's hand, and, perhaps unconsciously, too, she felt the responsive quiver, the sudden stillness of perfect understanding, and sympathy. 'These days – things are so – uncertain. I'm scared, Maggie. I want to be with him.' Maggie gave a small sigh, and the young girl was flooded with a feeling of warmth and closeness as they hugged tightly.

It was not surprising, therefore, as the April shower shook and rattled the window panes up in the roof, behind the draught-sealing thickness of the black curtains, that Helena should turn to the landlady who had become her friend and confidante now that she faced the greatest crisis, and greatest joy, of her young life.

'There's no doubt?' Maggie Turner said automatically, stroking the back of the dark head, feeling the wetness of tears through her blouse. She felt the head shake. 'When's the baby due?' she asked next, refusing the word 'it', stepping round it in her mind.

'November. About the middle of November.' Helena raised her face, still kneeling, pressed against Maggie's legs. Her tearstained cheeks, her brown eyes, were only inches from Maggie's gaze. She blushed, but didn't look away, or flinch. 'It must have been that weekend in February. You remember. He had that forty-eight-hour pass.' The colour deepened. 'It wasn't the first time. That was at Christmas. Christmas Day, in fact.' Her head dipped, she looked at Maggie so sheepishly, with such an innocently guilty, crooked little grin, that they both burst into tremulous laughter, their brows touching, the tears starting again from both of them.

The confession went on, on genuinely tender ground now. 'He came back,' Helena murmured softly. 'That Friday night. He waited, and I sneaked down. Let him in.'

Maggie nodded. Her dark eyes shone with the sparkle of her tears. 'I know, love. I heard you.' Is it my fault? the older woman asked herself, then gathered the weeping girl to her once again, squeezing her in a longing to shut out all the pain she knew lay ahead. She nuzzled at the salt of tear drops, brushed with her fingers at the damp tendrils of the black hair.

'I'm not ashamed!' Helena declared fiercely, when they had recovered sufficiently. 'I want his baby more than anything else in the world. I just don't want him to be worried by it all. He's got enough to be worried about, keeping himself safe for us.'

'You've got to tell him, though, love.' Helena stared, a little surprised at the passion in Maggie's voice. 'I mean, he'll be able to get leave soon, won't he? So's you can be wed. That's the important thing.'

'I'm not ashamed of this baby!' Helena repeated vehemently. 'We love each other—'

'I know, I know,' Maggie crooned, holding her again, stroking. 'But for the baby's sake – for all your sakes. He'll want to marry you, as soon as he knows, won't he?'

Helena smiled radiantly, nodded. 'Yes. There's plenty of time, though. Before November. He'll be getting some more leave in the summer—'

'You have to let him know right away, Helen! You owe him that. Tell him you're all right. That everything's going to be fine. You can stop here. We'll take care of you. Just tell him. Right away. Promise me.'

'Yes, all right, of course I will.' Helena smiled fondly at Maggie's anxiety, then her face assumed a deeply serious expression as, once more within inches of Maggie's, the eyes filled with new tears. She leaned forward, offering her lips, and they kissed gently, slowly. 'I love you,' she whispered unsteadily. 'I'm so glad I've got you.' She thought of her own parents, and the drops fell, sparkling, down the glistening curves of her cheeks.

2

Helena stood facing her parents, like a prisoner at the bar. Her face was almost grey, drawn with her anxiety, her eyes red, the shadows emphasized, the lids swollen with her grief. The small handkerchief she was twisting about her fingers was soaking. Her gesture, and the careworn lines on her tragic face, made her look younger than her years, and she felt as helpless as a child before the weight of their hostility. She had her back to the glow of the fire; she could feel its heat falling on the backs of her calves through her stockings, on her body through the thickness of winter clothes.

The heavy comfort of the front parlour, the solidity of the deep armchairs, the long sofa, with their pristine, lace-backed rectitude, was a solemn setting which was perhaps appropriate for this important moment. Helena would have preferred the weekday, cosier warmth of the large kitchen, where they generally took their meals, and sat around the high fire of the range, reading, or listening to the wireless. But then, there was no warmth in this occasion. It had been building up for weeks, from the time she had left home nearly two months ago.

The setting was, after all, doubly appropriate, for it was here that they entertained guests, and certainly she felt, had been made to feel, that she no longer belonged here, to them. Her mother had cried when Helena had ruined the already tense atmosphere of the Christmas holiday by announcing her intention to move out. She had expected, or even hoped somewhere in her mind, for an outburst of fury from her father, but Joseph Barr was too controlled for that. 'Let her go,' was all he had said, contemptuously. Good riddance, he might have added, his daughter felt.

He was sneeringly dismissive of her plans. 'You're giving up a good job, with good prospects, to go scrubbing floors and emptying bedpans at the hospital? No wonder Philip Surtees thinks you're barmy! He's not far wrong. You think that's going to make a more worthwhile contribution to the war than what you're doing?'

She wished fervently then that she could get much further away than the nine miles down the dale to Whitby, thought desperately of going to see if she could volunteer for one of the women's services she would probably be conscripted into when the time came. Briefly, she envied Ernie, in spite of the harsh routine, the discomfort, of life aboard ship, with the long patrols in the brutal northern waters, where the enemy was the savage weather, and returning 'home' meant the windswept bleakness of Scapa. But at least in Whitby she would be ready for when he could make his precious escape for a few days. They would be together, and that was all that mattered to her.

' She was more committed than ever, absolutely sure of herself, and him, after that wonderful, uncomfortable, momentous Christmas night in the strangeness of that musty bedroom, in a stranger's bed. She had grown up then, for sure, was able to face her mother's weak tears, her father's contempt. To stand up to him, which she had always been afraid to do as a child.

'Why on earth do you need to move out? You already work in Whitby. It's not as if you're not used to the travelling.'

'I'll be working shifts,' she explained, striving not to sound sullen in her answers. 'Maybe nights, or late turns. The trains are hopeless these days, you know that.'

'Got it all worked out, haven't you?' her father concluded. 'No point in arguing.'

But now, with February winds shaking the solid red brick house high on Kilbeck Side, dug in solidly near the top of the long hill over the village below, Helena was sinkingly aware that there would be argument in plenty. She had felt it from the moment she climbed up from the station, with her small case. She had paid several duty visits to her home. This one was for a whole weekend, and the dragging reluctance in her steps, before which the shaded torch flickered over the familiar ground, was not caused solely by the breathtaking pull of the long climb.

That Friday night, late as it was, they were careful not to approach the chasm that lay yawningly between them, but tiptoed around with polite caution. 'And how's Ernest?' Lizzy asked, with that ringingly false brightness in her voice, as though she were enquiring about someone she knew from the WI.

'Fine. Except for the atrocious weather they're having when they go out.' She smiled bravely. 'At least it keeps them from danger – of bumping into any enemy, I mean. He says they can hardly find their own way about, let alone find anybody else.' Diplomatically, she steered towards safety. 'How's things at school, Dad? How are you coping?'

The expected, and in many cases, dreaded, influx of evacuee children had begun, soon after the first raids had started the previous September on London and the south of England. Joseph grimaced, and shook his greying head. 'We're up to thirty-five extra now. And only Miss Gibbons as extra staff. Most of them are from Tyneside, so there's the language barrier as well. Little heathens, most of them! How on earth they cope, teaching in the cities beats me!'

Joseph studiously refrained from including her when he gave the summons for Elspeth to go 'off to bed' at ten o'clock. Kit, their young brother, had already dragged reluctantly up the stairs an hour and a half previously. There was a return of the tension crackling in the warm air of the kitchen when Helena was left alone with her parents, but still no one said anything. Her father's paper rustled loudly. Helena scooped up the playing cards from the table cloth, patted them together and slid them into the packet. 'Actually, I think I'll go up, if you don't mind. It'll be a change to get an undisturbed night.' Already, people had become blasé about the siren out here in the countryside. They rarely bothered to get up, even if they heard its wailing.

Joseph was reaching for the clock from the high mantelshelf, under which the tea towels were hanging. She went to him unthinkingly, then crimsoned as she sensed the tension in him, his stiff stillness. It was too late to withdraw her gesture, and she stabbed a hasty, pursed-lipped token at his right ear, before swinging away to her mother, who put her hands out briefly, touching her elbows. ''Night, dear. God bless.'

A night light was burning, and she wriggled swiftly out of her clothes, shivering violently, her breath steamy in the cold. She was glad of the winceyette nightgown, and even gladder of Elspeth's curved and accommodating back, into which she snuggled. Her younger sister put her hands over the wrists which were crossed at her waist. Elspeth was wide awake, and eager to chat. With the self-centredness of someone who was only three weeks away from her sixteenth birthday, most of her talk at first was concerned with school and boys and the latest scandals of the village. It was only after these were exhausted that her thoughts turned to her sister and her problems. 'And how's Ernest? Still the grand passion of your life?' She wriggled round suddenly, and, thrusting a leg between Helena's thighs, pressed her body in lewd parody against her, chuckling salaciously. 'You going to give your little sister some tips on how to make love to a man?' As Helena struggled free of her embrace and shoved her vigorously away, she felt the gulf of experience which now divided them, and the clutch of trepidation at the thought of how completely she now belonged to him, body and soul.

A thin covering of snow fell on the moor tops the following day, and Helena, Elspeth and Kit went for a long, rambling trek over the high curve of Kilbeck Rig. They came back weary and laughing with carefree youth, and Helena felt nostalgically at home again. Until, late at night, after brother and sister had gone up, the summons had come, and she faced her mother and father in the inquisitorial atmosphere of the front room.

'We have to talk, Helena,' Joseph began portentously. She had started by sitting, rather nervously perched on the edge of the big armchair, while they sat, as though to emphasize their solid alliance, side by side on the sofa. After a while, when the discussion grew emotively heated, Helena jumped up, swung angrily to and fro in the confined space.

'You seem to be absolutely besotted with this young man,' her father exclaimed. 'You obviously find it impossible to think clearly. I can understand you feeling flattered. The first man ever to pay you any attention. To find you – attractive.'

She felt herself colouring up. 'Attractive?' She spat the word back at him. 'It's not just—' She paused, her face flamed. Oh, why, why couldn't she speak honestly? she cried inwardly. She could say it all so eloquently to herself, inside herself. 'I've known – I've had boys who found me attractive before. It's not just that. It's – it's much more.'

'You're eighteen, Helena,' her mother said, in that gallingly reasoned tone. 'I know you think you're very grown up, sophisticated even. Girls do, especially nowadays, when everything's so unsettled. But you've got to realize – you've had no experience at all. Just wait—'

'I don't want to wait. I love him. He loves me. We're certain. It doesn't matter how long we wait, it won't—'

Her father pounced, like a lawyer seizing a chance. 'Well then! If it doesn't matter, then that's just what you can do. Wait. I must say he seems a very impatient young man. You know he's written to us?' He made a soft click of disgust, for which she hated him, felt sick, then deeply ashamed, at the pure loathing spreading through her, crawling over her body until she could feel the hairs standing on end. 'If you could call it a letter! More like a note to the baker. Saying he wants to become engaged! Huh!'

'Yes, I agree,' she returned, the tears flashing, her head held up aggressively. 'It's ridiculous. Why bother with all that? I just want to be married to him. A special licence. We can do it when he gets leave. In the summer.'

Her mother gave a muffled exclamation of horror or distress. Joseph gave vent to his explosive anger. 'Stuff and nonsense! Married? Good God! You're a child, still, and this stupid behaviour proves it beyond all doubt. You'll not get married as long as you're under our jurisdiction. And we can stop you, don't think we can't, young lady! Of all the harebrained schemes I ever heard, this takes the biscuit! All right. So you've never made much of the opportunities we've given you. Threw away the chance of a higher education, of bettering yourself. I've had to stand by while you wasted those opportunities. You've no idea what a bitter disappointment that was to me. Not that you care about such things, I realize that. I see very clearly just how much you value our opinions, our advice. But to watch you positively lowering yourself—'

'Oh, yes! That's it, isn't it?' Her head tossed, her eyes flashed now with rage, she stood there in front of the hearth, struggling to express herself over the anguish building within. 'He's not good enough for me, that's what it is! You think he's common! A common fisherman, too low for us high and mighty folk! Let me tell you, he's worth ten of – of – anyone I've met round here before!'

Her father stood, quickly, then, ashamed perhaps at such an abrupt display of feeling, moved with elaborate courtesy around her, and, with careful precision, shovelled out needless coals and spread them on the fire. 'Oh, I don't know,' he said, in that cold, perfectly controlled sneer. 'From the way you're behaving right now, I can see you fitting in admirably with the other screeching fishwives of Kingstaith. Tell me. Will he expect you to wear a bonnet and sit on the doorstep selling crabs? You'll have to get used to having your picture taken in the summer.'

She began to sob. 'You cuh-can ask him yourself!' she cried, feeling wretchedly childish and beaten. 'He's coming in a fuh-fortnight's time. He's got a weekend leave!'

'I don't think so,' her father replied coldly. 'I won't have the likes of him in my house. Nor you, as long as you continue to consort with him.'

3

Helena crept in an agony of fear down the dark staircase, keeping the small disc of light from the torch close to her frozen, stockinged feet. The measured tick of the clock in the hall was appallingly loud. One for every hundred thumps of her racing heart, it seemed. The rings on the heavy blackout curtain squeaked as she drew it slowly aside, and she felt the cold sweat inside her clothing. The click of the key turning in the half-glassed door leading to the porch, the protesting screech and thud of the bolts in the outer door, boomed and echoed in the guilt-ridden dimness. The cold swept in, enveloped her.

'Ernie!' she whispered, gasping with fright, yet felt tearfully weak with relief at his black shape which loomed immediately on her summons. 'Don't make a sound!' she breathed needlessly, going through the ritual of locking up once more with fresh, agonized slowness. She led the way, clutching his hand, towing him along, up the softly creaking minefield of the endless flights of stairs. By the time, they were behind the locked door of her own attic room, she was drenched with perspiration, and shivering jellyishly.

She put her finger over his lips, then they were crushingly pressing together, their mouths roughly open, worrying at each other in the desperation of their passion. Oh God, she prayed, don't let there be a raid tonight, please, please! The coal fire was glowing redly, she had lit several candles, and the room was a rosy haven, a heaven, the first they had ever shared. She was swept by a deep embarrassment, and a helpless anger at herself for feeling thus, but unable to do anything about it, until, with a clumsy but new and wonderful tenderness, his large hands moved worshipfully, struggling with buttons, sleeves, tugging, lifting, dealing even with the intricacies of girdle and suspenders, and stockings, while she lay compliant all the while, trembling, as much with her need as her embarrassment and fear.

Presently, she was naked, glowing pinkly in the firelight, and she watched shyly, fascinated, while he undressed. It was the first time they had seen each other's bodies properly. She *was* afraid, initially, at the unmistakably evident sexual desire for her, but wondrously loving, too. Then it was rapture, the feel of warm flesh, bodies stretching, touching, exploring, secret no longer, lips touching, tongues tasting, the feeling growing, frightening, wonderful, thought slipping to hungry need, to melting sensation, and he was in her, touching her until she knew she was wet and ready for him, and his thrusting hardness was in her hand, and she was open, crying with the need for him.

The pain did not matter, she wanted it, didn't want him ever to leave her, then all her awareness, even of him, was shatteringly gone for an eternal instant, and she shook and sobbed, torn and lost in a blaze of terrifying release, the awareness coming back to a briefly fearsome crushing, plunging ordeal, then the surge of him coming, and the love flooded back, with his fluid, and hers, and her tears of total joy and union.

The bed sheets were like icy water, for she had forgotten to put the hot-water bottle in, but they giggled and hugged, as close to each other as bodies could get. She tried and tried to push the idea of time passing out of her mind.

She had met him from the train in Whitby station, they had drifted happily through the already blacked-out streets, up the hill, slipping on the frosty pavement. She made a point of taking him along the passage when she let them in to the house, to Maggie, who was sitting as usual in her kitchen. Vicky was there, and he had teased the girl gallantly, enjoyed the romantic image he cut in front of the females.

Upstairs, alone, they had kissed, passionately, and longed to do more, but, by mutual consent, resisted. 'Come back at eleven,' Helena told him. 'I'll come and let you in.'

Now, deliriously happy at the feeling of his protective, enfolding body about hers, she tried to keep telling herself not to think of clocks, of time moving inexorably onward. An eternity, they had. All day tomorrow. All night, too, if it were possible. His train did not leave until noon on Sunday. Thirty-six hours. An eternity. She clung to him even more tightly.

They were dozing when the siren sounded, and she clung to him in fright and indecision. There was still a strong glow from the fire, and she struggled with great effort out of the cocooning warmth of the nest they had made, fumbled in a drawer for a nightdress, pulled it on, then slipped on the thick, check dressing-gown, as she heard movement below.

She held up a warning finger, went to the door as a door below

opened, and Maggie's voice called, 'Helen! There they go again.'
There was a fractional pause, a beam of light swung up at her
fleetingly, left her again. 'Listen. I'm shattered. I'm going back to
bed. You can go down to the cellar if you want, but I'm risking it.
I'm going to let Vicky sleep on, too. Why don't you nip back to
bed? Keep warm? If they choose tonight of all nights to drop a
bomb on Prospect Mount, too bad! I'll see you in Heaven, right?'

'Right.' Happily, convinced that fortune, or God, smiled on
lovers, she dived back into the warmth, his waiting arms.

4

'Still walkin' out, then?' Sophie Wheatley asked, the disapproval
clear though unexpressed. Helena glanced down at her fingers,
twisting away in her lap, and blushed miserably.

Ernie leapt in to the fray gallantly. 'Aye, that's right, Mam. An'
ah know 'ow lucky I am an' all!'

'And what do *your* folks think of you goin' out with our Ernie?'
she pressed, ignoring his interjection.

Helena stammered, reached for the flowered teacup, with its
gold-painted rim, part of the 'best set', saved for ceremonial
occasions, then wished she hadn't, for her hands were shaking
badly. 'Well, they think I'm a bit young,' she temporized, feeling
like a prisoner pinned down on the rack, aware of the implacable
eyes on her.

'Ah'll bet the' none too pleased, eh?' May, Reg's wife, put in
sharply. 'Yer da bein' the 'eadmaster at t' village school, like.'

'The'll come round,' Ernie said bluntly, striving to end the
interrogation.

'Yer not livin' at 'ome now, that right?' May pursued
vindictively. She paused, just long enough, then went on with
wicked innocence, 'What time did yer train get in this mornin',
Ernie?'

'Before *you* were out of bed, that's fer sure!' he retorted hotly.

'Eh! Watch it, young un,' Reg growled. 'Don't come the big 'ard
matelot, sonny Jim. Yer still nobbut a bairn. Like 'er.' He nodded

at the mortified Helena, who felt as though she were on fire. She remained staring down at the cooling tea, her eyes stinging. 'Yer'll be comin' into t' Anchor tonight, won't tha?' Reg continued. 'The's a crowd o t' lads lookin' forward t' seein' thee. Yer mates,' he added, with heavy emphasis.

'Naw, ah doubt it,' Ernie answered dismissively. 'I'm off over to Helen's place tonight. Might stop over if it gets too late.'

'Oh aye?' May commented, with blatant disbelief.

'You can probably get back late!' Helena blurted, her dark eyes large, wounded.

'Ah should 'ope so,' Sophia murmured reproachfully. 'Ye've 'ardly set foot in t' door an' yer off out agin. We shall 'ave 'ardly seen yer, an' yer off back temorrer.'

Helena hurried ahead, down the uneven, wide steps, and the treacherous cobbles when they made their escape. Ernie came after her, reached out to catch her arm. 'Whoa there! Hold yer horses, missus!' She didn't meet his gaze, looked away, to the closing white mist which hugged the shoreline in the gloomy afternoon. They turned left, forced to slow as they started the steep climb up the High Street. 'Sorry about that,' he offered awkwardly, holding on to her arm.

All at once, she turned, pressed herself against him, uncaring who should see, and wept on his chest, hidden in the big lapels of his service greatcoat. 'Oh, Ernie! Isn't there anybody who can be happy for us? Doesn't anyone want us to—'

'Yes! There's us. We're 'appy fer us, aren't we?' He pulled up her jaw, kissed her hard on her upturned mouth. 'And that's all we need,' he said fiercely, squeezing her to him. She nodded, sniffled back her tears, and took comfort in the strength of his arm which now looped round her waist as they trudged on, up the long hill, past the Bethel Chapel, and the Wesleyan on the opposite side, to Bank Top, and the red brick of the station buildings.

From the gritty black cobbles of the yard, they went into the damp of the waiting-room, no larger than a hut, with the scored, paint-chipped benches round three of its sides. Two giggling girls, about their age, were huddled in there, hair crimped and waved into place, their scent strong in the confined space. Clearly they were heading for a Saturday evening out on the town in Whitby.

'Listen,' Helena said bravely, her knees touching his on the narrow seat. 'Why don't you stop here? Just put me on the train. It would please your mam. She's right. They're hardly going to see anything of you. It isn't fair. I can understand how she feels.'

She saw the line of his jaw harden, stand out. He shrugged slightly. 'Ah've told you, lass. It cannot be helped. You and me's what matters. There just isn't time. If they'd made the effort it'd be different, mebbes. We're a pair, you an' me. We go together. And if they don't like us, they'll 'ave ter lump us.' He ignored the sidelong, sniggering glances of the girls, and put his arm boldly over her shoulder, pulling her into him.

'Your folk are just as bad,' he said, into her dark hair as she leaned against him. 'They're spitin' themselves. If it wasn't fer the war an' that—' He sat up straighter, as though shaking himself, and smiled at her. 'They'll come round to us eventually, love. Meantime, we've got ter mek the most of it. And in the summer we're gettin' married, whatever 'appens. Yer dad can't stop us. We can get a special licence. Just you and me. That's all we need ter be there, eh?' He kissed her, and the two girls went into a paroxysm of giggles, shoving at each other in delight.

When they went out onto the little platform, already hazy in the mist closing in all the time, one of the pair came up boldly, saucy eyes flashing, looking with smiling challenge at Helena. 'Can we touch yer collar, Sailor?' Her companion snorted through her nose in scandalized glee.

Ernie flipped open his heavy coat, slipped it back a little way so that the blue jean collar with the three thin stripes showed. 'Go on then, but be gentle wi' me, won't yer?'

5

'Yer know what they say about this fuckin' place, doncha?' Eddie Collinson came clattering down the steel companion-way to Mess 35. He was clad in a towel which was draped round his hips like a loincloth. His jutting belly, liberally covered with the black curls which spread over most of his body surface, hung over his sole garment proudly. 'Nine months winter and three months very bad weather!' He dropped the metal bucket full of dhobi in front of his locker. The towel slipped, fell at his feet.

'For Christ's sake, put it away, Eddie,' someone called from the group at the wooden mess table which ran almost the whole length of the mess along the curving outer bulkhead. The two scuttles were firmly clamped shut, their covers fastened, so that the only light, apart from the shaft of filtered daylight which came from the hatchway at the head of the ladder leading to the deck above, was provided by the overhead bulbs, which were wreathed in their customary fog of thick smoke. The tobacco smells mingled exotically with the subtly lingering aromas of the lunch of several hours ago. In one dimmed recess of the mess, angled off by the gleaming, silver-coloured double rows of lockers, several hammocks were up, the inhabitants of which, watchkeepers, slept on through the din.

Eddie Collinson turned to face the assembly, spread his legs, knees bent, and gyrated his hips, shook his belly like an eastern dancer. His squat red penis, under the luxuriant black bush, waggled and rotated obscenely as he thrust his loins forward. 'Gettin' you excited, dearies, is it?' he cooed.

Ernie Wheatley gave a mock groan, turned from the wooden bench at the inboard side of the table, glanced over his shoulder. 'Careful. Yer brain's showin' again.'

'Watch it, yer gormless fuckin' fisherman!' Eddie stooped, picked up the damp towel and flicked it at Ernie's neck. He swung round, staggering as he tried to rise and grab at the towel, but Eddie had turned away, was rummaging in his locker. 'Bet it'd drive that posh lady friend of yours wild, this would. Bet she's seen nothin' like it. Not from you, anyways.'

'Yer right there, old son. Ah'm not a sick old pervy like you. Some of us are decent, not that you'd know owt about that.'

Eddie shook his head sadly. He bent, stepped into a pair of pusser's underpants of hugely generous proportions. 'Of course! I should've known.' He appealed to the other members of the mess emotionally. 'The poor young sprog 'ere still thinks it's for pissin' out of.' He moved towards Ernie, his arms held out to embrace him in a bear hug. 'Come and let your old sea daddy tell you the facts of life, me boy!'

'Stay away from me, you old beefer!' Ernie yawned loudly, stubbed out his cigarette in the large metal spitkid half filled with sand, one of several dotted about the messdeck. 'Christ! I 'ope we can get ashore temorrer. We've got that game to play with Comms yet.' They had been at anchor back in the wide reaches of Scapa Flow for two days now, enjoying the break from the exhausting and dreary routine of patrolling the inhospitable waters of the North Sea as the flagship of Vice Admiral Holland's squadron, to prevent Germany's capital ships, such as the *Scharnhorst*, *Gneisenhau*, *Bismarck*, or *Prinz Eugen*, from breaking out into the Atlantic and wreaking havoc on the vital convoys.

But though they were always initially glad to thread their way through the narrows and drop anchor in the windswept expanse of water off Hoy, with the small islets strung out around them, there was little to offer in the way of runs ashore. A few bleak soccer pitches, a fleet canteen with ropy beer and ropier hours, and an old fleet auxiliary which sometimes housed variety shows. Apart from that, there were impromptu pulling and sailing contests between chummy ships, and films which could be shown on board.

Ernie decided to clear his head by taking a turn on deck, pulling on his thick seaman's jersey before he made his way on to the upper deck. Though this was the first week in May, and the sun was shining brightly, the stiff breeze could still cut murderously through clothing. He found a sheltered spot under the lee of X turret, and stared out at the low, green and brown humps of the land off to his right. This large metal box against which he was leaning was his action station. He was part of the turret crew, along with the 'bootnecks', the Royal Marines, who made up the majority of the gun crews on a ship as large as *Hood*, even in wartime.

She was a self-contained community. Ninety-five officers, over 1,300 men. That must be more than the number of folk that lived in Kingstaith, he would guess. And a darned sight more varied, coming as they did from all parts of the British Isles, with a few Paddies thrown in. She was old now, originally laid down in 1918 to take part in the last lot – a spanking new battle cruiser, 41,000 tons, eight 15in guns ready to hurl enormous death more than twenty miles, with an admitted speed of twenty-five knots, which meant considerably more at full ahead.

He looked up at the twin monstrous barrels under which he was sitting. Canvas covers were stretched over their gaping mouths, to lessen the effect of spray damage at sea. They were not removed now when they sailed into harbour. Not when word could come through at any time to get up steam and head out again. They didn't bother removing them for action, either. Flimsy canvas didn't impede the progress of the lethal projectiles, and was cheap enough to replace.

Gazing up at the vastness of them soaring way overhead, it was hard to imagine that such steel and iron solidity, a miniature city with over 1,400 inhabitants, could be anything but invulnerable. Yet if he cared to make the long climb up the series of ladders leading to the lofty height of the flag deck he would be able to see the spot where the *Royal Oak* had been sunk eighteen months ago in October '39, by a U-boat which had penetrated the 'impregnable' defences of the remote anchorage. The battleship had been 'dead unlucky' they said. The anti-submarine defences had not been completed at that early stage. It couldn't happen again, they said. Ernie was inclined to be a little sceptical of such assurances. In the words of one of the most popular choruses he liked to bellow at the sods' opera sing-alongs the ship's welfare committee was forever organizing – 'Oh no, not fucking much!'

Still, no good worrying about torpedoes punching holes below the water-line. They were probably right. You probably were dead unlucky if you happened to get in the way of one of those things. In the wrong place at the wrong time, that's what it amounted to. And chances were, unless you really *were* in the wrong spot, you'd have time to get into one of the boats or grab hold of a Carley float before she went down anyway.

No, the real problem was the one they were out there looking for, and getting chucked about like peas in a tin can – the Jerry battleships and cruisers reputed to be penned up in Brest and the Baltic. And long may they stay there, he wished devoutly. It was funny to think of all those Jerry matelots, spitting and polishing, doing their dhobi, writing letters home, going out on the piss. And all praying for exactly the same thing. That they didn't have to go out and face some British bastard lobbing 15in shells at them.

He was facing the stern. Below him was the top of Y-turret, with its periscope sticking up – they'd really be in the what's-it if they ever got to the stage where they had to rely on that thing for sighting the flaming guns – and beyond, the quarter deck, with the ensign flying from the stern because they were in harbour. Although he was a 'Hostilities Only' rating, he knew well that things would have been vastly different in peacetime. Officer of the Watch in frock coat, telescope under his arm. Side boys and other flunkeys in attendance, boats whizzing up and down, scoured white planking.

Thoughts of the upper deck brought his mind back to the unpleasant contemplation of enemy action. The popular 'buzz' was that the armour plating of the upper deck was far too thin, and this would be a grave problem should they be unfortunate enough to be hit by an enemy bomb. 'Straight through and out the fuckin' bottom, mate!' was how Eddie Collinson, Mess 35's comedian, put it. He had grinned at Ernie. 'Us lads next to the magazines! Well.' He shook his head and clicked his teeth expressively. 'Won't be enough left to put in an envelope to send home.'

Ernie stood up, glanced across the water, coming out of the shelter of the turret, to stand near the guard rail for a last look around. He could not help a stirring of appreciative pride at the sleek lines of the *Prince of Wales*, at anchor well away from them on the starboard quarter. The towering superstructure of the bridge and flag deck was already scarcely more than a dark silhouette against the cream and pale yellow of the spring sky. It looked slender and delicate, and from it rose the slim pointer of the foremast and its two horizontal yards, with the webbing of the radar aerials, the modern magic eyes which would make the vital difference in hunting down their enemies. The destroyers were low shapes in the pale waters, dwarfed by their bigger sisters.

Oh well. Picket boat would be back with the mail soon. Ernie felt his heart leap, his stomach hollow with that strangely sweet, empty feeling he got whenever he thought about Helena. Funny, he always used her proper name in his thoughts, but when he spoke, he usually dropped the final 'a'. There would be a letter from her this evening, he was sure. There had been one waiting when they got in two days ago, but that had been lying there ashore for another two days before that. So there was bound to be one for him today. She wrote a bit to him every day, never missed. Always put the day and time as a heading. She posted at least two a week. He tried to do the same, though sometimes he was forced to miss the odd day, and other times he had to struggle to find anything to tell her. If only he could get down on paper all that filled his heart, the bursting quality of his love for her. She could. She made his eyes sting, his throat close up, with the power of her writing.

He savoured the anticipation of reading her words. He always tore open the envelope straight away in the crowded, noisy mess. ''Ey up, Ernie! Bet it's a Dear John, oppo!' Eddie invariably called, but Ernie was oblivious to the racket all around him as he drew in the words avidly. He liked to get away somewhere quiet when he got the chance, to go over them again. On the upper deck if the weather wasn't foul. The unsavoury solitude of the heads if he was desperate.

As soon as the pipe was made announcing the postie's return and that mail was ready for collection, he was up off the bench like a sprinter at the gun. 'Ah'll get it!' he yelled, diving for the ladder. It was there, he saw the envelope, recognized the writing, sorting it from the bulky pile he was holding even before he climbed back down to the fug of the messdeck. The duty cooks were swabbing down the table and the deck beneath. Several people were already at the metal grille behind which the hammocks were stowed. 'Fuck all else to do except get your head down in this hole!' was a frequent complaint.

'An early night with the five-fingered widow, eh?' Eddie quipped. Ernie was scanning the pages, his dark eyes flicking rapidly along the lines, his lips faintly moving. 'Bugger me! It really *is* a Dear John!' Eddie cackled. 'I'm sorry, oppo, really.'

'Fuck off!' Everyone round them glanced up in startled surprise. Eddie staggered back from the vicious blow Ernie delivered to the shoulder before he almost trampled him down as he flung himself at the foot of the ladder.

6

'Quick march! Ordinary Seaman Wheatley, sir! Request for compassionate leave, sir!' The master at arms stood back. Ernie pulled in his back, stood ramrod straight before the lectern. The commander gazed down at the papers, gave a quick half glance to his left, and the gunnery officer, Ernie's divisional officer, stepped forward, spoke briefly, in a low voice, to his superior, who nodded and frowned. His patrician face lifted, gazed at Ernie with undisguised contempt. 'So. You've got your girl up the duff and you want to go off and sort it out. Nice little break for you to get up to more mischief, eh?'

Ernie felt his rigid body clammy with sweat. His fingers curled, he forced his arms to stay stiffly at his sides. Keep yer temper, he urged himself desperately. He had an almost overpowering urge to smash a fist into that sneering face, to scream obscenities at him. It was as if he had done unspeakable things to Helena. Three-ringer or not, he deserved a good sorting.

The gunnery officer bent forward again, murmured more urgently, clearly making a case for his charge, and the commander's expression softened slightly. 'Well? What have you got to say for yourself? You going to do the decent thing?'

'Yes, sir.' Ernie stared ahead, tried not to look into his cold eyes, knowing that he would give away the hate he felt. 'We're sort of engaged anyway. Planning to marry in the summer. Soon as we can. Now, it'll – that's why I need ter get 'ome, sir. We 'ave ter make plans. We'll need ter get wed as soon as possible. That's what ah want, sir,' he added strongly. Now his eyes did meet the commander's.

'When's the sprog due?'

'Baby's due November, sir.'

For an instant, the commander locked gaze, wondering whether to take offence. 'Well, at least you're not leaving her in the lurch,' he conceded huffily, in what might have passed for an apology. 'But we are fighting a war, you know. There are plenty of girls getting into trouble these days. You've got plenty of time to get things sorted out.' He turned to look at the first lieutenant, who was at his other side. 'When are those dockyard mateys due on board P of W, Number One? We'll be in again then, I expect.' The first lieutenant came close, murmured softly. 'Right.' The commander directed his gaze at the master at arms, ignoring the sweating figure in front of him. 'Put him down for a forty-eight from the twenty-first.' He turned back to Ernie. 'That's two weeks from now. You can wait till then.'

'But—'

'Silence!' roared the master. ''Bout turn! Quick march! Lef' right, lef' right, lef' right!'

1 AUGUST, 1915

1

''Appy birthday, Miss Alice.'

She saw the pain, and the tenderness, so clearly revealed in Tommy's eyes that her own misted with tears. She ached with the heavy sadness. 'Please!' she cried, as though he had physically hurt her. 'Don't be like that! Not now! Not when we're alone!' Her voice dropped to a low, husky murmur, as she moved in close to him, put both her hands on his shoulders. She moved her head forward, until he could feel the warmth of her breath, his gaze fixed on her pink, slightly parted lips. 'Give me a birthday kiss. Wish me luck properly.'

She saw his mouth curve, approach hers, and she closed her eyes, shivered with her longing to feel him, then they were pressed urgently together, and she couldn't breathe, didn't want to. The tears were there, glinting on her lashes, when they broke the embrace, her eyes enormous, soft with love, and all the confusion and doubt and fear of the sensations racing in her blood that made her want to stay like this for ever, made her want more, so much more, that she didn't understand. All the emotions that were mirrored in his troubled look.

She tried to laugh, it came out more like a trembly whimper. She put her hand on the top of her woollen beret, with its big, central pompom. She was wearing a light coat, buttoned at the tight waist, with a triple flounced, dark layer of silk around the wide hem which ended at mid calf. The skirt underneath was short, too, so that the lower portion of her black-stockinged legs, her ankles in the shining, soft boots, could be seen. These were her normal, everyday clothes, and gave her the schoolgirlish appearance she suddenly found herself wanting to cling to. She had kept her hair down, too, brushing it out so that it hung in thick, black waves softly folding at the ends, over her shoulders, nearly to the middle of her back.

Her mother had stared at her in surprise when she had appeared dressed like that after lunch. 'I just want to go for a walk, Mama. Be by myself a bit.'

'But don't you – I thought you'd want to rest this afternoon. Be fresh for tonight.'

There was to be a party this evening. Nothing too lavish, about a dozen young people, plus a few older relatives, and friends of her parents. It was not considered good taste to hold lavish affairs at this turbulent time in history. Besides, most of the young men just a year or two older than herself had answered the call to the Colours. Like both her brothers.

Alex Junior was a lieutenant in the 'Koylies', the Yorkshire Light Infantry, had been shipped off to France only two months ago after completing his training. His father had been bitterly opposed to his volunteering at first, even though Mr Guthrie had played a prominent part in the recruitment rallies and was on the local war committee. 'Of course we need volunteers,' he asserted, 'but there are plenty of young chaps doing nothing worthwhile. We've got a mine to run here, boy! Vital war work. I need you here.'

And Alex had lingered, dutifully miserable, while his younger brother, Herbert, just down from Oxford a month before the outbreak of war and cheerfully vague about what career he wished to pursue, had hastened off to enlist in the navy. He was a sublieutenant on a destroyer, HMS *Thirlmere*, part of the Grand Fleet's 13th Flotilla, stationed up in Rosyth. Alice had witnessed one or two harsh exchanges between the brothers, and had felt sorry for Alex. As the eldest, he had a far rougher time, she acknowledged. Sort of son and heir; his path narrowly channelled out for him – school, and the mine. He hadn't even been allowed the freedom of four years at university, not that he had shown any inclination towards academia. But she knew Bertie had had a high old time at Oxford, without any of the pressures his older brother had been subjected to. But then, Alice would reflect, why didn't Alex stand up to Father more? Tyrants ruled because people allowed them to.

As she grew into her teens, Alice had enthusiastically declared herself a supporter of the Women's Suffrage movement, and had had a number of blistering clashes with the family tyrant herself, several of which had ended with her being ordered to silence, and, once, to be confined to her room, a prisoner, for a whole, long, tummy-rumbling day. She had welcomed her martyrdom almost cheerfully at first, hugging her nobility to herself, thinking of the sufferings endured by the Pankhursts and others, the shocking death of Emily Davison, trampled under the king's horse at Epsom. 'Poor deranged woman,' her father had said dismissively. 'She's tried to kill herself before.' Mrs Pankhurst's autobiography had been published only last year. Alice had read it, smuggling a borrowed copy into the house and carefully hiding it from her parents and Evie, her mother's maid.

But the morning after her own imprisonment and forced fast, Alice had tearfully apologized to her father and begged his forgiveness. The humble pie was bitter, but the food that followed was not. Eventually, it was one of the women who supported women's suffrage, her passions diverted by the war towards a fierce patriotism, who changed Alexander Guthrie's mind, when she forced a box containing a white feather into his son's hand and spat into the tortured, beet face.

Not for the first time, Alice found herself envying the male sex. The war had at least spared her what would have been for her the chafing restrictions of a continental finishing school, though she would probably have accepted the chance to broaden her horizons, if only physically. But if her older sister, Olga, who only two months ago had celebrated her twenty-first birthday with a series of lavish events which even the exigencies of war had not dimmed, was to be upheld as a typical result of such 'finishing', Alice could only be thankful it had been denied her.

Olga had returned in 1913 and gone through the modified version of coming out which the north's industrial aristocracy had established. It had worked. There was a chinless wonder, some cousin of the Powers' family, Daddy's sleeping partner in the mine, to whom she was now engaged, the union announced at the dance held at her twenty-first, thus cleverly killing two birds with the single stone.

With the boys away, it was easier for the girls to be accorded the comparative luxury of their own rooms, for which Alice was profoundly grateful. Olga had long ceased to be fun, and had never relished the role of companion or confidante. On Alice's oftimes stormy journey through adolescence, her one true friend, her 'parfit gentil knight', had ever been her faithful Tommy.

It was a relationship neither could acknowledge, one they were forced to maintain in increasing secrecy as they grew older. Not long after her fourteenth birthday, her mother had sent for her one afternoon. She was sitting in her chair in her favourite spot, at the edge of the lawn on the seaward side of the house, surrounded by patterns and balls of wool and knitting needles. A second curved, high-backed wicker chair was for Evie, who sat and kept Mrs Guthrie company. Diplomatically, the maid now withdrew, and Alice soon understood why.

'Alice.' Her mother's quiet voice had that patient tone of suffering that made Alice wince. 'There's some gossip going round the village. You were seen romping about with Tommy Cousins down on the beach. Somebody said the two of you have been going to that awful artist woman's place in Kingstaith. It's got to stop. You're not a little girl any longer. It isn't right.'

'Someone?' echoed Alice scornfully, her face flaming. 'Who? You mean Evie, don't you? She's got ears a mile wide, and a nose just as long.'

'Be quiet, girl! It doesn't matter who said. It's all over the village. I told you I didn't like you visiting that woman. All that nonsense about painting you! Your father would have a fit! And this business with Tommy. If I told him, he'd be furious. You don't want to get the lad into trouble, do you? He's left school now. Isn't he coming to work here, for Gough? You've got to start conducting yourself properly, Alice, really!'

After that, they were more circumspect. To her delight, Alice found a new accomplice in her innocent deception – Dora, Tommy's sister, who had now been promoted to the rather grandiose title of under-housemaid. Though it occasioned her many uncomfortable moments of doubt, the pretty girl, only three years older than Alice and Tommy, often acted as messenger or intermediary. "E sez 'e'll be down at t'jetty at five, miss,' Dora would whisper, pink-cheeked.

At home, she would remonstrate gently with her brother. 'Yer daft, our Tom. Ye'll both get inter trouble one o' these days.' It was partly stubbornness that made Tommy carry on with the almost lifelong friendship, because of its flouting of the social code. But only partly. There were other, more frequent, times when he acknowledged the sense in Dora's words, the foolishness of continuing to meet Alice on terms which could not be recognized in their narrow society. True to his vow, he had not sought a job in the gardens of the hall, but instead had got taken on at the mine, working on the surface at the landward end of the mile-long tunnel which emerged out on to the cliff at the port, then, at his sixteenth birthday, going underground to mine the ore itself. Ah'll pack in seein' 'er, he promised himself stonily. Tisn't right. But, somehow, he couldn't bear to give it up. Give *her* up. It disturbed him to dwell on how much she meant to him.

When the war came, in keeping with the general instability of the times, he dreamed that things might be different. The war would bring enormous changes. Everyone said so. He could join up. Become famous. A hero. Maybe he and Miss Alice....

Even the war seemed depressingly far away, at first. 'Yer too young, lad,' they said. Then his dad grudgingly conceded, 'Yer can join up when yer sivventeen.' He would and all, he fumed. Then, one grey December morning, a workaday Monday, just a week before Christmas, they heard strange rumbles, rolls of thunder reverberating in a weird manner. Word spread quickly through the mine. 'Invasion! Bloody 'Uns! Their bloody fleet standin' off the coast!'

Still black with dust, all work suspended in the feverish excitement, men began to jump on the wagons, to run through the damp chill of the black tunnel to the coast. The dark grey of clouds away on the eastern horizon was lit rosily by flashes, then came the boom of firing guns, the thud of shells falling. The sounds of rolling gunfire had been heard earlier to the north, hence the rumours of an invasion force. Plumes of dark smoke, distantly small, drifted up from behind the headlands stretching down the coastline behind which lay Whitby.

In fact, only three German battle-cruisers, from the High Seas Fleet, had carried out a bombardment of Hartlepool, Whitby, and Scarborough. It did not last long, but there had been considerable damage in all three towns and a number of fatalities; 122 in Scarborough alone. It brought the war uncomfortably close to home, and trains and charabancs in the area did a brisk trade carrying sightseers to look at the gaping, rubbled ruins.

Through all these excitements, Alice and Tommy continued to meet, to hold hands, to walk along the narrow shore of the shallow wyke into Kingstaith. One of the few places they could be sure of a welcome was along the three-foot wide passageway of Gutter's End, and in the tiny, cramped rooms, littered with finished and half-finished canvases, of Salmon Cottage. Rosie Dwyer was intrigued, and privately enchanted, by this unconventional alliance.

She had managed to persuade them, Alice gladly, Tommy with great reluctance, to pose for her – dressed, of course – usually outside the cottage, where the rough alley petered out against the louring slope of the red cliff. 'Light's bloody useless inside,' Rosie grumbled, while boy and girl sat, extremely self-consciously at first, hand clasped in sweaty hand. 'She won't bite you, boy!' Rosie bellowed, guffawing at the reddening Tommy. 'Get hold of her! Don't tell me you don't want to, 'cos if you say so, you're a ruddy liar!' He would have been, too, but he didn't want to make a public declaration of his feelings.

Each time they walked, Alice was reminded, powerfully, of the first time he had really kissed her. How shocked she had been, and how scared. And how thrilled, too. She could never forget it, that hard, demanding, almost cruel mouth, her own blazing response to it. She had experienced that sensation many times since. It had grown as she grew, as her body changed, transforming to a woman.

It had caused her many solitary, genuinely frightened tears, and there was no one she could confess to, no one in the world, not even Tommy. Perhaps him least of all.

It's love, she told herself, disturbed, ashamed, altogether uncertain. Love was supposed to be of the heart. She thought she knew that feeling, knew the sweet, tender ache of it. This was different. Dangerously different, located far from the heart, deep in the base of her churning belly, between her trembling thighs. Sometimes, shockingly, she felt it when Tommy was far far from her thoughts. Like, for instance, when she looked at Rosie's pictures of the young boys she had painted – and young men, and women, too – all entirely, gloriously, naked. She couldn't love them all, could she? But she loved Tommy. She was sure of that.

The kiss for her seventeenth birthday was special. When he released her mouth, she clung to him, gasping for breath, sucking in air, leaning trembling against him, rejoicing in the feel of his arms, his body, supporting her. Then she wanted nothing but his mouth on hers again, the thunder of her blood. She had thought only fictional heroines swooned, but now she believed she was close to it, the world was giddily insubstantial about her.

There was a fold of rocks halfway along the narrow shore, remnants of some ancient cliff spill. They formed a fingery shelter, a roofless screen from the seaward edge and the land. She led him to it, tugged him, sensing his half reluctance, and understanding it. Danger clung to them. She picked up some large stones, cleared a space in the gritty sand, sat, and pulled him down beside her. They were still holding hands. Her knees were drawn up, she saw him staring at her boots, her ankles neatly side by side.

'Ah'm joinin' up!' he blurted, his eyes lifted desperately to her face. 'Navy. It's all fixed. I leave in two weeks.'

She nodded, lifted his hand, with her fingers laced in his, to her cheek, rubbed its red, roughened back, along the smoothness of her skin with great tenderness. Her big eyes filled slowly, the tears hovered on her lashes. One slid down with a miniature splash. She used his hand to wipe her cheek. 'Oh, Tommy,' she wept. 'I shall miss you so much. I love you.'

'Don't! Don't say it! Tha mustn't!'

Then they were lying on the damp sand, hands on shoulders, clinging, their blood, and their straining bodies, taking over. His hand left her shoulders, clawed with a life of its own up from the laces of her boots, up the warmth of her black-stockinged leg, dragging through layers of ruffled, stiff cloth, burying, scrabbling, up over cotton-covered knees, feeling the catching lace ruffles of underwear, feeling the thin linen, the solidity of her thigh. She sobbed and shook. 'We mustn't!' she wept, unconsciously echoing his cry, yet clamping his hand to her, squirming, moving it even, to the beating dampness of her crotch, clamping it fiercely to the shrouded centre of her raging desire.

2

'Pa insists that I finish my third year at Cambridge before I enlist. I'm afraid the bally war might be over before then!' Philip Surtees' thin face was set into the conventional mould of manly regret. 'I feel it so badly, you know. Now that Alex is over there. And Bertie. I feel so left out of it.'

Alice smothered her sudden urge to slap him. 'Don't,' she answered coldly. 'I don't know why everyone's so anxious to rush off and get themselves killed all of a sudden. It's madness.'

'Oh, come on, Alice! A chap has to do his bit, hasn't he?'

'And what about girls? Shouldn't they be doing their bit as well? I might run off and be a lorry driver. I heard they're taking on girls down in London. Some of them are even going over to France. Why should you boys have all the fun?' She blushed at the crassness of the last word. 'Anyway, I was reading in Daddy's newspaper that we're going to run out of bullets and shells soon. This fellow Lloyd George is going to stir things up with this Munitions Ministry. Soon we'll have to be doing for ourselves. He's going to take girls off to the factories. There'll be no maids or cooks left.'

'I'd hate to think of you wearing a boiler suit and getting covered in oil,' Philip grinned. 'I rather think you'd be far better staying at home to tend the wounded heroes.' He reddened, bravely reached out to capture her thin hand. She did not help him, but sat woodenly while he held her wrist stiffly. 'I must say, you look jolly nice tonight,' he braved, feeling the thin line of sweat beneath his hairline. 'So grown up and – well, grown up. Lovely. With your hair up, and everything.'

Now she blushed too, sensing his quickly flung glance over the slight round of her bosom, the suggestion of the divide of her breasts which showed above the low bodice. She felt herself grow hotter, tried desperately to divert her thoughts from the memory like a brand of that madness down among the rocks, the terrifying loss of her senses, except the rush of physical excess that had left her twisting and turning – madness was the only word for it – and wanting him to do things to her, to touch her, there, in that spot where she was melting with her longing for him. The very thought of it was like being on the rack now.

His hands had been there, at her centre, rough, pressing, and she had wanted it, lying there, her clothes up round her hips, and he had pulled her wrist, his hand like iron round her, dragged her hand to his loins, and she felt that great, mighty thrusting hardness, guessed what it was, shivered with fright and lack of understanding, wondering how it could possibly be put to her.

His cry had been like an animal when he flung himself off her. She had struggled to push down her skirt over her new knickers, lain there, shivering violently, half hidden on her stomach, then, suddenly, panicking, had leapt up, flung herself at him, wild, tears streaming. 'No, no, no! We mustn't be like this! I don't know – I love you, Tommy! I don't know about the – the sexual side – I don't know about anything. But I love you, Tommy. Hold me. Just hold me. Please. Don't leave me now.' And he had held her, they had sat down again, and she had lain half across his knee, her head on his chest, and he had cradled her, rocking her like a baby. She had felt so warm and soft and protected. It was as if she had already given herself. She had, she felt. The sex bit was scary; they were both lost and so ignorant. But one day they would learn it together. She was sure of it. 'We'll go away,' she murmured. 'When all this war is over, we'll go away. I want to be with you, Tommy, that's all I know.' He had said nothing, but held her, went on nursing her, holding, rocking.

Philip Surtees, the solicitor's son, set to carry on the prosperous family business in Whitby, leaned in more closely, allowing his knee to press against Alice's. His palm was damp with sweat, but his eyes were large and gentle, full of the uncertainty she could feel. Nice eyes, she thought distractedly. Like Tommy's. But they were not Tommy's. 'You know I think you're jolly nice,' Philip stammered, his face even redder than before. 'And I know you're only seventeen—'

'You're only a year older, aren't you?'

'Yes, yes,' he replied hastily, as though apologizing. 'But things the way they are – if this war isn't over, I'll have to go next year. I want to!' he added, so fervently that she felt her heart well with sympathy for him. 'To do my bit. But – I'd like to think you – you were special – to me. Could you – well, before I have to go – if we could be—'

He couldn't finish the sentence, and she felt sorry for him even as the shock of his halting words registered with her. He was asking her to be betrothed! The old-fashioned prissiness of the word that came to her startled mind almost made her giggle. Engaged! Yes, that was better. But not now, not on her seventeenth birthday! She could just imagine what father would have to say to that! Then the thought hit her, like a blow in the pit of her stomach. Not now, no. But, as Philip had hinted, later. Later, in a year from now, her parents would probably be only too glad to give their consent. Especially her mother. Alice almost glanced around the luxurious room to seek her out, to see if she was watching the young couple clutching hands. She pulled free from his grasp, Mama would be delighted with such a match.

He was gazing at her with a worried look, those eyes soft with his anxiety and unsureness. 'There isn't anyone else, is there?'

She shook her head quickly, glancing down at her lap. 'No,' she murmured, hating herself for the lie.

3

'Don't! Don't touch me – I'm ticklish!' Alice gasped, shrugged her shoulders away from the gently reaching hands, and crossed her arms over her breasts. She was blushing profusely. 'I wish I'd never said I'd pose like this! It's – too embarrassing!'

The sun was shining strongly through the open skylight, under which the chair was placed. Alice could feel it, its warmth shockingly strange on her naked body. The hard roundness of the wooden seat was pressing her buttocks flat. She could feel the rim digging into the backs of her thighs, feel the sticky dampness of perspiration. She'd have a red mark there when she stood up, she thought inconsequentially.

The muscles of her legs were aching, too, from the unnatural coyness of the pose, one knee crossed primly over the other, the toes of one pointed foot resting on the wooden floorboards, the other hovering a few inches above it. A white sheet was draped with elaborate carelessness about her hips, its folds placed to hide her loins, the dark triangle of her pubis, but falling away either side at her thighs, to hide little else.

The tiny room at the top of the cottage was bare of all furniture, except for the chair, placed under the skylight to catch the full brilliance of the shaft of sun penetrating from above. Around the walls were stacked canvases, leaning on the floor. A battered kitchen table was full of pots and jars and brushes and rags, while an easel stood by the sole tiny uncurtained window.

Alice had felt both reluctant and excited when she came to the appointment. She was blushingly shocked by her daring, thrilled by it, too. Nevertheless, it had taken quite a bit of coaxing, and laughing reassurance on the part of Rosie before Alice had at last consented to pose in the nude. 'Please, please, please! Promise – swear – you won't tell a living soul!'

Rosie had laughed heartily. 'Don't be such a namby-pamby, for God's sake! You're a young woman now. Seventeen for God's sake! I thought you were all in favour of the Women's Movement? Was it all just fine talk then? Are you ashamed of what the good Lord has given you?'

'No, of course not! But it's – it's—'

'Immoral? To show beauty as it really is? Is Michelangelo's *David* immoral?' She shook her head. 'I thought you'd got beyond all this old-fashioned prudery, girl.'

Alice agreed, but remonstrated when Rosie stood grinning and waiting in the chaotic untidiness of her bedroom. 'Don't stand there watching me!' the embarrassed girl squealed, shooing her out. 'And where's that sheet? You promised me I'd be wrapped in a sheet!'

She had managed to sit still, had even giggled nervously, while Rosie arranged her, though she was deeply embarrassed at displaying so much of her body, even to another woman. 'I don't even let my sister see me like this!' she protested.

'What? Don't you share a bath? I thought girls loved to romp together!' The notion of Olga enjoying a bathtime 'romp' with her sent Alice into fits of snorting giggles.

She sat motionless while Rosie worked quickly, first with charcoal, then with paints on the large sheet of paper she placed on the easel. The sight of the cloud-flecked blue square of sky over her head, the unaccustomed feel of the sun on her bare skin, the strangeness of sitting there in still silence, unclothed, in that bare room, stirred her deeply, roused her. Her mind drifted to Tommy. She was meeting him that afternoon. What if he were to see her like this? What if she were to see him?

She squirmed, eased her aching buttocks, broke the pose. She grabbed at the sheet which threatened to fall from her lap. 'All right. Take a break.' Rosie groaned, straightened, holding her hands in the small of her back. 'How's your young man?'

Alice's face pinked. 'He leaves on Friday.' She had already confided in Rosie his enlistment in the navy. Now, she lifted her brown eyes, luminous with her sadness.

'Come on! Cheer up! He'll come back a hero, covered in medals.' Her light words did not comfort the girl, and she came forward quickly, with a small sound of sympathy, moved behind the chair and let her hands fall on the thin fragility of the shoulders. Then she lifted a palm, cupped the side of the slender neck caressingly, her fingers playing with the earlobe revealed by the swept-up style of the black hair. Her normally gruff voice was hoarse with compassion. 'Don't fret, my sweet. Listen. If it'll help, you can use this address. I mean he can send his letters here. It might be easier.'

'Oh, Rosie! Thank you! You're such a brick!' Alice swivelled round, her eyes shining with tears, rising impulsively to grasp at the older, bulkier figure. Then she gasped as she realized she was standing naked in the other's tightly hugging embrace, and she wriggled free, diving for the bedsheet which she wound awkwardly about her.

She sat for another lengthy interval, while Rosie worked almost without talking. Again, she moved inadvertently after a while, and Rosie came to her to rearrange the pose. This time, the large, suntanned hands moved with more familiarity, and touched the slight breasts, causing Alice to twist violently away. 'Don't – don't touch me! I'm ticklish!' She had folded her arms over her bosom, but now she clutched at the sheet, pressed it to her loins.

Stung by the girl's unthinking rejection of her intimate gesture, Rosie fought to keep her voice steady and light. ' "Me thinks the lady doth protest too much"! Are you this squeamish in the arms of your beloved?' She nodded at Alice's breasts. 'Why, look. Your titties are quite hard.'

Alice's face flamed. She grabbed the folds of the sheet in her lap, pulled it up to hide her chest. 'It's – I'm a bit cold.'

'Warm as toast, my dove!' Rosie smiled. She gave a playfully vigorous shove at Alice's head and turned away, moving back to the easel. 'But perhaps you'd better go and get dressed. Don't want you to catch cold, do we?'

When Alice came back, dressed in the calf-length grey skirt and white blouse, with a light summer overall drawn over them and left open, Rosie was tidying away. 'Can I see?' Alice asked timidly, still aware of a residue of awkwardness between them, disturbed and puzzled by it, for she could not understand it.

'Certainly not! You'll see the finished article, my lady. If it ever gets finished,' she added significantly.

Alice felt her cheeks glowing a little. 'Well, just tell me when you want me,' she said, not meeting Rosie's look. The older woman came forward, seized her hand and drew her to the head of the tiny staircase, which led down to the front room. 'I'll have plenty of time,' Alice continued. Her throat closed, her eyes filled with tears as she thought of her loneliness with Tommy gone.

Rosie held her before she opened the front door. 'Bring your young man round to say cheerio.' Alice nodded speechlessly, her eyes huge. Rosie leaned forward, kissed her lightly on her lips. 'Go well,' she whispered.

4

'I want to come to the station! I want to see you off properly!' Alice wailed, clinging to him, pressing her head under his chin, tears pouring down her face. He could feel the convulsive sobs shaking her slim body as he held her to him, and the ache of his love for her, and the desire, even now, which made his manhood stir and throb inside the tight clothing.

'It's better 'ere, love,' he whispered, swallowing hard, his own eyes stinging with his tears. He lifted her face, tilted it so that he could reach that curve of mouth, place his lips over it, seeking to imprint it on his memory. His head jerked to take in the splendid, ripe summer beauty of the cliffs, the deep blue of the placid ocean. 'This is ours, all of this. This is where ah'll be rememberin' you.'

'Tommy!' She couldn't speak. Could only cling to him, desperately, torn with her love and her sadness. 'Come back to me! I love you!'

He nodded. 'I love you, lass,' he whispered, tears on his lashes. And what the hell is going to happen to us? his reeling, misery swamped mind wondered as he held the sobbing girl crushingly to him.

'Alice isn't well,' her mother said, with that slight emphasis which expressed so eloquently what must be left unsaid, and Mr Guthrie, at the head of the dining-table, nodded, with a fleeting grimace of distaste. 'Evie can take her something up later.'

But it was not Evie who took the tray up to the room Alice now had to herself, whose windows looked over the greenhouse roofs to the tennis court beyond the wall, and the distant orchard. 'Lazy young bitch!' the lady's-maid declared in the kitchen. 'There's nothing wrong with her. Can't be her time of the month. That was a couple of weeks ago. No mistaking that!' she added feelingly.

'Ah'll tek it up,' Dora volunteered, straightening her white cap and apron. 'Then ah'll be off 'ome.'

She tapped at the door, waited, and then went in. Alice was sitting up, propped on pillows, her long black hair flowing down at either shoulder. She had been dozing. An oil lamp on the bedside table cast a soft glow over the dark room. 'Shall I put the light on, miss?' Dora asked. She came forward, carefully placed the tray over Alice's knees. Then she caught sight of the swollen eyelids, the young face stamped with grief. They stared at each other mutely, and Alice reached up, seized Dora's hands. Suddenly they were clinging to one another, Dora sitting awkwardly on the bed, leaning forward, crying together.

'Don't tek on so, miss,' Dora urged presently, drawing back, dabbing at her cheeks with a white-cuffed sleeve. ''E'll be all right, will our Tommy. 'E can look after 'isself.'

'Please! Dora! Can't you call me Alice? At least when we're alone. I—'

The capped head shook rapidly. Dora got up, smoothed the coverlet, her face flushed. ''T'isn't right, miss,' she answered, shocked.

'How's your mother – mam?' Alice corrected herself quickly.

Dora gave a sad smile. 'She's right upset. Tommy bein' the youngest an' all.'

'Bert hasn't gone, then?' Tommy's older brother was the first born of the family, already thirty, and married, with two children.

'Naw, miss. 'E's not that daft.' Her mouth opened; she blushed anew, thinking of Tommy, and the young girl in the bed. 'Not that ah mean—' She paused, flustered, then carried on. 'It's just that 'e's got a lot ter think about, Bert. With the bairns and everythin'.'

Alice nodded. 'Quite right. There's a kind of madness about.' She frowned heavily, sighing. 'All these recruiting rallies. Those stupid women! The women are the worst.' She stared up at Dora, her sorrow still plain. 'You heard about what happened to Alex? Outside the offices?'

Dora nodded. 'Ah know. Daft, i'n't it? Ah just 'ope none of 'em come near our mam. She'll belt 'em one in the gob!'

Alice couldn't help smiling, in spite of her heaviness of spirit. She reached out a hand again, and sought Dora's. 'You'll be my friend, won't you?' she said simply.

Dora swallowed hard, nodded. Inside, her mind screamed, No, no, it's all wrong. You can't! Not you and our Tommy. You're a lady. It's madness. Real madness. It can't work. Nothing can come of it, not in a million years. But she said nothing, squeezed the soft hand in her own short-nailed, work-chapped fingers, unable to stop herself from the automatic little bobbed curtsy before she left.

5

Alice had another friend, one who became closer to her than anybody, during the long weeks, then months, following Tommy's departure. The cramped, untidy little cottage in Kingstaith became a haven to her, the only place where she felt she could truly be herself in another's company. Their intimacy was sealed by the physical bond between them, for Alice continued to sit for Rosie, and even to enjoy the secretly disturbing excitement the freedom of being unclothed gave her.

There *were* moments of unquiet, especially at first, when Alice saw something in the way Rosie would look at her, with that lingering appreciative frankness in her gaze which somehow seemed, even to the naive girl, slightly improper. She was still stiff and awkward when Rosie touched her limbs or body to arrange her, though the older woman was always careful to make the contact lightly, and always with some quip to ease the tension. And then, as long as Rosie was doing no more than looking at her, there was the shameful acknowledgement within Alice's confused mind of the pleasure those admiring looks could give her.

No doubt of the bond of friendship, though, which Alice shared, expressed eagerly, in the embraces, the kisses on gladly yielded mouth, when they met or parted. The portrait was long finished, and Alice had shriekingly giggled and protested when Rosie teasingly declared she was about to sell it locally. 'Not here, Rosie!' exclaimed the wide-eyed girl, in shocked delight at the contemplation of the scandal it might cause. 'What if someone recognizes me?'

'I hope they do. I'm not *that* bad, am I?'

The idea was, again, disturbingly titillating. The thought of it being seen, perhaps hung in a public place, hundreds of strangers' eyes turned upon it. Upon her, for Alice thought it was remarkably good, was undoubtedly her, captured in all her youthfulness. Both innocent and temptingly wicked at the same time. She liked to look at it. It was like looking in a mirror, only excitingly different. Another self, with a mysterious life of its own. She wished it was hers, she would have liked to have it hidden somewhere, so that she could contemplate it at leisure. She blushed as she wondered if Tommy would ever see it, if she would ever dare to show it to him.

Rosie often teased her. 'Your young Thomas will love it! When's he going to get some leave?'

And the scandalized girl would squeal with embarrassment, slap at Rosie's fleshy arm in outrage. 'Don't you dare! You must promise me! On your honour!'

The sunlight on the thick daubs of the cream and ivory, pink-tipped flesh became a poignant reminder of the summer, as a wet autumn slid into a damp, miserably cold winter. The second Christmas of the war came. No one predicted now that the war would soon be over. The name of the Gallipoli Peninsula once again captured the headlines, as it had so often throughout the spring and summer, as, one week before the festive season, the evacuation began, and the name of Churchill, too, newly resigned from the Cabinet, was muttered like a curse.

The gloom of the war news and the weather was lifted magically by a telegram which arrived on Boxing Day. When Evie came in, with the buff envelope on a tray, and bobbed at Mr Guthrie's elbow as he sat reading in the drawing-room, close to the wide windows to make the most of the grey light, Alice heard a soft gasp, and looked up to see her mother's face completely drained of colour. Only her eyes, brilliantly etched in a fixed stare of utter anguish, stood out. Alice felt her own heart lurch even before she understood what was wrong.

Her father's hands shook slightly. His face was set in rigid control, and, again, Alice felt that wave of hatred at him for his block-like inhumanity. But then she saw the rigid lines relax, saw the emotion flicker cross the strong features, and she was deeply ashamed of herself. 'It's all right, Meg,' he said quickly, using the diminutive to his wife which he only used in private. 'It's from Alex. He's coming home. On leave. Tomorrow, he hopes.'

'Oh God! thank God!' Her mother burst into tears, sprang up, rushed, not to her husband, but to her maid, whom she embraced like a sister. 'Evie!' she wept.

Everyone began to talk excitedly, all at once. 'Margaret!' Mr Guthrie said, with his habitual quiet firmness. 'Steady, dear.' It was a command, and she reached sniffingly for a handkerchief in her sleeve.

Alice knew almost at once that Alex was frighteningly different. He was not wounded, as his family had at first feared when they had had time to digest the sudden news of his coming. He looked mainly tired, his face pale. And old, Alice suddenly realized, with a deep sense of shock. He looked old, acted old, moved slowly, seemed to take ages to comprehend the simplest remark and to reply to it. Again like an old man.

He said so little that it became nerve-racking after a day or so. He would sit staring ahead of him, then glance about bewildered when someone repeated a remark, touched his sleeve lightly to gain his attention. In the drawing-room, after dinner, when they were all gathered amidst the clutter of decorations, the bowls of festive food which war shortages had not apparently undermined to any great extent, he got up and helped himself to whisky from the decanter on the sideboard without waiting for his father to offer it. Alice saw the momentary expression of shock on her father's face. There was a slight frisson of embarrassment. Alex turned, his glass almost full, then lifted it slightly in his father's direction. 'You don't mind?' he said abruptly, his speech sounding jerky. 'I've really missed this.'

He made many such trips, while everyone affected not to notice, but the more he drank the more he seemed to shrink into himself, his face pale and abstracted. Alice quivered with shame at Olga's bright, cutting voice, when she said, 'Come on, Brother. Tell us what it's like. All those mamzelles parlez-vousing. What's it like out there?'

His dark eyes were turned on her and he stared as if he didn't know her. Abruptly, he shook his head. 'I can't,' he answered, with similar abruptness. 'I can't tell you!'

Olga gave a little, mocking laugh. 'My goodness! Is it *that* bad then?'

'Yes,' he said baldly, and there was an awful second of silence.

1916's first day brought some snow flurries. Further inland, on the moors, it lay thickly, but along the coast it was a mere dusting which, next day, had gone. The winter was wet and chill, with white rolling fog banks which penetrated far enough inland to settle about the house like snow itself, out of which the tall chimneys of the hall loomed disembodied. Alice fretted through the interminable dreariness, and somehow managed to keep secret her lonely love, shutting herself in her room and writing sheet after sheet of her thoughts and emotions, adding some each day, posting off the fat letters at Kingstaith, or further afield when she got the chance.

She succeeded, too, in keeping her friendship with Rosie Dwyer undiscovered by her family. Since Alex's short leave at Christmas, Mrs Guthrie worried even more about her two sons, and spent most of her days shut up in her own room with Evie to keep her company. Alice was allowed to do as she pleased. Father was fully occupied at the mine, so there was no one to object or even be curious when she pulled on thick coat or cape, stout boots, and headed off into the shrouding mist for the muddy walk along the clifftop. 'Is there a letter?' she would cry eagerly before she even greeted Rosie, and would swoop on the blue envelope with cries of joy whenever the tall figure would hold one out to her.

Tommy's letters were generally short and rather stilted, though she hated to admit it. But he always ended 'Yours forever' and plastered crosses all over the remaining space. 'He's been transferred to a ship,' she told Rosie, with pathetic pride, on receipt of one missive. She always vowed she would save them to open when she got home and was alone in her room, but she could never resist tearing open the envelope and quickly scanning the contents while Rosie prepared the tea in the cluttered tininess of the narrow galley kitchen. 'It's a battle-cruiser. The *Queen Mary*. He's up in Scotland.' She peered again at the page. 'At Rosyth. He's with Admiral Beatty.'

'Oh, tell him to give him my regards when he sees him next,' Rosie called, carrying in the tray, and, with difficulty, finding a spot large enough to deposit it on the littered table.

Alice glanced up, her eyes wide. 'Oh! You know him, this admiral?'

Rosie aimed a mock blow at the dark head and Alice drew back. 'Goose!' the older woman chuckled fondly.

But Alice now gave a wild scream and leapt up so swiftly that Rosie nearly dropped the teapot she was holding. 'Good God, child!' she roared, genuinely startled. 'What—'

'He's coming home! He's coming home!' She grabbed at Rosie, hugging her shoulders, swinging her round in her enthusiasm. 'Next month! April 4th!' Laughing and crying, she fell into the other's welcome arms, and they both spun round and round in the enclosed space. 'Mmf! I love you!' Their mouths closed in an eager kiss that went on and on, until Alice broke free, panting, her cheeks glowing. But her eyes, brilliant with tears, were alive with her happiness, and she didn't mind, enjoyed the sensual feel of those lips planted on hers, loved the whole world at that moment and didn't care who knew it.

6

'Come on. As quiet as you can.' Alice, eyes dancing, held a finger to her lips. 'We don't want anyone to see us.'

But she didn't really care, she was giggling with excitement and fear as she fumbled with the heavy old key, until Tommy said with fond exasperation, ''Ere, give it 'ere, lass. Ah'll do it!' He got the front door open, then they were inside, in the safety of the untidy little front room. 'Yer sure none of 'er mates'll turn up?' he said cautiously.

Alice leaned against the locked door, smiled shyly. 'No. She said we should use it. She's away till Monday.' All at once, there was an awful constraint of silence between them. Alone, entirely safe from prying eyes, safer than the rocks on the beach, or their spots along the cliff. This was their real time together, she knew, the only time they could truly have to themselves. Three days' leave. Seventy-two hours. One day gone, and tomorrow must be spent with his family, before he caught a train in the evening to begin the long trip back to Rosyth Dockyard.

They had of course met the previous day. She obviously could not be waiting for him at the station, but she had found an excuse to send Dora off along the lane back to the Cousins' cottage in Mine Row. She had come back red-cheeked, eyes alight with happiness. ''E's 'ome, miss. 'Bout an hour ago.' She lowered her voice, blushed. ''E sez four o'clock at the old beacon.'

They had met on the clifftop. She was there far too early, her heart thudding, trembling with anticipation. She hadn't dressed up, worn her everyday skirt and blouse under the heavy top coat, kept her hair down, a woollen tam pulled on her head. She didn't want to arouse suspicion by putting on smart things. It didn't matter, anyway. She just wanted to see him, be with him.

She was afraid. Afraid there would be an awkwardness, an embarrassment, after the passionate freedom of the letters they had written, the declarations they had made. But when she saw him coming along the path, slim and romantic in his jaunty uniform, she raced to him, and they said nothing, only hurtled into each other's arms, crushed their mouths together until they were forced to break for breath.

She blushed when she told him about Rosie's cottage. 'Can you get away tomorrow? All day? I've already told Mama I'm going out. They don't expect me back until just before supper.'

He had lied, too, eagerly, and was there on the path at almost the same instant as she was. Now, secure, they were gripped by shyness, by fear, and uncertainty. Alice moved bravely to him, put herself in his arms, lifting her mouth to be kissed. 'I love you,

Tommy. I want to belong to you properly. With my body as well.'

He had said nothing, but his eyes were burning as he gazed at her, drinking her in. 'Are ye sure?' he whispered huskily. She nodded.

Then suddenly her dark eyes danced with all their old mischief. She grabbed his hand, pulled him to the steep little staircase. 'You want to see me with all my clothes off?' She snorted at the eloquent look of shock on his face as she tugged him along.

In the bare room that acted as studio, he stood before the portrait, stared at it solemnly. Alice's face was flushed, she was still giggling, deeply embarrassed, then she saw the almost awed look he gave her, and she was quiet, and very still. 'Yer beautiful, lass,' he told her wonderingly, shaking his head. His gaze reflected all the pain and splendour and unsureness of the love they felt.

She kissed him gently, again took his hand. 'Come.' She led him to Rosie's bedroom. The single bed was neatly made, the coverlet turned back. The tiny space, amazingly, had been carefully dusted and tidied. A large bunch of daffodils stood on the window ledge in a glass vase. Alice unbuttoned her blouse, then tugged at the fasteners on her skirt. 'I want to be yours, Tommy.'

He wanted to cry out, to stop her, knew that he should, that he was doing her untold harm by allowing her, this, to go ahead. So many lonely nights, in his hammock in the crowded mess, he had vowed he would set her free. Vowed that he would save her from herself, from him, before it was too late. And now, at the very moment of decision, he could not do it. He watched her undress, his eyes stinging, his heart aching with love for her. His body beating, throbbing, hardening, with his desire for her.

The clothes rustled, she dropped them on the small wooden chair against the wall. He saw her step out of the long white knickers, peel off the black stockings. Her legs looked pale, and thin, her body so delicate, as she drew off the chemise. Her voice caught on a sob as she forced herself to look at him.

'Am I as good as the picture?' she said shakily, the tears starting to her eyes. She moved at the same time as he did, throwing herself into his arms, their cry of need uttered simultaneously in the small haven of the bedroom.

24 MAY, 1941

1

'Enemy in sight! Range 36,000 yards!' the turret captain shouted over his shoulder, from his position by the breech. Next to him stood his layer, and the sightsetter.

'Gun ready lamp on!'

Ernie glanced across at Eddie Collinson, who was facing him at the other side of the hoist which lifted the giant shells up from the magazine below, to be loaded into the breech of the gun. Eddie's face looked pinched and small, enclosed by the white anti-flash hood, with the steel helmet pulled low over his brow. Ernie was reminded of a picture he had seen in a school book of a medieval soldier. He wondered why everything suddenly seemed brilliantly outlined in the artificial light. There was a humming; they felt the deck swing as the turret moved, locking on to a new position, then the thudding vibration began again, shaking everything, transmitting itself up through their feet, which seemed to rattle on the steel plating.

'Christ, we must be shifting now! This is it, me old fruit.' Eddie's smile was forced, his eyes looked big. He's scared, Ernie thought. So am I. Do I look that scared?

'Altering course,' the setter called, his shape dumpy as he squatted in the metal bucket seat at his post, the headset clamped to his ears. Ernie remembered the jokes they had made one drill when he had had to do the setter's job, translating commands to and from gunnery control. 'No good having a bad-speaking bastard like you!'

Eddie had protested. 'Nobody can understand a word you say at the best of times. You need a southerner for that job. Somebody who speaks English!'

Not for the first time, Ernie wished that he was not in the gunnery team, but had a post at action stations that was on the upper deck. Bridge lookout, or with the bunting tossers on the flag deck. They would have a superb view from up there. 'Yes. And they'll be the first to have their bollocks shot off when we get strafed.' Everyone seemed to be most afraid of an air attack. Eddie was no exception. 'While we're tucked away with armour plating as thick as a barn door all round us, those poor sods'll be trying to climb up their own arseholes for shelter, you mark my words.' But Ernie disliked the feeling of being shut away, the smell of the oil, then the cordite stink and the massive plunge of the gun when a salvo was fired. And salvoes were certainly going to be fired now. Eddie was right, for once. This *was* it. The big one.

He wondered for the nth time what Helena was doing, laughed at himself for his foolishness. She was doing what he would be doing if he had the chance, sleeping, for it was just after dawn. In the bed he might, *would*, have been sharing with her, if fate, or God, or whatever you wanted to call it, hadn't played its perfectly timed hand and brought news of two big Jerry ships coming out, on the very afternoon that he was due to take his longed for forty-eight to go to her.

The sense of disappointment and frustration was as keen as ever when he thought about her, imagined the tears when she realized he wasn't coming. He had let her down. That's what she would think. That's what he felt, too, even though he knew he wasn't really to blame. He just wanted to be with her, so much, to tell her how much he loved her, that everything was going to be all right, more than all right. Everything was going to be wonderful, they would have the best baby the world had ever seen and he would take care of both of them.

He knew what he wanted now, knew where he was going. No more messing about with the coble, with Da and Reg. When he got out of this lot, he was going to make something of himself, he owed it to Helena and the child. If only he could have been with her, to tell her! She'd be so worried, not knowing what was going on, why he hadn't turned up. He hadn't had time to get a message off to her, not that he would have been allowed to. There had been such a mad panic to get up steam and out again. Some of the lads had had a good chuckle over the fact that there was still a bunch of dockyard mateys aboard *Prince of Wales*, putting right the numerous defects that had been brought to light during her work-up period. 'Bet those civvy bastards didn't reckon taking part in a poxy sea battle, eh?' Eddie chortled.

Nor had I, reflected Ernie bitterly. Not when I was all shoe-shined and tiddly, ready to jump into a liberty boat and go off home to Helena. Instead, most of his forty-eight had been spent cooped up in X-turret, at action stations, or sitting about the deck outside, when the stiff breeze and driving rain showers had permitted. The Denmark Strait could be inclement even in late May.

At first, they had wondered if this was another false alarm, but as they headed west from the Orkneys, the vice admiral spoke over the tannoy, telling the ship's company of the aerial reconnaissance which had confirmed that *Bismarck* and *Prinz Eugen* had left Kiel and were heading for the Atlantic. As well as their own squadron, Admiral Tovey, the C-in-C Home Fleet, had set sail with his main units. After nearly two days of tension as they ploughed north-westward at full speed, came the news that *Suffolk*, a cruiser, had picked up *Bismarck* on her radar, and was shadowing the enemy, along with her sister ship, *Norfolk*.

They had gone to cruising stations after supper last night, which meant that the two watches, Red and Blue, were again subdivided into 'parts'. The pipe, 'First part of Red Watch to stand down', meant that Ernie and Eddie actually enjoyed the luxury of going below to a, for once, sparsely populated messdeck where they got their heads down on the narrow benches. Other bodies crashed out on the mess table. Nobody slung hammocks, not when the alarm bells for action stations could sound off at any minute. In any case, soon after midnight, the whole ship's company was closed up again, and nerves were once more running high. Now, with the morning brightening every second in the east, the smudge of smoke on the horizon was changing into the tiny points of a ship's superstructure. A big ship. An enemy ship.

Ernie jumped as the turret captain swore loudly. 'Why the fuck have we changed course? We were bearing on the target fine and dandy! Now we've lost her! There's only the forward turrets locked on now!' It was a question puzzling a considerable number of more senior personnel. Even more puzzling was Vice Admiral Holland's next signal to the *Prince of Wales*, ordering her to concentrate her fire on the left-hand vessel of the two German ships they were approaching. On board the British battleship, they had correctly identified this target as the lesser of the two, the heavy cruiser, *Prinz Eugen*, and ignored the order, keeping their guns trained on *Bismarck*.

As it was, because of the angle at which they were approaching the enemy, and the fact that they were tucked in so close astern of *Hood*, the *Prince of Wales*, too, could only bring her forward turrets to bear on the enemy. 'Why don't we open fire?' the turret captain shrilled, to no one in particular. Ernie and Eddie stood there, gazing at each other mutely, their nerves stretched to a finely thrumming tension, as long minute after long minute ticked by, with the four deadly ships rapidly converging on one another in the brightening morning.

It was as though time had been stopped. Trapped in an eternity, they stood at their posts, sweating, shivering. 'Some fucker start shooting!' Eddie almost screamed at last, and the turret captain snarled him to silence without glancing round.

The klaxon blared, startling them all. the setter began to chant his figures. 'X-gun clear for firing!' the turret captain shouted loudly into the mouthpiece about his neck. They felt the quiver, the checking of momentum that indicated the forward guns had fired. Surely now they must get the order to commence firing? But it didn't come. 'Christ knows where *that* went!' the turret captain relayed back to them, after listening to the reports from the gunnery director behind the distant bridge. 'We're only firing at the wrong fucking ship!' he burst out, a few minutes later.

The ship heeled deeply, and everyone clutched at the nearest support. 'Change of course!' the voice sang out from the breech, and the setter up there beside him droned out a new set of figures.

'You don't fucking say!' Eddie muttered, hanging on to the chains of the hoist, and, despite his fear, Ernie smiled broadly. He felt a sudden, emotional wave of warm comradeship for Eddie, and reached over to punch his arm.

'Now we'll show 'em!' he said strongly. He looked down the shaft where the shells lay gleaming sinisterly on the tray, ready to be slung up to them for reloading. He could see the helmeted top of one of the bootnecks down below. As if to emphasize his words, the turret buzzed and swung violently through an arc, locking on at last to the target. 'X-turret clear for firing!' the turret captain yelled again, and they knew this time they would be in on it.

'Range 26,000 yards!'

'Fire!' The klaxons and voice shrilled simultaneously, and the turret leapt and shook at the thrust of the great gun. The sharp sting of the cordite filled the air, the chains of the hoist rattled loudly, drowning out all other noise for Ernie and Eddie, who swung the great tray round. No time to think now. Work, sweating away inside the thick clothing, the sealing hoods which added to the discomfort in the enclosed fug. Except that Ernie *did* think, confusedly, as his body worked. Why can't I see what's happening? his mind protested, trying to visualize the scene outside. What on earth will I tell Helen? How can I describe any of this? This isn't what a battle should be like, shut up in a metal box, machinery whirling all around you.

He stood panting, saw the charges rammed home, Helena still vaguely in his mind, the last thought before he was obliterated, in a blinding, silent, white heat which wiped out him and his companions in an instant.

The great flash, and subsequent roar, stunned those who saw it from the *Prince of Wales* and the other ships, both British and German. It was probably the biggest explosion of the war, until *Enola Gay* dropped her deadly load on Hiroshima one August morning four years later. The blinding flash originated in the after magazine, about thirty feet below Ernie in X-turret, where the shells were stored. Too lightly armoured. Badly designed. Poor tactics on the fatal run in to engage the enemy. Superior gunnery skills on the part of the Germans. All that was to come later, to be haggled and torn over around the world. When it happened, there was only disbelieving, gut-wrenching shock, and horror.

A huge, dark column of smoke rose in a brief, impressive monument. The dark, tortured hulk was half gone almost immediately, settled, other explosions sounded across the water, she rolled and was gone. Three minutes after *Bismarck*'s shell had struck, seven minutes after *Hood* had fired off her first wild salvo at the wrong ship, there was nothing left except the clearing pall of smoke, the oil and debris on the surface of the sea. And three survivors, plucked out of the water by HMS *Electra*, a destroyer. Three, from a complement of 1,419 men.

When the news of the catastrophe buzzed around the corridors of the Admiralty, there were several senior figures who shook their grey heads, and suppressed a tiny shiver, as they heard the echo of Beatty's words, pronounced a quarter of a century before, only a week to the very day. 'There seems to be something wrong with our bloody ships today.'

2

'He must have been delayed. Red tape or something. There *is* a war on.' Even as she spoke, Maggie Turner winced at her own crassness, but Helena gave a pathetic, twisted little smile, and nodded, almost gratefully. Her eyes were red, puffed slightly underneath, the skin around her cheeks looked blotched. At least she had stopped that regular morning retching, the awful, bitter acid bile feeling as she hung over the toilet bowl, with little to bring up. She could still be spectacularly sick at other times, with very little warning. Such as the other night, when Vicky had gone out for fish and chips, and Helena had wolfed them down with voracious glee. Feeding two and all that. Not for long, though.

This morning, she had felt sick with excitement, for a change. All day at work on the wards, the churning in her belly had had nothing to do with the baby growing inside her, only her desperate joy, and need to see Ernie, which would happen in a few hours, she kept on telling herself incredulously. It would be one of the three evening trains from Middlesborough, probably the last one, he thought. He told her in his hastily written letter that he would get a 'make and mend', and get away after lunch on the Friday, which should enable him to get to her some time that evening. *Don't hang about the station*, he had written anxiously. *It'll probably be the last train, sods' law, so just stay in at the flat and I'll come straight there.*

Stay at home! Fat chance! But she had waited, heart racing, at the barrier, for all three trains, and when, in the bleak ten o'clock dimness, he had failed to materialize through the wreathing smoke and steam that hung about the end of the platform, she had sat down on the slatted wooden bench and sobbed heartbrokenly, until a middle-aged porter's concern had driven her to move, handkerchief to her face, into the dark night.

Maggie pushed another cup of tea at her across the kitchen table. Helena smiled again, bravely. 'You get off to bed. Don't wait up. There might be another air raid.' In fact, the 'moaning minnie', as the siren had long been known, had not sounded for more than a week, and optimists had dared to begin to hope that, after eight long months and 40,000 civilian deaths in London, Coventry, and other major cities, as well as the destruction or damage of more than a million homes, Hitler had finally realized that the British were not to be bombed into submission.

'I'll sit up a bit longer. Just in case.' This time, Helena's smile was apologetic, and Maggie's heart went out to her again.

'It's all right. I'll keep you company awhile, if you don't mind. It's funny. I'm still not used to sleeping by myself. You'd think it would be the other way round, wouldn't you? That it'd be Alf I couldn't get used to, he's been away so long.'

Maggie kept up the light chatter, all the while trying to dismiss that sick feeling in her own gut, and the black terror of the memories she kept fighting determinedly to push away.

At half-past midnight, Helena was struggling to stay awake. Her face looked forlorn, and pinched, and she was shivering with cold. 'He's not going to be able to get here now, love,' Maggie said gently, her hand on the thin arm. 'It'll be in the morning, you'll see.' Helena nodded. The brown eyes gazed with weary helplessness at her, and made Maggie feel like weeping. 'Listen,' she said, 'you're frozen. Why don't you come and get in with me? I told you – I hate sleeping on my own. We can snuggle each other. Come on.'

Helena went up to change and use the bathroom, then came down in her dressing-gown, which she slipped off shyly before climbing in beside the waiting Maggie. She was wearing a thin cotton nightdress, sprigged prettily with flowers. For a few awkward seconds, they lay there, careful not to touch, then almost simultaneously, they moved. Helena gave a low, shuddering cry, clung to Maggie, shaken by a fit of violent grief, comforted more than she would have thought possible by the warmth of the arms that held her, and the body that lovingly enfolded her.

The 21st was a Wednesday, and Helena had arranged to have the Thursday and Friday free, though she knew Ernie would have to leave on Fridy morning, in order to be back on board his ship some time in the evening. Thursday morning seemed endless, as she sat in the station buffet, drinking stewed tea until her bladder would force her to make frequent trip to the Ladies' on the platform. The red chocolate machine still stood outside, with the gold lettering proudly proclaiming its wares, even though it had been empty for months.

By lunchtime, she could no longer stem the tears, and her handkerchief was a sodden, twisted wreck in her hands. Frantically, she wondered if she should try to contact his family at Kingstaith. But Ernie had told her he hadn't let them know he was coming home, because he wanted to spend all his time with her. *If there's time we can pop out and see them. And your folks*, he had added, with brave defiance.

At one o'clock, she was back in Maggie's kitchen, and in her arms, sobbing once more in desolation. 'He's not coming. Something's happened.' With a tight, sinking feeling she made certain she concealed, Maggie turned on the wireless in the front room, but there was nothing relevant on the news bulletin.

'He'll get in touch as soon as he can,' she assured the distracted girl. 'Don't get yourself in a state. They'll have had to go off somewhere, I expect.'

'I don't know what do do,' Helena said helplessly. 'I don't know who to get in touch with to find out.' Her tired eyes brimmed with fresh tears. 'There's a train at four from Middlesborough. I ought to be there.' She sounded crushed and defeated.

'You stay here,' Maggie said strongly. 'I'm going to go and see if I can find out anything. I'll go to the Docks Office by the Lifeboat House. There's a navy chap in there now, I'm sure.'

Maggie was patient, but resolute. After more than two hours, and a lot of earnest persuasion, she received the information that units of the Home Fleet, including HMS *Hood*, were indeed at sea. 'That's classified,' the port officer, an elderly wavy-navy lieutenant, told her sternly.

Maggie smiled, resisted the sudden, girlish temptation to snap out, 'Aye aye, sir!' and salute smartly. 'Thank you. I appreciate all your help,' she said instead, and hurried home. Helena was pathetically relieved, the tears now a release of pent-up emotion. Oh God, Maggie thought, an inner chill clutching at her, spreading creepingly through her blood. Why can't I feel relieved, too?

On the Saturday, Helena was on the early shift. Maggie was up, in her dressing-gown, when the slim figure came downstairs on her way out. Helena seized her hands, smiled at her. 'Promise me you'll send word if – you hear anything? If there's a letter – please!'

'Yes, all right. I'll send Vicky up. I promise.'

'You're an angel.' She leaned forward, kissed her quickly on the lips and turned away.

It was on the one o'clock news, in a special communiqué at the end of the bulletin. 'It is feared … heavy loss of life....' Maggie rose from the chair near the window, gave a very quiet cry, her knuckle raised to her mouth, experiencing once again all the flood of pain she knew she could not save Helena from, aching with the inevitability of it, the certainty of the young man's death.

Would Helena know? She was due to finish work at two. Would she hear of the disaster before she left the hospital? Maggie hurried out to the hall, which was lit by the early afternoon sunlight in a burst of incongruous cheerfulness. She sought the number of the Docks Office, tried to get through, but the operator told her the line was busy, advised to wait and try later. Of course, *Hood* was a big ship. There must be hundreds of men aboard, probably a good many from this area. She could imagine all too well the sickening anxiety of the relatives, their prayers, the desperate need to find out. She began to cry, went back into the kitchen, where Vicky stared at her in puzzled alarm. 'What's wrong, Mam? What is it?'

The coldness inside was spreading, and with it a hopeless inertia. She sat, made tea, couldn't drink it. Waited, for almost an hour, until she heard the front door open, heard the light footsteps, coming straight along the hall and passage. 'Hello. No news then? I—'

Maggie couldn't push herself up, and Helena stood gazing at her. The colour drained from the young face. Helena leaned against the chair, her knuckles white on its back. 'No,' she whispered. 'No. It's—'

Then Maggie found the strength to rise, to reach out, and they clung together and shared the pain which locked them together in a dreadful intimacy as close as the tenderness they had come to feel for each other.

3

With the ferocity of a drowning man to a lifeline, Helena clung to the hope that Ernie would have survived. She strove to transform that hope into a belief, which Maggie pretended to share, all the time enduring that terrible inner knowledge of the tragedy. It was Maggie who got through, eventually, to the Docks Office, explaining her quest to a stranger, describing her visit of two days previously, her interview with the RNVR lieutenant. More interminable waiting, until she was able to speak to him. It was terrifyingly simple. He gave her the names of the three survivors.

Ashen-faced, she turned from the receiver, shook her head, flinched at the raw loudness of Helena's revolted cry, hoarse with agony and unacceptance. 'No! No!' She fought, struggled against Maggie's hold, until the older woman had to fight in return to keep hold, force her down into the wooden chair, waiting for the threshing figure to collapse, which she did after long seconds.

'I know, my love, I know,' she wept, crouching, cradling the bent shape, pressing her wet face against the untidy, dark springiness of the hair.

In the early hours of the morning, Helena looked up at her. The face, ravaged as it was, looked absurdly young, as though the stamp of grief was too great to assume expression. She blinked at Maggie with exhausted bewilderment. The tears had stopped. 'What am I going to do? I'm on my own.'

'No, you're not! Don't say that!' Maggie almost shouted, grabbing at her, shaking her forcefully. 'You're not on your own! Do you understand that? You've got me! Us! Alf and I. You'll stay here, you'll be with us.'

Helena didn't return to work, forced herself on the Monday morning to take the local train out along the coast, staring out at the placid sea. She looked down from the high viaduct to the level stretch of the beach at Sandsend, remembering how she and Ernie had walked along the shore from Whitby, until the rolls of barbed wire and warnings of danger had driven them inland, through the golf links, to the coast road. Looking out through the glass, the heat of early summer warming her face, she thought how appropriate it was to do that. Stare out at the world from behind a thick sheet of glass. Cut off from it. That was how she felt. Strangely remote.

Her thoughts about the new life growing inside her frightened her, the way they jumped about, from one extreme to another. One minute hating it, feeling the curse of it, most shockingly, hating Ernie for doing that to her, taking possession of her, condemning her to it and leaving her alone to face the consequences, deserting her. You needn't have gone, her mind screamed at him. Reg was still safely at home, still working on the boat with his father. Rupert, five years Ernie's senior, had only just received his call-up papers and been posted to the army camp at Catterick for his basic training. You didn't have to go, she condemned bitterly. We'd already said we loved each other. And still you went away.

Then, sweeping in like a tidal wave, remorse, and guilt, and an aching immensity of love that made her thank God, and Ernie, for giving her the life within her, the most precious gift she could ever have. He had given her that; it was his, part of them, which she could cherish the rest of her life.

But everything was pain now, everything that assailed her eyes with the grief of her loss. The Virol advert on the fence at the back of the little platform, the smiling young matron on the poster superbly moustachioed by a vandal. The green door of the waiting-room where they had sat, with the two sniggering girls, that cold February afternoon, knees touching, her body still sore with the baby they had just begun. Every house front, every shop, every elaborately carved pigeon loft in the steep gully of the beck to her left as she picked her way carefully down the steep, uneven slope, to the harbour and the huddled cottages.

She went along the cobbled High Street, passing the two chapels, on either side, grimly facing each other, enemies even in non-conformity. As she turned into the shallow-stepped alley leading to the blue door at its end, she saw that the small windows of the neigbouring cottages had their curtains drawn. The sickness came again, and she wished that Maggie had come with her. She felt hurt when she recalled the clear reluctance Maggie had shown, the excuses – at least, that's what Helena had felt they were – about the domestic chores, the washing day that couldn't be postponed. 'You'd better be on your own. They won't want a stranger intruding at a time like this.'

I'm a stranger, Helena thought, but didn't say. 'You could wait for me. Outside, I mean,' she suggested instead, childishly pleading. But Maggie was determined. She was not going to Kingstaith. And, belatedly, Helena recognized her own childishness. Maggie was right. She had to face them, face his mother, alone. Tell them that she was carrying his child, that part of him lived on, in her.

She proved to be unequal to the task, even though she upbraided herself with bitter tears afterwards for her cowardice. Reg's wife, May, met her at the door, her thin face closed, sharp as a hatchet. 'Oh, it's you.' There was even a hint of reluctance in the time it took for her to move aside and let Helena in to the gloom of the crowded front-room, made somehow dimmer by the light filtered through the curtains. Sophia Wheatley was sitting before the gleaming range, in whose small, high grate the fire glowed redly. She was in a dark dress, with a spotlessly white apron covering the front from chest to hem. 'It's that lass that Ernie – you know.'

Helena swallowed, the tears came readily, spilled over. 'I'm sorry,' she choked. Mrs Wheatley nodded. The high-backed chair seemed to add to the upright sternness of the figure. Her hair was still dark, with little trace of grey, pulled back severely off the strong face. Helena began to cry more loudly, the sounds amplified in the ticking silence, while the two women watched her. 'I loved him – very much,' she stammered appealingly.

His mother grunted. 'So did we,' she answered starkly.

May interrupted, with that sharp accusation in her tone. ''Ow did yer know? When did you 'ear?'

'I heard it on the wireless. Then I rang – my friend rang – the office in Whitby. Saturday night. Late.' She hesitated. 'They said families had been informed.'

'Aye.' May nodded, with grim acknowledgement, as though honour had been satisfied. She gestured at the envelope still propped by the black, pillared clock on the high shelf.

'You must have a cup of tea,' Mrs Wheatley pronounced, and May moved obediently. Helena noticed that there were cups and saucers set out, a clean cloth spread over the table. The silver-hooped, oak-coloured biscuit barrel, with its miniature embossed silver shield, stood at the centre. The crockery was the best flowered, dainty service. They were obviously expecting a series of callers.

How do I tell her? Helena thought, with a sense of panic. She felt as if the words were struggling to escape from her, and again came that sudden resentment of Ernie. We should have been doing this together. But he would have found it just as difficult, she admitted honestly. But I wouldn't have been alone! her racing mind screamed rawly. We would have had each other, it would have been all right.

There was a loud noise outside, the rattle of equipment tossed down in the yard. She was relieved when the door opened and the bulk of Reg blocked the oblong of light, followed by his father. Billy Wheatley nodded his acceptance of her repeated, stumbled condolence, not even taking the pipe, which was not alight, from his clenched teeth. He moved out to the kitchen, closed the door behind him, did not return. Had he ever spoken to her? she wondered miserably.

Reg was now the one who carried the burden of politeness,

questioning her about her life, her work, with a rough, jarring heartiness. 'Our Rupe's comin' 'ome tonight. Cliffy's at sea. 'E'll prob'ly know by now, though, ah reckon.' He shook his head and made his first reference to the tragedy which had brought her to this close-knit, alien world. It should have drawn them together. Instead, she felt even more of an outsider. 'Bad business, eh?' Reg said.

Misery clogged her throat. And a cold recognition of her defeat. She wouldn't tell them, couldn't give them the news of her pregnancy. Later, when some weeks had passed, she promised herself. But now all she wanted was to get out, escape from them. Just like she had felt the last time, and the time before, she acknowledged leadenly.

They were as eager as she was to see her go. 'Ah'll walk yer up t' station,' Reg said. 'Ah need ter call in at Stamps'.'

'Afraid she'll lose 'er way, are ye?' May jabbed at him. Helena blushed, stumbled the goodbyes, made no reference to seeing them again, and neither did they. She was breathing deeply with relief when she got out at last into the open, was surprised to feel Reg's large hand close round her arm above the elbow and hold on to her. In the High Street, eyes regarded her curiously, then moved embarrassedly aside from Reg, Ernie's loss placing an awkward restraint over the greetings.

'Will there be – a funeral service?' Helena asked him diffidently, wondering if she could face such an ordeal.

He shrugged. 'Dunno. S'pose not, wi' no body or owt.' The blunt horror hit her in the pit of her stomach. 'Mam went te St Peter's – the Mission church – yesterd'y. She said they 'ad prayers fer 'im. Our Ernie. Daft beggar!' he added, with sudden, explosive emotion, and she began to shake, and cry. They were halfway up the steep bank out of the village, and he clumsily pulled her into him, leaning against the stone wall. The strength seemed to have gone from her, her legs were rubbery, and she leaned into him, her head pressing against the roughness of his jersey, wetting it with her tears, comforted by the smell of him, his strength. His hand felt huge, holding the back of her head to his chest, his breath was warm as his nose and lips rubbed on her hair.

'Yer not in any bother, are ye?' The sharpness of his words, the abrupt bluntness and suspicion of them, were like another blow, and she stiffened with loathing, shaking her head violently, levering herself off his bulk. But he was still clutching her waist, pressing his knees against her. His fleshy face peered down at her. Appalled, she saw the desire in his grey eyes, the frank, probing lust of his expression, felt the physicality of their contact. The mouth swooped, his lips touched her cheek, lightly, but with an intimacy that made her shiver with revulsion. 'Yer a fine lookin' lass,' he rumbled. She could feel his low tones transmitting their sensuality through to her as though he were caressing her. 'Ye've filled out a bit since ah fust saw yer. Yer were nobbut a bairn then. Remember? That day ye came seekin' our Ernie. Just a bit of a kid.' His head ducked again, he smiled. ''E could pick 'em, could Ernie.'

She wriggled free, pushing herself off him, swung away, striding out up the slope. She was trembling violently, wanting to scream, to spit obscenities at him. He fell alongside, laughed deeply. But he made no attempt to get hold of her arm again. At the gate leading on to the platform, she stood well back, watching him warily, saying nothing. He smiled again. 'Listen, yer a young lass. Nice lookin'. Ye'll meet somebody soon. Ye've got to 'ave fun, eh? Specially nowadays. Anything can 'appen. Mebbes we could meet, eh? In Whitby some time. 'Ave a drink together. Just you an' me. Our Ernie would 'ave liked that. Friendly like. No need ter tell anybody, eh?'

Oh God, God, why didn't she hit him? Why did she just stand there, in absolute silence, even when he thrust his face into hers and kissed her again, slobberingly trying to find her mouth, which she only just managed to pull away? He went quickly, with that deep, hateful laugh of his. He must have sensed her revulsion, surely? She wept all the way back in the train, which, thankfully, was not crowded. She kept her face turned to the window, her brow pressed against the glass, her handkerchief like a veil, and saw nothing at all of the familiar shoreline which swept past her a few yards away.

4

'Your mother rang.' Maggie tried to meet Helena's gaze directly, unable to confess that it was she who had rung the Barr house in Kilbeck, had spoken, almost in tears, of Helena's grief, her need for solace. 'She needs her family now,' Maggie had said, feeling that well-remembered sense of desolation, and hopelessness, even after all the years.

The faint but unmistakable reserve, and offendedness, had saddened Maggie, even though it didn't surprise her. 'Of course,' Lizzie Barr answered stiffly. 'We've heard the news. We guessed – that that boy was – we knew he was on that ship. I was going to call. Tell her please, we'd – we'll expect her home. As soon as she can.'

You were going to call, Maggie thought. But it's Monday. When were you going to call? How long have you known? Helena had told Maggie about her parents' opposition, how her father had even said she was not welcome in her own home as long as she was associating with Ernie. Maggie wondered if Helena had ever reflected on the immediate and unreserved bond which had sprung up between the two women, despite the age gap of nearly a quarter of a century, the compassion, and the love, which meant, Maggie knew all too well now, as much to her as it did to Helena. She would tell her soon, when the cruel rawness of the wound had begun to heal over a little, share the last secret which was an indissoluble part of the bond.

'They want you to go home. They want to see you,' Maggie urged. 'And this time you've got to tell them about the baby,' she went on gently, reaching out to take Helena's hand. The girl had tearfully confessed her inability to pass on the news to Ernie's family. 'They'll want to help.' She prayed hard, over her own sickening doubt, that that was true. She gripped the thin hand tightly, transmitting her feeling into the hold. 'In any case, you've got us, don't forget. We won't let go so easily.'

The wireless on the Tuesday evening, and the banner headlines on the Wednesday morning, were all blaringly triumphant over the sinking of the *Bismarck*. 'The *Hood* avenged', one paper shouted, and Helena felt only the magnification of her sorrow, imagining the telegrams going out to German homes, the cancerous spread of pain, the devastation of more and more lives. Rather grudgingly, for she had already taken two days' sick leave, the hospital allowed her to juggle shifts so that she would work the weekend, and thus got Thursday free. To her dismay, the equally short ride on the train, this time up through the Esk Valley to Kilbeck, was as painful and nerve-racking as the one she had made to Kingstaith three days previously. Except that, this time, she was resolute that she would somehow break the news of her pregnancy.

She had to pass the school on the long climb up the hill to Kilbeck Side, the row of dwellings and farmhouses that stood high above the dale where the village itself clustered about the shallow-running river. She was glad that her father and Elspeth and young Kit would be out. It would be easier to tell her mother on her own first.

They both cried, hugging each other silently, close again after the barrier of the months since Christmas. Helena was startled at how emotional she felt at seeing the familiar comfort of these surroundings, the pictures, the fireplace, the furniture of her home. The strength of their security wrapped itself about her warmly. 'I've got something to tell you, Mum,' she started bravely, when they were sitting at the kitchen table, cups before them.

She knew afterwards that her mother had guessed before she got the words out. She was angry with herself for not being able to hold back the tears when she told her. But all that was soon forgotten with the shock and the pain of her mother's reaction. Lizzie Barr wept more bitterly than her daughter. 'How could you? How could you do – something like that to us? The way we've brought you up – a decent home! What on earth will we do? Your father! The disgrace!' Helena sat there dumbly, stunned by the onslaught of panic-stricken horror.

'How far on are you? There must be something – we shall have to see someone. When was it?' She stared at Helena in fresh horror. 'Oh God! Not Christmas?'

'February. It was February,' Helena muttered. 'I told you – the last time he was on leave. He was going – he was due—' She could not go on, a huge sob shaking her. 'I want this baby!' she shouted, her eyes glaring at her mother. 'It's all I want! I'll take care of it!'

'You stupid stupid fool! How can you? The shame – you'll have to go away somewhere. Until it's over. Your poor father!' They wept together, in ugly, contrasting grief.

'I'll go,' Helena sighed, a long time later, when they had both recovered. 'Don't worry, I won't bother you again. I—'

'You're going nowhere, my girl!' Her mother sprang forward so quickly Helena flinched automatically, expecting an attack. 'You'll wait for your father. Sit down!'

She heard her mother in the front-room, speaking hurriedly into the telephone. 'I've told your father to come up as soon as he can. He's usually quite late these days. But he'll be up soon. Elspeth and Kit won't get back until five.' They returned on the train from Whitby, where they went to school. 'I don't want them caught up in all this.' Her voice quavered. Her face was creased with worry.

'I'm not ashamed, Mum,' Helena murmured unsteadily. She wanted to go to her, put her arms around her. She needed desperately to feel the love she had always assumed would be there for her.

'You ought to be!' The stricken face was screwed up with her disgust. 'I can't believe you – you could be so – so wicked! So easily led to do that! And that wicked boy! I know he's not here to take the blame, but he should be! I could never forgive him, not—'

'Be quiet!' Helena yelled in a tortured voice. 'Just shut up! I won't listen!'

Lizzie darted forward, and hit her with her palm across the head. The dark hair swung, Helena instinctively put up her arm, took the next swinging blow on it. It left an angry red mark on her pale skin. They both cried wildly, panting for breath, shaken equally by the eruption of violence. Resolution, fight, drained from Helena. She folded her arms on the table, hid her face in them, torn by her weeping, feeling totally alone and longing to be with Ernie, even in death.

Rather like a punch-drunk fighter, she endured the onslaught of her father's reaction almost numbly, though in its way it was more devastating because of his rigid control. Disgust showed in the curl of his mouth, the set of facial muscles locked in cold contempt. 'You can have the child in the workhouse. You won't blackmail us. I warned you. It's your disgrace, not ours. We'll face the shame, whatever people say. And they'll have plenty to say, no doubt. Not that that will worry you, I suppose. Shameless already, what harm can it do you?'

For the first time, emotion showed, dimly, in the thick tremor which caught at his voice. 'I can't believe we went wrong. It's something – evil. Or sick in you. I can't look on you as ours any more.' His tone steadied, modified. 'We can have you seen by a doctor. You're under age. Yes. We can have you committed. In an institution. Clearly you're unsound. Dementia, that's what they call it.'

She stared at him, her face a ghostly pale, her eyes dark and huge. 'Committed?' she whispered. 'You mean in an asylum?'

'They'll take care of everything. They have hospitals. The child, all that. They arrange adoption. It's for your own good—'

'No! No!' She jumped up, her face working. 'It's not me that's mad!' Her arm flew up wildly. 'There's people out there – half the world – trying to kill each other! This baby – Ernie's and mine – I'm going to take care of it!'

'Are you indeed? You can't even take care of yourself, can you? I think you've proved how unbalanced you are. You can stay here in your room until we get medical help. Just don't try to disrupt—'

'No! What makes you think—'

'Then get out now!' he cried, and she flinched at the enormity of his foam-flecked, frightening release of rage. 'Get out of this house! Go back to the scum you wallow with! We don't want to see you again!'

'Gladly!' she screamed, and turned and ran, tears streaming, not stopping to pick up the attaché case she had brought, expecting, as she had, to stay overnight and catch the early morning milk train back to the coast. Her things were sent on through the post to Prospect Mount next day. There was no note with them.

5

'Come on, young lady! School tomorrow. It's late enough.' Alf Turner swiped playfully at his daughter, who pulled a reluctant face, then flung her arms round him.

''Night, Dad. See you in the morning.'

Alf sighed with the luxury of sitting in his own kitchen, curling his stockinged feet in contentment. He had got back from a journey across country made difficult by wartime timetables, and let the prospect of a whole day's slippered ease at home wash over him like a warm bath. It had been awkward meeting Helena. His heart had gone out to her when they embraced briefly and he had felt the start of a weeping fit shake her slim frame, but she had quickly stifled it, brushed away the tears with determined courage. 'I've got some letters to write if you'll excuse me,' she said, soon after his arrival. 'And I'll have an early night.' He knew she was tactfully withdrawing, leaving him with his family. He already knew how friendly she and his wife had become, and guessed that the girl spent more time down here than up in her own flat.

He sensed that Maggie was awaiting an opportunity to talk seriously to him about something. He suspected it had something to do with Helena and the tragic death of her young man, whom he had never met. He was shocked by Maggie's revelation about the baby, though he hoped he disguised it well enough, chiding himself for his narrow, old-fashioned attitude of what was proper. He knew immediately how deeply Maggie must feel about the poor girl, how her heart must be torn with sympathy, and so he understood perfectly when she said, looking at him with those compelling brown eyes, 'You know why we've got to stick by her, don't you? You understand how I feel? I've told her she can count on us. She can stay here, have the baby here. We'll look after her.'

He smiled sympathetically, nodded. 'Yes, love. Of course. She'll be all right here, never fear.'

Those eyes softened, misted with affection. And remembrance. 'You're a good man, Alf Turner. You know that, don't you?'

'And you're a right fine-looking wench. You know *that*, don't you?'

That night, in the private darkness of the bedroom, Maggie lay with her nightie rucked about her waist, enduring the sweating weight of Alf as he lay on top of her, his heavily breathing mouth blowing in her ear. 'Was it good, eh?' he whispered, his words muffled in her dark hair. 'Was it all right for you?'

She eased a little under him, and he moved. She felt the cold, wet emptiness when he withdrew, and clutched him back to her, pressing her bosom to him. 'Lovely,' she sighed comfortably. And it was now, she thought, enjoying the gentle strokes of his hands on her, happy that his brief passion was spent, praying that he was really happy, because she wanted to make him so.

Next day, a little gruffly because of his embarrassment, Alf added his own affirmation of his wife's promise. Pink-faced, he made sure of waylaying Helena before she went off to work. 'I just want you to know, Helen, love, we hope you'll stay here, with us. Maggie's very fond of you – and me – I am, too,' he blurted hastily, causing Helena to smile through the tears she could feel were close to the surface. 'She knows what it's like. She's been through it herself. There's always a place here for you.' After another little pause, he ploughed on, 'She told me about your folks. Give them time, love. Mebbe they'll come round, once they've got used to the idea.' He saw the black hair shake vigorously, and didn't pursue the idea. Uncomfortably, he wondered what his view would be if Vicky were to come to him in a few years' time with a similar tale. How would he feel about her? One thing he was certain of: he could never throw her out, tell her he didn't want to set eyes on her again.

A few days later, Helena came in from work, her face bearing evidence of the strain she was under. Maggie had her tea ready for her, had looked forward to her return, to this quiet time they shared together, just the two of them, in the kitchen. Vicky was usually either up in her room or out with friends until later. Maggie felt a secret twinge of guilt at the closeness, the tenderness she felt for the girl sitting opposite her. It was too intense, it wasn't right, she tormented herself. Then she remembered again that far off time which was all being brought to life once more, uncannily, through the pretty, tragic form, and the feeling of compassion and love was so strong it swept aside all the guilt, all the discomfort of her feelings.

'I hope you don't mind,' Helena began now, tucking into her food with an enthusiasm that pleased Maggie deeply. 'My old boss is coming round later. I called in to talk to him. What with the way things went at home, Dad going on about me, about me being put away and everything.'

'They can't do that,' Maggie said anxiously. 'I'm sure they can't. We won't let them do that.'

'No, I know, it's just – only being eighteen. I don't want anyone to interfere – to take away my baby,' she added fiercely.

'They won't, love.' Maggie patted her arm. 'If necessary Alf and I will adopt it. Just to make sure.'

Helena's face lit up in a smile so warm and loving that Maggie felt her heart stabbed by it. The girl put her workworn hand over Maggie's, kept it there. 'I couldn't manage without you,' she said simply. 'Anyway, Mr Surtees couldn't talk much at the office. He said he'd pop in this evening. Talk to me. He'll be able to put us in the picture, legally, I mean. He knows all the ropes.' She smiled again. 'I'd like you to be there. You're – well, closer to me than anybody in the world.' The eyes filled, the lower lip quivered, and Maggie saw the slim throat swallow hard.

'Yes, love, of course. That's fine by me.' She stood up, her face flushed. Helena glanced up at her in some surprise, at her suddenly flustered air. 'You finish your tea. I'd better tidy myself up if Philip – Mr Surtees – is coming. Front-room job, that is.'

'He's fine, really,' Helena reassured her. 'He's a really nice man. Offered to help straight away.' She stared at Maggie curiously. 'Do you know him?'

Maggie's colour deepened a little. She nodded. 'Yes. I knew him a long time ago. We were friends when I was a girl.' She felt again that squeezing pressure, the memories and the sense of the inevitability of it all as the skeins pulled about her heart.

31 MAY, 1916

1

'Better get one o' them Dr Cassell's pills down you now, old fruit!' Tommy smiled at Paddy Foley's remark, deriving a measure of comfort from the very familiarity of the tired old joke which had gone round the messdecks of the squadron ever since the advertisements had first appeared in the papers. 'A sailor's nerves,' the inscriptions were headed, and promised benefits for everything from 'spinal paralysis' to 'brain fag'. The reason they had caught on, become such a joke among the men of Beatty's battle-cruisers, was that they were enthusiastically endorsed by a stoker (first class) from their very own *Princess Royal*. Many fierce arguments had raged aboard Tommy's ship as to whether the mythical figure existed in reality. Some claimed to know him; no one had conclusive proof.

I could do with something, Tommy acknowledged, recognizing the clenching, hollow sickness in his gut. He squinted up at the bright sunlight, enjoyed the warmth striking through the serge uniform, glancing outboard to the dazzle of it on the placid North Sea. The morning had been chilly, with great patches of that white, swift rolling mist he knew so well, imagining it drifting in along the clifftop back home, blotting out the sea, billowing like smoke over the fields at the edge, scudding in over the gardens round the hall.

'Just another sweep,' Paddy Foley had predicted confidently, before they had snatched a hasty, makeshift meal of corned dog sarnies and tea slopped from the tall jug into their tin mugs, on the quivering deck plates outside B-turret. Most people had agreed. It had happened so many times in the long months since he had joined *Queen Mary*, adding to the growing sense of frustration which dragged morale down. Only last month they had been called out at seven o'clock one evening, to head off frantically into the North Sea, uselessly searching, while four German battle-cruisers had sneaked past and bombarded Lowestoft and Yarmouth and escaped scot-free. There had been several loud arguments, and fist fights, in the pubs of Fife after that fiasco.

Then, last night they had just got settled round a table in the crowded fleet canteen at the naval base, with the first round of drinks going down nicely, when an officious PO had leapt on to the platform at the end of the long room and bawled everyone down to silence. 'Signal from flagship. "Raise steam for full speed. Clear for action on leaving harbour".' Of course, there was a great roar, before the general haste to swig off the beer and join the crush for the doors, but still with the feeling that it had all happened before, that they would be back in a day or two to sit drinking and grumbling once again.

Not now, though. 2.20 and one of Vice Admiral Beatty's light cruisers in the scouting screen had sent the signal, 'Enemy in sight'. HMS *Lion*, the flagship, had hoisted these flags to alert the other five battle-cruisers of the squadron, and altered course to intercept, ordering full speed ahead.

Tommy's post was in B-turret, the upper of the two forrard turrets housing the 13.5in guns. 'Lay out those dressings, Cousins. Those water bottles full? Good. Foley! Bully beef? Biscuits? Where's the ruddy piss bucket? Right-oh. God knows when we'll get out of here again.' The nervous anxiety of the gunner's mate did not help to ease the palpable tension. Although Sublieutenant Tomms was nominally in charge, the young officer was more than happy to leave things to the experienced Petty Officer Halliday, as they went through these nerve-racking moments.

Tommy had tried to tell Alice about his shipmates. About Paddy, and how, since the troubles in Dublin last month, he had had to put up with a lot of stick, and how Tommy had determined to stick by him. *He can't help being Irish*, he had written, then crossed it out heavily, feeling that it carried a hint of undue criticism. He didn't tell her very much about service life. In fact, though it pained him to have to admit it, he didn't tell her very much about anything.

When he struggled with pencil and paper, seeking out the rare privacy that was so hard to find living in such close proximity with more than 1,200 other men, he would feel more keenly than ever the gap dividing him from Alice. The gulf of social class, of education, that yawned between them. And then came the bitter attacks of conscience, and of dread, now, since that miraculous, foolish leave nearly two months ago.

There was still a feeling of dazed bewilderment, an air of unreality about that magical day, that poky bedroom in Salmon Cottage, with the squeaky bed where all that wonder had taken place. The way she had exposed herself, given herself to him, that sweet, fragile nakedness. It made him want to weep when he thought about it, which he did, so often, couldn't stop himself from thinking about, until he grew shamefully hard with wanting her.

He had been scared, probably as scared as she was, with the passion that had caught them both, shaking them with its intensity. Both of them fumbling, frightened virgins, driven by their hunger, somehow getting over all the ignorance and fear – the pain, too, for he had hurt her, he could still hear that gasp, the whimpers of her pain – to the love and the tenderness they had shared for so long. Just as precious was the feel of her next to him, her smooth warmth, her happy surrender of her shy body to his embraces after their first fury, lying together, in peace.

The fury had returned, had occurred twice more, as though they wanted to cram everything into those hours, to store up the passion of their love through the long months of separation ahead of them. He winced, yet smiled, at the secret intimacy of the memories. The sight of her slim body, bent over, the bruises darkening on her pale skin, hobbling like an old woman, giggling tremulously even at her discomfort. 'Tommy, love. Do you mind?' Her face and neck steeped in blushes now, as she continued with breathy embarrassment, 'Will you – I have to use the pot. I can't – will you wait outside?'

He had stood naked, staring at the pictures propped against the walls in the other bare room, shocked at himself, yet thrilled at the sound of her urinating. Then the sharp gasp of her breath at renewed pain had made him blush with remorse. Automatically, his hands moved to cover his genitals when he came back, and then she had shocked him by coming to him, and moving his hands, touching him there, his flesh throbbing and stirring. 'No, don't,' she protested softly, at his move to disengage her touch. 'It's lovely. I love it.'

That was a day all on its own. Her letters always referred to it. She could make him blush even in her letters. *Take care of my little friend. I hope he'll grow for me again next time we meet.* He smiled, but he couldn't help feeling deeply shocked. Girls – Alice – weren't supposed to think like that. Even though he did, so often, torturing himself with the memory of her.

He thought about that picture of her, of her sitting there, with nothing on, Rosie staring at her, getting it all down. Another strange one, Rosie. The village lads told terrible tales of her, not that he believed any of them. But she was strange. The picture was beautiful, it was Alice all right, beautiful, but shocking, too.

They had been so foolish that day, he kept telling himself. Now he wondered what would happen, how they could solve the enormity of the problem facing them. What would happen if he simply went to Mr Guthrie and told him? I want to marry your daughter. I love Alice. What would they do to him? To her?

'Right! Get inside, lads! We've got some fighting to do!' PO Halliday pushed Tommy unceremoniously in the back, and he left the bright sunshine, the heavy steel door clanging shut on it, the clamps turning to seal them within.

It was over an hour later before they fired their first salvo, at 3.50. Subby Tomms called out information as he picked it up from the gunnery director high above the bridge behind them. *Queen Mary* had the reputation of being the best shot of all the battle-cruisers, a reputation she upheld now in the first real exchanges with the enemy. Hampered by the reappearance of the patchy white mist caused by the humidity, and by the funnel smoke which drifted across in front of them, she nevertheless scored two quick hits on the German cruiser, *Derfflinger*, whose gunnery officer was later to describe the British ship's firing as 'superb'.

Everyone was working flat out now, sweating with the excitement as well as the effort of loading and training the heavy guns, but they were conscious of the sublieutenant's words, yelled shrilly above the noise. 'Bloody good show. We've hit 'em.' A few minutes later, he called out, 'Damn! *Lion*'s taken a hit.' That was the flagship, carrying Beatty himself, and they waited for more news, which was slow in coming. 'She's all right,' Tomms told them, speaking over his shoulder. His eyes were glued to the periscope raised above the turret roof.

Ten minutes later, over the confusion of noise and voices, they felt a perceptible quiver, and a muted thud. 'We've been hit!' Paddy Foley exclaimed, and Halliday shook his head. 'Naw. That wasn't us.'

'Christ!' Sublieutenant Tomms turned away from the scope to the hazy interior of the turret. 'She just blew up. Everywhere. I can't see her!'

'Who for fuck's sake?' Halliday's hoarse voice smashed through years of discipline and training.

'*Indefatigable!*' Tomms mouthed, not even aware of the breach of good order.

'Ready for firing!' The bellowed call sent them all jerking like marionettes into co-ordinated action once more.

There was a tremendous crash, and blackness. Tommy's spinning mind thought the gun itself had blown up, but then he wouldn't be here, would he? The blackness had picked him up and dashed him down again, and it was so hot. Even inside him it was hot; he couldn't breathe. Then he managed a tortured, sobbing breath, and felt an agonizing pain in his lower back. The darkness was blowing, drifting. He was lying over something hot, burning into him, but he couldn't move. But he could see. He saw a jagged, ripped lump of steel plate, torn like a piece of thin paper, sticking up right in front of him.

A voice was speaking, but it was far away, he couldn't pick it up. It was a shape; he could sense it rather than see it. 'Get out of it! Quick! She's going over! He's had it! Look! Leave him! Get out!'

He wept quietly with relief at the way the pain drained away all at once. The movement was gentle, flowing now, pleasant. Who was leaving? He stood at the bottom of those rickety, narrow stairs, knew Alice was waiting for him at the top. But who was leaving? 'Get the picture for me!' he called, smiling. He didn't care. They could all see it. He was so proud of her. She was beautiful. 'Bring the picture.'

On the bridge of HMS *Lion*, herself fighting to bring the dangerous fires below under control, Vice Admiral Beatty turned to his flag captain, as the great gout of metal and incongruously fluttering pieces of paper rose and descended at the spot where *Queen Mary* had been, and said, 'There seems to be something wrong with our bloody ships today.' Behind him, someone scribbled in the log, '4.20. *Queen Mary* blew up'.

2

The grey light of dawn filled the window recess. Alice felt as though she had not slept at all though she knew she had, for the weird dreams were still vividly with her. The crazy, worried thoughts crowded in on her as soon as she was fully conscious, and all at once she flung back the bedclothes and got up. She went over, drew aside the curtains at the dormer window. Out of the side window to her right, she saw the pale yellow wash in the east, the delicate shading of pale colour which made the thin streaks of cloud stand out all the more darkly. It was another splendid sunrise, and though she had no idea how many such she had witnessed from this familiar spot, she was comforted greatly by it. Yet again, she wondered if Tommy would be watching it from the deck of his ship.

The sea, too, was lightening now, especially along the line of the horizon. It would be warm. The glorious first of June. That was a sea battle, wasn't it? Poor Mr Swales. She had never paid enough attention to her history lessons. They never seemed to deal with the things she wanted to know, the real details of everyday living it fascinated her to think about. Instead, it was all kings and queens and dates and battles. The thought of battles made her breathe her silent prayer for Tommy to start her day. Not that she formulated it in words, even in her mind. It was a feeling, like her love. It didn't need expression.

Oh dear, Tommy. She *did* address him now, in silent speech. We have a problem now, my love. She sighed, tried to fight down that rising sensation of fear. She turned back, glanced at the sheet, turning the blankets down, with little hope. She put her hands on her belly, pressed lightly, but knew she felt nothing, no discomfort. She bent, gathered the hem of her nightgown, drew it up over her head. She walked naked over to the long mirror of her dressing-table, stood contemplating herself solemnly. She touched her breast, shivered slightly, caressed the nipple gently, blushing. Was it more sensitive than usual? She parted her legs slightly, carefully touched the folds of tissue beneath the small dark triangle of her pubis. Nothing, apart from the shameful shiver of pleasure the contact gave her.

Definitely the second 'monthly' was late now, by a week. Did that mean that she was pregnant? How could she find out? She would have to tell Rosie, ask her what to do. Yet, somehow, she shrank from such a disclosure, even to Rosie. The fact that it had happened in her cottage, in her bed, made Alice oddly even more reluctant. Especially as Rosie had scarcely even referred to it afterwards, as though she did not wish to talk of it.

Though she blushed when she thought of it, she acknowledged that she must write soon and tell Tommy. He should be the first to know, after all. They would have to be married. And quickly, too. Surely they would allow him some leave in such circumstances? If only she could be absolutely sure that she was pregnant! One day. Just one day. Was it possible? Surely it was highly unlikely? How many times had they done it? Three.

Standing gazing at herself, she shivered suddenly, more violently, felt that wicked desire stealing into her to touch herself properly. She moved hastily to the washstand near the window, poured cold water into the basin, bent and washed her hands and face, then breasts and between her legs, drying herself quickly. She would get up, saddle Kitty, go for a ride before anyone was stirring.

She peered at her watch on the bedside table. 5.30. And the sunlight was already starting to penetrate. Would it have been darker before this new Daylight Saving thing? What had they done? Brought the clocks forward? It still confused her. Dora had told her there was one shopkeeper in Whitby who simply refused to have anything to do with it, just opened his shop an hour later than everyone else, and closed it an hour later. Were you allowed to do that? Wasn't it law now, an Act of Parliament? Anyway, it was going to be a lovely morning, and she could never go back to sleep again.

She dressed quickly, pulling on a thick woollen jersey, and the thick cycling knickerbockers, buttoning them and tucking them under the three-quarter socks before sliding her feet into her riding boots. She knew Papa would blow his top again if he saw her. 'You look like a boy,' he told her accusingly. She would have to be careful. Still, she could slip in through the kitchen and get upstairs while he was breakfasting.

She made her way down through the fields of the adjoining farmland, avoiding the lane and the road down to the harbour, coming on to the clifftop track north of the village. She could see the twin points of the cliffs between which Kingstaith nestled. Because of the steepness of the gorge where the beck flowed into the sea, around which the cottages were clustered, she could see only one or two of the roofs of the uppermost dwellings, but there was a thin layer of light grey smoke, as insubstantial as the morning mist, hanging almost horizontally above the village, indicating that a good many people were already up and about, with fires lit. She grinned, almost tempted to ride down there and call at Salmon Cottage. Rosie would certainly not be one of those early risers, and she could imagine her friend's shockingly robust language if she were to put her idea into practice.

But the path down from the cliff was far too narrow and steep for Kitty, even if she led her. She turned towards the sea, lightening now, sparkling in the morning light, and negotiated the tricky little descent through the clinging brambles on to Dalton's Meadow, and enjoyed Kitty's sedate canter up and down the level stretch of tussocky grass. She wasn't much of a horsewoman, she admitted freely. Not like Olga, who had even gone over and ridden with the Kilbeck Hunt on occasions. No longer, though.

As Mrs Luke Powers, she was far too involved in playing the little housewife among the doilies and the teacups to do anything so energetic. Besides, it smacked too much of fun. Alice felt guilty as always when she reflected on how pleasant she found home now that Olga had removed herself from it. With Alex and Bertie both away, too, it was a fairly lonely place at times, but she preferred it that way. She was pretty much allowed to do as she pleased these days, as long as she showed up for meals and was ready for church on time.

She was determined this life of ease wouldn't go on, though. Two months from today she would be eighteen. Time to do something with her life, to make some useful contribution. With Tommy away, there was nothing to keep her here. She wanted to learn to drive a motor car, had been pestering Dougie Palliser, who drove her father to and from work, to teach her, until Papa had sternly ordered her to leave him alone. But she was determined to do something – there were women joining the services now. She fantasized the delight she would derive from turning up as a uniformed member of the Women's Royal Naval Service at Rosyth and seeing the look of utter amazement on Tommy's face.

The remembrance of her present disturbing reality was like a slap. She wouldn't be going anywhere if there was a baby growing inside her. Forget your silly daydreaming, she scolded herself. You've got to find out. Then plan what to do.

Kitty had stopped and was grazing. Alice swung herself lithely off her broad back and moved towards the edge of the strip of grass, where it fell away to the steepness of the cliff face once more. Suddenly, she stared with new attention out to sea. A low, dark shape had appeared round the nab, quite close inshore. She realized at once it was a navy vessel, though not a large one. She saw the ensign streaming proudly from the mast, and a gaily coloured string of signal flags below. But then, just aft of the mainmast, she saw the jagged rent in the superstructure, the gaping black tear in the forrard funnel through which the black smoke was pouring, billowing out behind her. Metal stanchions were twisted like bits of thread, there were other jagged holes in the hull, as though a giant hand had flung a handful of peppering shot.

Small figures were gathered about the upper deck. Two of them stood high on the bridge, their arms bent as they waved vigorously.

She snatched the scarf from her neck and held it high, waving back. Others along the length of the ship saw her and waved; she heard the faint sound of cheers carried away thinly on the breeze. Her heart beat quickly as she noted more evidence of the damage that had been done. The ship swept on, a brave sight, hugging the coastline, steaming close to Port Hilda, heading in the direction of Whitby. She saw other dark smudges on the horizon.

All at once, she felt nauseous and she began to tremble, her legs weak. She sat down in the grass, listening to the soft tearing as Kitty plucked at the grass. A hot, bitter liquid burnt in her throat, and she knelt, doubled up, and retched dryly, spat into the fronds of long grass, gasping and holding herself, until the fit of sickness passed. Shaken, and frightened, she climbed on to Kitty, let the pony walk slowly back up through the fields, keeping to the hedgerows.

'Are you all right, dear?' Her mother's question was occasioned, not by Alice's look, but by the fact that her plate held only two thin pieces of toast at breakfast. Freshly washed, this time in warm water, her hair neatly pinned, and in skirt and blouse, she had come into the dining-room just as her father was disappearing behind the crisply ironed pages of the morning paper.

'I took Kitty out this morning,' Alice remarked. 'There was a navy ship. It came right in close. It had been badly damaged.'

The paper crackled, her father's carefully groomed head appeared again. 'What was it?'

'I don't know. Not very big, I think.' She saw the worried expression set into her mother's face, knew she was thinking of Bertie at once. Mama's war was very personal. But then, so was hers. She had thought of Tommy right away, her heart had thumped with fear for him for a moment. Perhaps that was what had made her sick like that.

Mother was going down to the village, to meet with the vicar's wife and the other local ladies, to roll bandages for the Red Cross. Alice felt bad, but only briefly, at the way she always made excuses to avoid accompanying her. Apart from the boring task, she could scarcely think of a more boring company to perform it in. She smiled to herself as she thought how shocked the good ladies would be if they could overhear some of the conversations she and Rosie enjoyed. As always, she was looking forward to the walk down to Salmon Cottage, in spite of her private anxieties. She wondered if she would tell Rosie her troubles today? She would have to confide in someone. And soon.

But when she came down the treacherous dirt track leading to the village from the heights of the cliff, she saw the gathered knots of fishermen, and their womenfolk, heard the animated buzz of talk. The atmosphere was charged. No one glanced at her amiss when she went over to a group of the shawled wives to ask what was wrong. Most of them recognized her, for there were not many days when she did not come to the village now. 'Been a big do, miss. Out to t' sea. The boats come in this mornin', said they 'eard firin' through the night. An' the's been loads o' ships comin' back, all shot up, like. Reckon the's been a big fight out there.'

In Salmon Cottage, Rosie filled the kettle, lit the spirit stove and placed it on the ring. 'Now don't work yourself up into a state, girl,' she declared, with gruff kindness. 'It's a big ocean. And hundreds of ships.' Alice smiled gratefully, and welcomed the comfort of Rosie's strong arms around her. She leaned against the sturdy shoulder, savouring the large, gentle hands stroking her hair and her brow.

There was no escape from the net of events closing in around her, though. They walked over the beck, and up the slope that led out from the northern end of the village, and up to the solid block of the nab, which stood like a natural breakwater over the village at its foot. Even there, they met folk eager to pass on news of a great sea battle. 'Reckon they've caught 'em at last!' an elderly man chuckled. 'This'll put pay to them wi' their bombardments an' their Zeppelins, eh?' The long traditions of Nelsonian might were firmly lodged in the majority of breasts, and people waited confidently for confirmation of another Trafalgar-like triumph. The truth came slowly, dribbling in with remorseless force.

Restlessly, Alice told Rosie she was going to go back home, to see if anyone could gather more information. Her mother was sitting, chalk-faced, in the drawing-room, staring unseeingly through the big windows to the neat circle of the rose bed and the immaculate lawns. The faithful Evie was in attendance. 'Your father's promised to find out what he can. He's coming home early.'

It was hard for Alice, pretending that her mounting dread was for her brother alone, especially when she saw Dora's worried features. As soon as she could, she clutched at the girl's hand and brushed her head close in brief contact. 'He'll be all right, Dora, I know he will.'

'Yes, ah know, miss. It's just a worry, isn't it?'

Unable to hide the strain she was under, Alice made excuses to retire to her room early. She was already changed into her night things when she heard the jangle of the telephone, and her father's voice, loud in the hall. Grabbing at her dressing-gown, she pulled it round her as she raced down the stairs in her bare feet.

Her mother was standing there, weeping, her hands twisting together, but Alice could see straight away that the tears were of relief. She turned, dramatically hugged Alice to her. 'He's all right. Thank God! He's all right!' Her father, rigid with the effort of listening over the distortions of the line, waved them away, and Alice led her mother into the lamplit drawing-room. 'Praise God, he's perfectly all right,' she wept. 'He's been trying to get a message to us since they got in.'

Mr Guthrie came in after some minutes. Alice could see that he, too, was affected by his emotions, though he tried hard to disguise them. Bertie's destroyer had been damaged, but he was unharmed. 'He's in Yarmouth,' her father told them. 'A lot of ships have had to make for various ports along the coast. That must have been what you saw this morning.'

Alice nodded, hesitated. 'You haven't – heard any other news? She blushed. 'I was thinking of poor Dora – her family. Tommy's—'

Her father shook his head, his lips pursed. 'Hm. Bad business. He was on the *Queen Mary*, she said. Battle-cruiser. They took the brunt of it. They lost several, I believe. Apparently *Queen Mary* was one of them. Blown out of the water, they say.'

3

It wasn't until three days after the Battle of Jutland that the Cousins received the official news of Tommy's death. In fact, Mr Guthrie's Saturday edition of the *Daily Express* also carried his name, in the disastrously long casualty lists inside, sombre and quiet reading after the glaring doom of the banner headline on the front. 'Unaccountable British losses – three battle-cruisers sunk. German battleship destroyed. Many smaller craft lost.'

'We're putting up a damned poor show!' Mr Guthrie said. 'On land *and* sea.' His wife was too guiltily relieved at the fact of Bertie's safety to take much heed, though she nodded her dutiful agreement.

Evie bobbed at his elbow. 'Dora's not in, sir. She says she's sorry. They've had a letter about their Tommy. Her brother, sir. It's definite, ah'm afraid.' She sniffed slightly, turned towards Mrs Guthrie. 'Miss Alice is still in bed, ma'am. Says she's still not feelin' well.'

'What's wrong with her?' Alexander Guthrie queried testily. 'We've seen nothing of her these past two days. If she's ill, we'd better have Dr Hanson in.'

'It's just a summer chill, I think, dear,' Margaret answered. 'She was up most of yesterday. I'll go up and see her in a minute.' She paused, her tone lowering to one of diffidence. 'And all this worry over Bertie – and young Tommy Cousins. She was fond of him, you know. They were pals. When they were children.'

His mouth tightened, and grimaced. 'I know! She needs a sense of proportion, does that one! You know, we'll have to do something with her. What does she do with herself all day? She doesn't seem to mix much. With friends, I mean. I've been thinking. Perhaps we should enroll her at that college in Whitby. What's it called? That secretarial place.' He grunted. 'Girls seem to want to do anything but settle down these days. They've even got this Women's Land Army now. Have you seen 'em? Joe Dalton's got two of them working for him on the farm. Strutting about like ruddy guardsmen, jackboots and all!' He shook his head despairingly.

The gravel crunched as the motor rolled up to the front steps. 'Will you be home for lunch?' his wife asked.

He stood, grunted noncommittally. 'I'll try. Saturday's just like any other day now. And I want to spend some time down at the port today.'

After he had gone, Margaret went upstairs. The house was so quiet nowadays with the boys and Olga away. She heard the muffled weeping as she turned at the head of the stairs. She went along the landing, pushed open Alice's door without knocking and went in. She saw the huddled shape turned on its side, facing away from her towards the window. The black hair was spread stragglingly over the pillow. When Alice turned, her face was swollen, swamped with her grief. Anguished sobs tore from her at the sight of her mother.

'He's dead, Ma! They've had the letter—'

'I know, I know!' Margaret came forward, sat down on the dishevelled bed, put her hand on Alice's shoulder. 'Don't take on so, love. It's sad, but—' She shrugged helplessly. 'This!' She gestured about her, taking in Alice's tragic form, the room. 'It's – it's not – proper!'

'Leave me alone, Mother!' Alice's voice quivered with a shocking disgust. She turned away rudely, burying her face in the pillow, her back turned dismissively.

'Well! You're behaving so – so foolishly. Your father's just been saying – you've got no idea of what's right. The way to go on—'

'You're right!' The slim figure swung round so violently that Margaret was startled. The streaming eyes flashed wildly. 'You're so right! You don't know! When you find out—' With a choking cry of rage, and despair, Alice flung herself into the pillow again.

'You're hysterical, girl!' Her mother was breathing heavily, indignant, but shaken by Alice's vehemence. 'I'll talk to you later, when you've got over this – this fit. I'll send Evie up, with some tonic. Dora's not here—' She left, closed the door quietly on the tormented weeping, deeply disturbed by Alice's emotion.

It was nearly noon when Alice forced herself out of bed, and got dressed. Evie had laid out some clothing, and Alice dragged on the garments without really noticing them. She felt worn out and empty, apathetic. But she knew the sorrow was there still, would always be there, would build up for release after release. I won't stop weeping for you, she told Tommy. She tugged a brush through her hair, separating it into untidy plaits which she pinned loosely on top, and thrust a woollen tam over her efforts. She slipped a cardigan over her blouse, then made her way downstairs, trying not to make a sound as she reached the hall. She didn't go out of the front door but turned back at the foot of the stairs and went out past the kitchen, using the short corridor past the butler's pantry, to pass out into the stable yard.

The lane was muddy. There had been showers earlier, and the clouds were still piled in the sky over the rising sweep of the land on her right. But over the sea to her left the sky was blue, and the sun had broken through strongly again. What was it Tommy said? If there was enough blue to patch a Dutchman's trousers, it would be all right.

She wondered whether to go to the front door, then decided against it. She skirted the long puddles of the back lane, went down the row of cottages until she came to the Cousins' gate. She stared at the tin bath near her head. That's what Tommy bathed in, had done since he was little. That's what they all bathed in. All in the room, in front of the fire. How did they manage? She felt herself blushing hotly, was ashamed of herself. Then she blushed again when the door opened, and the tall Louise stared at her blankly.

'Oh, it's you.' For a second, Alice was afraid she wasn't going to let her in, then she stepped back. 'Oway in. Ah thought it might be our Mary. We're expectin' 'er any time.' They passed through the small back kitchen to the front living-room, which was oppressively hot, for the fire was burning in the high range. The curtains were drawn over the front window. Ginny Cousins was baking. The big table where they ate was covered with newspapers, and there were jars and bowls scattered everywhere, and the sweet smell of freshly baked scones hung fragrantly in the air.

Ginny wiped her hands vigorously on her apron. She looked confused, and deeply embarrassed. 'Oh, Miss Alice – ye'll·'af to excuse us. Just doin' a bit o' bakin'. The'll be folks comin'. And our Bert and them'll be comin' fer tea.'

'Yes, yes, it's all right. I won't stop. I just want to say – to say – I'm sorry—' Her throat sealed up, she couldn't hold back the huge sob. She dashed forward, clumsily clutched at the startled woman, felt her standing stiffly in her embrace, then, suddenly, the arms came up, the stiffness relaxed, and, for a few precious seconds, they were close, united.

'Aye.' Ginny nodded simply, very dignified, wiped at the tear on her cheek with the back of a hand. 'Ah know ye were fond of 'im, miss. An' 'e was, too. Of you.'

But then there seemed nothing to say. She refused a cup of tea, was heartily glad when Dora came down the narrow staircase. She looked soft and pretty in her dark frock. 'Would you like a walk?' Alice blurted suddenly, her face crimson. She could feel the tears starting to her eyes again. She was so like Tommy, Alice thought. The girl nodded quickly, didn't even look surprised.

'Yes, ah could do with some fresh air. Ah'll not be long, Mam.'

They said little until they were past the Far Row, and the road down to the harbour. 'Me da's gone to work,' Dora said. ''E'll be knockin' off after dinner. 'E were just under me ma's feet at 'ome.'

'Dora! I've got to talk to you! To someone! It's—' She started to cry, noisily, shaking with her grief. Dora held her, their faces rubbed together, until the fit had eased a little. 'I think I'm going to have a baby. Tommy's.' She was shaking, but the tears were of relief now. She could feel it, the comfort of having shared it with someone else.

Dora's dark eyes were enormous, for the moment her sadness spirited away by the shock of the news. 'Are ye sure?' Alice nodded, dabbed at her cheeks. ''Ow far on?'

'It was – when he was on leave. In February. I've missed twice. My second – it should have been over a week ago.'

'Ye'll 'af ter do something!'

'No!' Alice cried out instinctively, shaking her head.

Dora caught hold of both her hands, held on to them tightly. 'Listen! 'E's gone! The's nowt 'e can do, miss! Ye'll just – ye can't 'ave a baby on yer own! 'E wouldn't want that – it'll ruin yer! Yer da! Think!'

She held her close again, waiting until the girl had cried herself out, her own eyes moist with compassion, her mind racing. Louise would know what to do. But how to ask her? She didn't want to trust her older sister with the truth. She would have to be clever, make her think it was for someone else. 'Don't worry, miss. Ah'll 'elp yer. We'll sort it out. Nobody'll know.'

Alice suffered deeply over the following days, her distraught mind a battleground of conflicting emotions. It's ours, Tommy's and mine. All that's left of him. 'But 'e's gone, miss!' Dora argued, with inescapable logic. 'Yer seventeen! An' yer'll be all on yer own. The baby'll 'ave no father. Your folks, an' mine. None of them'll 'elp. Ye can't do it ter the poor mite! It 'ud be bad enough if Tommy 'ad been 'ere. The'd still be against yer. Yer couldn't 'ave married 'im.'

Alice nodded in fierce contradiction. 'We loved each other! We'd have gone away.' Dora was silent. No use pursuing that argument. It would not arise.

'Yer can't ruin yer whole life! An' the baby's! Better put a stop now. Even fer Tommy's sake, miss. Think what the'll all say about 'im now – when the find out—'

That was the hardest fact to fight against, as Dora knew. She laid plans. Asked discreet questions, 'Widder Welch's, miss. There's pills. An' gin. And an 'ot bath. That'll do the trick, the reckon.'

Alice gave her the money. 'Aren't you – you know? Worried? Getting these pills? They'll think it's you that's – in bother.'

Dora smiled. 'Naw. Could be fer anybody. Any road, the not bothered as long as yer pay. Now listen. When can yer do it? When's yer mam out? Be best of a mornin', miss. When she's out at 'er village meetin'. Nosy drawers Evie'll be out the road then an' all.' They giggled like guilty schoolgirls.

'I want you with me, Dora. I'm scared.'

'Aye, right-oh.' The older girl was scared, too, but she smiled reassuringly.

When Mrs Guthrie went out the following week, Dora already had the boiler full. As soon as Evie went off to the room over the stables, Dora turned the brass tap, filling the bucket with the hot water which she ferried upstairs to the bathroom. 'As hot as yer can stand it,' she cautioned Alice. 'You 'op in. Ah'll bring more water.'

Alice squealed softly when the sweating girl tipped the last pail into the clawfooted tub, sending the steam billowing. The tiles and the mirror over the basin were clouded, running with condensation. 'No! Don't run any cold in!' Dora chided.

'I'm like a lobster! Look at me!' Alice couldn't help sniggering. She had swallowed the two pills, her heart racing with fright, and now she started on the gin, snorting and shuddering with disgust at its sharp, burning taste, despite the water with which it was diluted. 'When will it – I feel it?'

Dora pulled up the small, cork-topped stool and sat. She leaned forward, her elbows resting on her knees. 'It'll be a few hours yet.' Her face, pink with her recent efforts, and the heat of the steamy room, reddened further. 'Ah've put a draw sheet on the bed. An' the's some more cloths underneath. The's the chamber pot. Ah'll come up after tea. See 'ow you are. Clear up. An' ah'll be in dead early temorrer.'

Alice gazed at her in alarm. 'Will it be – will there be much mess?'

Dora tried to meet her gaze squarely. 'A bit. Like an 'eavy flow, the woman said.' She paused. 'It'll 'urt a bit.'

The brown eyes reflected Alice's trepidation. 'I wish you could stay with me.'

'Ah'll keep lookin' in. Ye'll be all right, miss.' She grinned conspiratorially. 'Now come on. Drink up. Ah want ter see yer drunk as a lord.'

'Join me,' Alice said. 'Get that tooth glass. Come on.'

Half an hour later, they were both giggling at every remark. Their cheeks were red. 'I feel wicked,' Alice confessed, gesturing at her pale body. She held up her glass. 'I'm a wanton, aren't I? Do I look like a wanton?'

'What's one o' them?' Dora asked, and they bumped their heads together as they snorted with laughter.

'You're a brick, Dora, you know that? The only one in the world I can rely on. My one best friend. I don't know what – without you—' Without warning, she began to cry, the tears pouring down her cheeks, and Dora wept, too. They kissed, and licked at the salt drops.

'I'm going crinkly,' Alice murmured, a little while later. 'And this water's nearly cold.' She stood, almost slipped, and Dora held on to her. 'Oh God, I'm drunk. I feel giddy. And I think—' She gave a wild cry, and lunged forward, brushing past Dora to fall on her knees over the toilet. She belched and then vomited copiously and long, while Dora bravely held her heaving, wet stomach, and resisted the urgent temptation to throw up herself.

Hurriedly drying her, Dora got her nightgown on her, and helped her into bed, placing a bucket close at hand, and spreading towels all round. She put a damp facecloth in Alice's limp grasp. 'Ah'll try an' keep yer ma out,' the distracted girl said. 'Try an' get some sleep. And don't make too much noise. The bucket's there.'

As the afternoon drifted into a beautiful summer's evening, Alice wondered dimly if she were about to die. Exhausted by the frequent fits of vomiting, she lay doubled in fiery agony, the pains tearing at her insides until she was biting at the sheets to suppress her cries. Dora was frantic, then panic-stricken. Tortured by doubt, she was ready to go to Mrs Guthrie and confess everything. Crying with fear, she slipped yet again into Alice's room. 'We'll 'ave ter tell 'er.'

'No!' Alice's face was blotched, shone with sweat. The sickly odour wafted up to Dora. 'I'm all right! Just wait! It can't be long now!'

But it was, interminably long. Dora hung on as long as she decently could, making an excuse of Alice's illness. Mrs Guthrie insisted on a strong dose of a patent cough mixture, purely for its sedative qualities. 'You're very flushed, love. I'm sending for Dr Hanson first thing if you're no better.' Amazingly, the sedative worked. Alice slipped in and out of a dream-haunted sleep.

When Dora came nervously tapping at the door before the rest of the household were up and about the next morning, Alice smiled wanly at her from the pillow. Her eyes were dark and weary against the pallor of her face. 'I'm all right. Apart from a horrid stomach ache.' She saw Dora's mouth open in enquiry, and went on quickly, 'No. Nothing's happened. Thank God!' She gazed steadfastly at the maid. 'I've been doing an awful lot of thinking lying here. And I know I've been so wicked trying to get rid of this baby. I just hope he's all right and I haven't harmed him. Because I want him, more than anything else in the world! We were mad to want to get rid of him. He's Tommy's, and I'll never, never be sorry. And neither will he!'

4

Alice's heart bumped painfully, feeling as though it was about to leap up into her throat. Yet she had to speak now. Now was the perfect time, in its own sick, twisted, logical way. Besides, she couldn't keep the secret much longer. Surely they would start to notice? She must begin to show signs soon. Her breasts were larger; they felt enormous, and sensitive, too. And she knew her belly was a little rounder, there was a distinct little pot. Her bottom, as well. That was fuller. It was ironic that it should take this to give her all the feminine attributes of a more graceful figure that she had wished for so often.

At least she had stopped being sick in the morning. Thank goodness Dora was the one who looked after her, and not Evie. Even so, she had been afraid someone would hear her one of these days. Dora looked almost as scared as she was. ''Ave yer told them, miss?' she would ask, her eyes big with worry. She had not suggested any further attempts to halt the pregnancy. 'Ah was that scared, miss. Ah was terrified! Ah thought ah'd be 'ad up fer murder!'

The only other person Alice had confided in, a few days after the incident of the pills and gin, was Rosie Dwyer. Rosie's open face had pinked a little, that was all, but she gazed levelly at Alice all the while. 'It was here, wasn't it?' Alice nodded. She was the one who lowered her head. 'You foolish girl!'

The black hair lifted, the vulnerable brown eyes showed pain, but spirit, too. 'I'm not sorry! I'm glad! 'Specially now. I want to have the baby.' And Rosie had simply nodded, in perfect understanding. No talk of secret arrangements, of getting rid of it, and Alice had been full of tearful, heartfelt gratitude. 'You've got to let your folks know soon,' Rosie advised. And Alice knew, sinkingly, that the moment had come.

Olga had arrived in a taxi cab all the way from Whitby, to declare theatrically that she was 'in a delicate condition'. Her mother, who had been expecting the pronouncement for at least the past six of the nine months since the wedding, gave a shriek of astonished delight, and rushed to gather her eldest daughter into her arms. 'Oh, my dear! What splendid news! Your father will be so pleased!'

Alice, who was at home at this time of the morning because Rosie had insisted she must have the first part of the day to herself to work on some sketches, went to her sister to add her congratulations. Olga offered her a cheek. 'Isn't it wonderful?' Mrs Guthrie exclaimed. 'I'm so excited! When is it due?'

'End of January, about. I've just been to the doctor.' Olga looked triumphantly radiant.

'Snap!' The stupid word was out before Alice could prevent herself. Her mother gaped. Olga made an impatient little click at what she thought a very vulgar and tasteless attempt at humour. 'Except I'm not sure when mine's due. About then, I should think.'

They both stared at her in almost comic surprise. An expression of slight pain flickered over Mrs Guthrie's pink features. 'Please don't be silly, Alice. Not now.'

'It's true. I'm sorry. I meant to tell you – before.'

'What?' Olga's lovely face was a parody of incredulity. Her dark eyebrows were curved halfway up her brow. 'You can't!' The hoarse whisper of her tone matched her expression.

'Stop it, you wicked girl!' her mother gasped, rallying. 'It's not at all funny! Stop being so – so wicked!' She gestured helplessly.

Alice could feel herself blushing. She faced them with trembling courage. 'It's true. I'm going to have a baby! It happened in April. When – I've been trying to find out – I'm sure now. That I'm pregnant.'

'No! Oh no! You can't!' Mrs Guthrie was chalk white. She clutched at the desk, then almost fell into the armchair. Both the girls sprang forward, for she looked as though she might faint.

Olga grabbed the bell pull. She turned on her sister, her face contorted with a snarl of pure hatred. 'Get out! Go up to your room! And stay there!' Evie came hurrying in, stopped in alarm at the three frozen figures. 'Go on!' Olga hissed, eyes blazing. 'Fetch some brandy!' she commanded the maid. 'Mama's not well.' Alice hesitated, opened her mouth, and Olga straightened, glared at her with such malevolence that Alice flinched, expecting a blow. She turned and ran out, raced up the stairs to her room, where she flung herself on the bed and burst into a fit of wild sobbing. I've done it, I've done it. Even in her distress, she felt glad that she had at last spoken.

The nightmare began soon after. Later, Alice decided that the circumstance of her older sister being on hand for the revelation was a good thing. It was easier to stand up to Olga's fury during the initial interrogation than her mother's bewildered sense of doom. And Olga appointed herself chief interrogator, with a vengeful eagerness. 'I didn't do this just to spite *you*, you know,' Alice retaliated strongly, despite her weeping.

'It was jolly perfect timing though, wasn't it?' Olga fired back, cheeks glowing, and Alice deduced that that was at least partly the reason for her sister's rage.

'Sorry if I've stolen your thunder,' she rejoined cuttingly.

But worse came when she revealed who the father was. Mrs Guthrie could add little but copious fresh tears, sobbing and muttering into her handkerchief. Olga was not so handicapped. 'You cheap, dirty little slut!' she hissed vehemently. The cords on her slender neck stood out throbbingly with her revulsion. 'You couldn't even – find somebody of your own kind – a – a labourer boy! From the mine! You're sick!'

'He's worth ten of your sort!' All the anger, and the hurt, and hopelessness of life itself burst like a breached dam inside her. She was choking, almost physically sick, with her disgust at the trick life had played on her, at the narrow hidebound rules of her society which had doomed their love from the start.

'A common worker's brat!'

With an elemental cry, Alice came up off the bed where she had been sitting. Her fingers hooked in Olga's elaborate coiffure, she clawed with her other hand at that insufferably lovely, contemptuous face. Her nail traced a red furrow down the cheek before the startled girl could turn her head away, and she screamed. She seized a wrist, and they tussled, wrestling, sobbing, until Mrs

Guthrie's screams brought them both to awareness. Evie came racing in, and at once flung her arms around Alice's waist and threw her bodily back on to the bed.

'You are mad! Quite mad!' Mrs Guthrie gulped, her hands raised to her face. 'I'll have Evie and Cook tie you down if you can't control yourself. I'm sending for your father!' Alice lay face down, torn by stormy grief. She was vaguely conscious of the key turning in the lock.

Hours tickled endlessly by. Now feeling weak and ill, her head pounding, she got up, washed in cold water, brushed her hair and tidied herself. She stood for more than an hour at the window, looking down across the lawn, the garden seat beside the flagged circle of stones with the sundial on its pedestal in the centre. Beyond the dark grey wall, the corn was already turning to its first pale hint of the ripeness to come. Beyond that, she could see one of the steamers leaving the jetty, hidden beneath the cliff. The dark smoke went almost vertically up into the haze of summer. There was not a ripple to be seen on the blue-green surface.

The window was open. She gazed down on the steep slope of the roof, the dark slates neatly laid in overlapping rows. If she stood on the stool, she could climb out easily. If she let herself go, she would roll down and drop over the edge. It was scarcely a proper drop at all, from the guttering down to the path. She could jump it, if she was prepared. But if she simply fell ... in her present condition, what harm would it do? Would it kill her? Not outright, she was sure. But it might cause some horrible internal injury. Kill her and the baby. Everyone's problem solved. She imagined their remorseful faces gathered round her deathbed, her eyes misting as she thought of her pale, tragic, forgiving figure.

Would Olga forgive? To her own shame, she sniggered at the vivid recall of her attack on her sister. Poor Olga! She really had stolen her thunder, after all. She was right to feel ashamed of herself. Oh, Tommy, my love. Can you hear me? Are you there somewhere? In Heaven? What's it like? Will we be happy, some day, you and me? She closed her eyes, kept still, her brow resting against the wooden frame. Why couldn't she feel him with her? Did she even believe in Heaven?

God might be in it, but all is not right with the world. The slaughter was staggering. Unbelievable. She saw the lists, day after day, in father's paper. On Tommy's ship alone, only twenty had been saved, out of more than 1,200. And three battle-cruisers sunk. One battle, so many lives. She shivered, thought of his body, all of them, tormented by the idea of bloody pieces of meat, unrecognizable lumps of flesh. And at the last trump, what would happen.

The tears came again, softly now, bringing a kind of relief. The child was there, growing in her. That was what mattered. She wouldn't die. Didn't really want to. She had Tommy's baby, that was all that mattered.

6 JANUARY, 1917

1

'It's a boy! Your niece is fine, Miss Dwyer. And the baby. He certainly seemed reluctant to make his entrance into the world. But he's here now and letting us know all about it. You can go up and see them both shortly.'

'Thank you, Sister.' Rosie could feel her legs trembling with relief. She blinked away the moisture from her eyes. Damned sentimental old fool, she chided herself. You'll be wanting to hand out cigars next! A boy, eh? Young Tommy. So Alice had been right all along. She had always insisted she was carrying a son.

A fierce pride swept through Rosie's breast, and that aching love which caused her both shame and joy at its immensity. She should not harbour such exclusive possessiveness towards Alice, yet she could not help herself, was dazedly grateful that the girl accepted it so unreservedly. They had done it, against all odds! She would take care of both of them, mother and child, with all the care and passion which the dead father might have lavished on them had he been given the chance.

And she had fought her good fight for her love, she could take private pride in that. Facing the wrath of Alice's father had not been easy, even though she knew she was providing a solution which would ease the stigma the family felt that Alice's pregnancy inflicted on them. Mr Guthrie had been fully prepared to have Alice committed to an institution and the baby placed in an orphanage. The girl might have been forced to linger for years, surrounded by the mentally ill, or those who had been unfortunate enough to find themselves in similar circumstances to Alice.

It was not guilt that prompted Rosie to act as she did, though she had felt some degree of responsibility for the girl's unfortunate condition. And unfortunate it was, she really did believe that. Had even been secretly angry with the poor dead boy for doing what he had. She shied away from the argument, put strongly and eloquently several times by Alice, that it was what the girl wanted, that she felt nothing but profound happiness and gratitude to Tommy for having given her the gift of the baby before he died.

However complex her own motives, Rosie had eagerly embraced responsibility for Alice's welfare. 'I shall pay for the confinement, and afterwards she can stay with me. As long as she likes. She has no wish to burden you with any of it,' she told Mr Guthrie resolutely.

'I can't begin to understand your interest in this sordid affair,' he answered icily, 'nor, quite frankly, do I wish to. The fact that you can condone such lewd behaviour speaks volumes. Suffice to say we wish to hear nothing further, from her, or you.' Rosie had not even set eyes on Alice's mother. The interview had been conducted with Mr Guthrie alone. From their subsequent silence, it was clear that her mother had no intention of going against her husband.

Rosie knew that, for Alice, her older sister's attitude had been equally if not more shocking. Her young face quivered with outrage even as she retold the incident. After the first days of shock and horror, Olga had come up with a solution of which she seemed almost proud. 'Philip Surtees!' she declared, with a note of triumph. 'He's keen on you. Has been for ages. He's down from Cambridge now. He's joining up soon. You must get him to propose to you.' She turned to Mrs Guthrie. 'We've got to get him over here as soon as possible, Ma.' She turned back to her sister, with an air of magnanimous satisfaction. 'And *you* must get to work at once. You know how to spoon. And these days all this long courtship and everything has gone by the board. No one'll think anything of it. A wedding before he goes off to the war. The babe comes early – so what! You'll be safely wed in any case. But we've got to act fast!'

'You are totally disgusting!' Alice gasped, disbelief almost as deep as her revulsion.

Olga was redly then palely furious. After managing nobly to forgive the little minx for her physical assault on her, it was just too much that she should now be verbally abused thus. 'Pa's right,' she replied cuttingly. 'You *are* mad!'

All Rosie's efforts had been more than amply repaid by the trust and love which her darling girl returned to her. What was for the older woman an idyll had begun with Alice's move to the untidy little cottage, which was transformed by her presence. Rosie even indulged in some semblance of housekeeping, fussing over her companion's health and regime with all the concern of a parent or a marriage partner. 'Milk, fresh fruit, and fresh air,' she pronounced implacably, and saw to it that her charge got plenty of all three. As the weather turned chilly and damp after harvest, and Alice's figure began to round out, the swell of her belly becoming more noticeable, necessitating the letting out of skirts and the purchase of maternity gowns, Rosie insisted that she should retire to the bedroom every afternoon after lunch, for a 'nap'.

'I'm not an invalid,' Alice laughingly protested, though she enjoyed being pampered. Sometimes, she would be assailed by a sudden, disturbing guilt at the thought of how happy she could feel, and at the knowledge that there were long hours now when the loss of Tommy did not occupy her conscious mind. Other times, she would look secretly at the plain, bulky figure of Rosie bustling about after her, and her eyes would mist with the tenderness and love which filled her for her truest friend.

She no longer felt shy at the physical intimacy they shared, revelling in the feel of the warm body and arms enfolding her in the cosy warmth of the creaking bed, the hands that cupped around her ripening breasts, or the increasing swell of her belly. The lips, too, that, in such intimate moments, would gently but firmly cover hers, and stay there, until they would both break, panting a little for breath, stirred by the contact.

The outside world was there, though, with its pain, waiting close outside the encapsuled warmth and security of the cottage. Rosie, after more than seven years in the village, had thought herself accepted, tolerated, by its inhabitants. She had come at first with several others, most of whom she was perfectly aware were merely diverting themselves with the notion of the life of the artist, 'playing at it', as one of her colleagues had remarked accurately. The accusation could at one time have been applied to her, she readily admitted.

But then she began to get something, a genuine pleasure, then thrill, from testing her considerable skill, though she had to confess still to an element of thrill also at the bohemian style of the existence into which she had been drawn. Certainly, she had swiftly realized, from a quite early age, that the conventional patterns of life – coming out, courtship, marriage, children – none of these held any appeal for her. Love, when it came, was both violent and shocking, for it was for one of her own sex – a pretty but manipulatively selfish girl, who hurt her and moved quickly on. So, escape to Kingstaith, and life in a colony of like minded individuals, was doubly appealing.

When the others moved on, Rosie was glad enough to stay. The natural beauty of the area, its ruggedness reflected in the lives of the folk who inhabited it, had captured her imagination. Its wild appeal held her. She didn't mind the sniggers, or the outrageously exaggerated rumours about her lifestyle, which the fisherfolk and others seemed to thrive on. She painted the wild landscape, and the untamed beauty she could discover reflected in the physique of the people, young and old.

True, she was sensually stirred by the beauty when she found it, in young bodies both male and female. And there were those greedy and vain enough to be quite willing to show themselves to her for a few shillings. There were even those, far away and from her own background, willing to pay considerably more for the pleasure of possessing such portraits. Not in sufficient numbers to keep her. She was lucky to have private means from a family fund which could have allowed her to live in comparative luxury had she chosen to do so, and which permitted her to pay for the expensive nursing home on the outskirts of York where Alice's accouchement took place, and the lengthy stay at the hotel which led up to it.

'I want to have the baby here – at home,' Alice had said, soon after she had moved into Salmon Cottage. This was where he had been conceived, where her and Tommy's brief love had passionately expressed itself. She did not say this, but both she and Rosie understood it. However, the village which Rosie had considered her home proved itself to be as hidebound and narrow-minded as other, more privileged places.

If Alice had noticed the sidelong glances, the whispers and sniggers, when they passed folk in the narrow streets, or along the little seafront at the harbour, she had thought little of it. Or of the fact that Rosie no longer had the regular stream of visitors to her door which she had previously enjoyed. Rosie herself chose to assume that it was tact which made the villagers, whose faces she knew well, avoid meeting her glance, or pausing to chat. After all, they must know by now who Alice was, and probably the sad facts of her recent history, given their normal, avid interest in local scandal.

Alice made no attempt to invent a history for herself. She was even brave enough to return to Port Hilda, to pay a visit to the Cousins' cottage in Mine Row. It brought a lump to her throat to glance along the lane leading to the gates of the hall, and see its tall chimneys reaching above the trees which fringed the gardens, and which, in their full summer splendour, hid the house itself.

The visit to Tommy's parents began in painful embarrassment, for she was met at the back door by Will Cousins, Tommy's father, in collarless striped shirt, and wide canvas braces. He was deeply shocked. 'Miss Alice! Ye'd best come in.' Her eyes were drawn at once to the black-edged photograph of Tommy, in his best uniform, staring with martial sternness from the high mantelshelf over the range. Ginny Cousins flapped about the crowded, tiny room, shifting things, urging Alice to the high-backed chair by the fire, fussing uncomfortably over her. When she sat, Alice felt the solidity of the child she was carrying shift burdensomely.

'I wanted – to let you know how things were,' she murmured inadequately, her face crimson. 'And to get news of you all, Dora and everyone.'

'Yer da's bin very good,' Mr Cousins answered heavily. ''E kept me down on the jetty. Our Dora's left. She's gone over Leeds way somewhere, Wi' our Lou. In one o' them factories. Meckin' shells an' things.'

'Oh, I'm sorry. I hope – it wasn't because of me, was it? What happened—'

'It were best,' Ginny said simply. 'She couldn't really stay on at t' 'ouse like could she? Not after – anyway, she's makin' a load of money. The both are.'

'Yer done wrong, ye know!' Will Cousins stated abruptly, his face reddening. His words fell like a small explosion into the tension of the room. 'Ah know our Tommy, God rest 'im, were wrong ter do what 'e did, but it were the pair o' ye. It wuz wrong of ye.' He shook his head. 'There! Ah've tellt yer te yer face as ah said ah would. Yer've broke yer mother an' father's 'earts, an' shamed us in t' village, an' all.'

Alice began to cry, quietly, her hands twisting in her lap. 'I loved – love – him very much. I wanted to marry him.'

'Doan't talk so daft, lass!' he said vehemently. ''Ow the 'ell—'

'Don't, Will,' his wife interjected. 'It's no good now, is it? Our Tommy's gone. Ah know you were fond of 'im, miss. And 'e felt the same—' Her voice quavered, but she went on strongly, ''E weren't a bad lad, ah know that much.'

Ginny Cousins insisted that Alice leave by the front door. She came out into the roadway with her, and reached for her hand, held it between both her own. 'I 'ope all goes well for yer. Are yer managin' all right?'

Alice nodded. 'Yes. I'm staying at Kingstaith. With a good friend.'

'Aye. That artist woman. I 'eard.' Her voice catching with emotion and embarrassment, she went on, 'Come and see us again. Bring the bairn – ah want ter see it. Ah'd like that. Very much.' She leaned forward suddenly and kissed Alice quickly on the cheek.

At the beginning of October, Alice went to Dr Freeman's surgery at Bank Top for her regular examination, Rosie accompanying her as usual. 'Don't you think you'd be better booking in at a nursing home for the confinement?' he said, when Alice emerged from behind the screen after redressing. 'There are several good ones I can recommend in the area.'

'Why?' Rosie asked sharply. 'Do you anticipate any difficulty?'

'No, not at all. Though you're slightly narrow hipped, Miss Guthrie. But I don't think the baby will be a whopper. Was the father a big man?'

Alice blushed furiously as she shook her head, hating herself for her embarrassment, and the doctor for his tactlessness. Or was it deliberate cruelty? she wondered. She wished, not for the first time, that she could have gone to Dr Hanson, the family doctor she had known as long as she could remember, though she knew it would have been impossible for him to continue to treat her after the rift with her parents.

'It's just that the folk round here are notoriously old-fashioned. Narrow-minded, some would say,' Dr Freeman was continuing, addressing his remarks as much to Rosie as Alice. 'I thought you might feel more comfortable being at a distance from the village for the event. It's a trying time emotionally, as well as physically. Still, it's up to you entirely, of course. I'll be available, if you need me. And Mrs Helliwell is an excellent midwife. You've booked with her?'

Mrs Helliwell was distinctly unfriendly when Rosie called on her a few days later, only accepting her commission with evident reluctance, a fact Rosie decided not to impart to Alice. However, she could not hide from her the evidence of the hostility displayed towards them which they found on returning from one of their afternoon walks. The word SLUTS had been daubed in large, blood-red capitals across the faded grain of their front door.

Alice was tearful, then angry. Rosie shrugged it off, and got to work with soap and bucket and scrubbing brush, though she could only eliminate all traces of the epithet by adding a new coat of blue paint to the door. 'Been meaning to do that for ages,' she told Alice cheerfully. 'Little beggars have done us a favour.' She convinced Alice that it was the work of children. 'It's not the first time I've been called that. And worse, as you know.'

A week later they were sitting before the fire, which was blowing back smoke annoyingly from the chimney in the almost gale-force wind, when they both heard a scuffling over the noise of the elements, and Rosie braved the freshly resplendent front door to hear the pattering of rapidly retreating steps. Next morning, on the rough stonework of the outside wall, in the same garish paint, were the letters PERV and a smear which marked the point at which the transgressors had been interrupted. That was even harder to remove.

The final straw came, soon after, as they lay sleeping securely in each other's arms. There was a violent crash which woke them in heart-racing fear. 'Wait!' Alice gasped, trying to keep hold of Rosie's hand, but she was already out of the warm bed and pulling on her gown. Downstairs, she found the window shattered, the room covered with shards of glass, and a solid stone lying on the rug.

'For the moment, they win,' Rosie declared grimly. 'I've never been happy about you having the offspring here, anyway. There's a place I know, outside York. We'll move into a hotel nearby and book you in for the happy event. That's what it's going to be. We've enough to think of without being plagued by these small-minded bigots!'

And that was what they had done. Rosie had insisted, too, on their present fiction, even buying her young charge a wedding ring. 'With this ring I plight my troth!' she had joked to the blushing girl when she slipped it on her finger. Privately, Rosie acknowledged that it was not a joke at all. She loved Alice very much, more so now than ever. So Alice became her niece, the tragically widowed Mrs Guthrie, whose husband had been killed at Jutland, only weeks after their short honeymoon.

Rosie's musings were interrupted by the arrival of a nurse, who smiled winningly. 'You can come up and see your grand-nephew now!' she announced.

2

'Isn't he absolutely beautiful?' Alice smiled up at her from the pillows with weary contentment. Her young face showed the strain of what she had endured. The flesh under her eyes was bruised dark with fatigue, and her skin against the dazzling whiteness of the pillowslip had a faint yellowish tinge. Her hair, though neatly brushed and arranged, had a dull, lustreless quality about it. But there was no doubting the depth of happiness and fulfilment which radiated from her.

'No, he's not! He's a red-faced, ugly little monster!' Rosie said gruffly, struggling hard to suppress the tears which stung her eyes. She leaned forward and, despite the hovering presence of the young nurse, placed her lips tenderly over Alice's, and held them there for a long, gentle kiss. Then her mouth brushed lightly against the tiny, screwed-up visage poking through the mummy-like shrouds enclosing the miniature form in a tight cocoon in Alice's arms. 'And as for you, you little brute! You gave my darling girl a bad time. Was it awful for you?'

Alice smiled. 'Agony! You don't know what you're missing!'

Rosie grunted dismissively. 'And I've no intention of finding out, my sweet. One mummy between the pair of us is more than enough.'

The infant began to give a wailing series of cries. The sister came in, smiling triumphantly. 'Now let's start feeding the poor mite up. Come on, Mrs Guthrie. We'll put him to the breast, shall we?'

'I'll go,' Rosie said hastily, getting up from the bed.

'No, no!' the sister protested enthusiastically. 'This is the best bit of all, I always think. Stay and enjoy it. It's a marvellous sight.' She was already unbuttoning the bodice of Alice's gown, and helping her up the pillows. 'Sit up. That's it. Let's get these bedclothes off. It's a wonderful experience. You must make the most of it.'

The pale, blue-traceried round of flesh was swelling full, the nipple enlarged and dark. The sister helped her to put the tiny, wrinkled face to it, and, after a few hesitant, exploratory turns, Thomas's countenance was half buried in the encompassing softness. Alice shivered, and giggled. She moved her legs slightly under the loose shapelessness of the gown, felt the damp, stinging soreness under the bulky pads. 'God! It feels – funny.' She looked down at the fragile miracle of the long skull, the beating of the fontanelle under the sparse and delicate hair. 'Tommy!' she whispered, and teardrops silvered on her dark lashes. Rosie saw, and ached with her love and compassion.

She soon became used to the sight of the baby at Alice's breast, and sat making sketch after sketch of them during the nine long days before the doctor finally pronounced that mother and child were well enough to leave. 'I've found a nice little cottage for us,' Rosie had told her, speaking with persuasive lightness. 'At Heslington. It's only a few miles from York. Pretty little village. Just two up and two down. Ideal for us.'

Their first night in their new home, which still smelt of the fresh paint and shone with the thorough cleaning Rosie had ensured took place before they moved in, when Thomas – 'I refuse to let anyone call him Tommy,' Alice pronounced. 'Thomas is much more dignified.' – was sleeping in his bassinet, and the fire, laid previously by the woman who came in to do, was crackling cheerfully in the small front-room, Alice came with tearful emotion to Rosie and stood close, face to face, looking up at the taller, bulkier figure. She put up her arms, linked her hands behind the sturdy neck, her large eyes fixed solemnly on the flushing, pleased face. 'I don't know what I would have done without you. I'll always love you for taking me in. Taking care of me. Some day I hope I can pay you back, somehow, for it all—'

'Don't you dare!' Rosie growled. 'I did it for me, I've told you! I'm getting far more out of it all than you could possibly imagine. So don't go all soppy on me now, you goose!'

'I have to, just this once. You're closer to me than anyone on earth, now that Tommy's gone. Closer than my own family. You're everything!'

Before Rosie's open mouth could utter its embarrassed objection, Alice kissed her, passionately, her own mouth open, turning, worrying, in the raw way Alice knew instinctively Rosie thrilled to. Her own body responded, throbbingly, with the excitement that still shocked her, and she pushed her shame defiantly away, pressing her body close, feeling the length of their contact, until they finally had to pull away, gulping, and gasping, and smiling through tears at one another.

'Do – do you think it's true what they said? That we're sluts? Perverted?' Alice panted.

For a very brief instant, Rosie's eyes flickered with a hint of pain, then she laughed almost harshly, and spun Alice round, slapping at her behind playfully. 'Of course! Great fun, isn't it?' she growled, her voice deep with mock sensuality.

3

'You ought to let your family know,' Rosie suggested, yet again, one afternoon when they were pushing the high perambulator in front of them, along the slush-covered path which ran along the edge of the uneven village green, whose muddy surface was beginning to show smearingly through the thinning layer of snow. It had been a brief but unseasonably late fall, for it was already spring, officially. They had celebrated Thomas's 'third' birthday two days previously. 'Three months old!' Alice told him proudly, and he smiled accommodatingly.

'Wind!' declared Rosie sceptically.

The event was marked by a more significant milestone on the greater stage of the world, for it was the day when America declared war on Germany and its allies, vowing to use 'force to the uttermost, force without stint or limit'.

The war had made its presence intrusively apparent a week earlier, when, in spite of the freezing cold, the two women had stood, with coats and shawls flung over their night things and their feet in clammy gumboots, together with a large congregation of their neighbours, in pre-dawn darkness, watching the sky away to the north-east lit with lurid ruddiness by the burning pyre of a German airship, which bent and broke and fluttered to earth, leaving a dying glow. Around them rose a spontaneous, ragged cheer. 'The've got these new bullets now, see,' a knowledgeable individual told all who cared to listen. 'Our airplanes. They can set fire to the gas. Got the measure of them now, I reckon.'

Safely snuggled once more under the eiderdown and heavy blankets in their double bed, hugging each other and rubbing their icy feet and ankles together, sharing each other's returning warmth, Rosie and Alice whispered in head-touching intimacy until greyness lightened the square of window. 'I can't hate the Germans,' Alice confessed, almost guiltily. 'I just think of those poor men up there, dying horribly like that.' She shuddered, and Rosie's grip tightened. 'Even with Tommy's death, I still can't hate. It's all such a waste of young lives. It's all so sad.'

'If only they'd let us ruddy women run the show, these things wouldn't happen,' Rosie grunted. 'They've got us doing all kinds of things now. The Forces. Driving. Farming. Factories. Surely when this lot's over, they'll have to give us a say in what goes on. There'll be hell to pay if they don't!'

Now, spirits were raised by this latest news of American intervention. Rosie returned to her recurrent theme of letting Alice's family know about the birth as they crossed the wide road leading to York, past the high wall of Heslington Hall's grounds, and made their way back to the row of small cottages. 'They don't even know where we are now. They'll probably know we've left Kingstaith, but that's all.'

'They probably won't even know that,' muttered Alice. 'Because they won't have bothered to find out. No. They threw me out. So be it.' She grinned suddenly. 'You're stuck with me, so stop trying to get rid of me!'

But she *did* get news from her family, as, at last, spring succeeded in breaking through, and the daffodils burst into their encouraging floods of colour, along the river banks, and beneath the walls of the old city. It was news which proved, joltingly, that she had not divorced herself as strongly as she might have thought from her family, at least on an emotional level.

It was a letter from Olga, which had been forwarded from Kingstaith, as Rosie had requested the post office to do. The curt formality of its tone added to the deep hurt Alice experienced when she read it.

Dear Alice

I trust this note will reach you eventually, wherever you are. I have some news which I feel ought to be passed on to you. Mother does not object. I have not spoken to Father.

You might be interested to know that your brother, Alex, has been posted 'missing presumed killed in action', on March 21st,

somewhere near Peronne, I think the place is called. Mother is
making herself ill clinging on to the idea that he is only 'missing', but
we have been told that there is no hope. His section of the trench was
heavily bombarded. The dugout where he was sheltering was wiped
out by a shell. It must have been very swift.

A memorial service has been held at St Hilda's. It's ironic that he
got through the Somme battle, only to be killed like that. Still, it's
happening to families up and down the land, and we are very proud
of him. Luke feels it badly that he cannot be released for war service,
but I thank God for it, and don't care who knows it. Your brother
Bertie is still safe as far as we know. He's still with the Grand Fleet.

It will be of no interest to you, I am sure, but I may as well tell you
that I was safely delivered of a boy, on January 27th. He was
christened last week. We have named him Alexander.

If you receive this, I should tell you that I do not think it would be
good to get in touch with Father and Mother, but I felt you should
know of Alex's death.

Olga

Rosie hugged her to her while she sobbed bitterly. 'He's buh –
been dead for over a month! And nobody got in touch with me!'
Despite her apparent brave acceptance of the family's rejection of
her, Alice was shattered by this cruel proof of it.

'There now! You don't know, sweetheart. They may have tried
to get word to Salmon Cottage, found we'd gone, and left it at that.
It's only because your sister wrote to the cottage that the letter's
been forwarded.'

'You've seen it. How cold it is! And she still says I shouldn't try
to get in touch. With my brother dead!' The weeping continued for
a long while, and Rosie sat rocking her gently in her arms, kissing
the dark head occasionally, and murmuring softly, to soothe the
pain.

That night Alice sat at the dining-table and wrote a short note
addressed to both her parents, telling them how sad she was at the
news, and asking if she might come and see them. She hesitated a
long time before she finally added, at the bottom of the single sheet,
You have a second grandson, a little boy, Thomas.

For a week, she watched eagerly, morning and afternoon, for the post, and Rosie's heart ached for the disappointment and the pain she saw each succeeding day in the beloved features. Every time Alice picked Thomas from his crib to feed or nurse him, she tried to picture her mother doing the same to her almost nineteen years before, and tried to understand her present renunciation of her.

Alice also wrote to Ginny Cousins, and was again disappointed, though not so bitterly, when no reply was forthcoming. She had put it out of her mind when, after three weeks, a letter came in a strange hand. When Alice got the envelope open and turned at once to the signature at the end of the letter, she saw, with a quickening of pleasure, that it was from Dora. She was writing, she said, on behalf of her mother, who was *not a very good hand with a pen and I'm not much better.*

They were all pleased that she and little Tommy were safe and well, and looked forward to seeing them both soon. *When are you coming back up this way?* Dora asked. It was a question Alice had asked herself already, a number of times, and, as they moved into summer, and her nineteenth birthday grew nearer, she put the question to her partner.

Rosie regarded her steadily. 'Aren't we doing all right here?' she asked. 'Young Thomas is thriving. We've no worries, have we?'

'We don't belong here,' Alice answered quietly. 'Salmon Cottage is our home. It's Thomas's home, too. You said when we left, "they win, for the moment". The moment's long gone. Don't you think it's time we went back?'

Rosie sighed, smiled crookedly. 'You're sure you're up to it, sweetheart? They'll still be there, those bigots, with their daubs, and their stones.' She nodded across at the cradle. 'And we have him to think of now.'

Alice lifted her head defiantly. She nodded. 'I know. That's why I want to go back. He belongs there, like his dad did. Like we do.'

4

The cottage was cobwebbed and thick with dust, and smelt unpleasantly of the mouldering damp, but they set to with a will, glad of the warm summer weather which enabled them to leave Thomas tucked up in blankets in the tiny square of yard at the front, where, in the morning, the sun penetrated hopefully between the leaning buildings. They got a fire going, and filled the side boiler, so that they had a plentiful supply of hot water. They worked down from the bedroom and the studio, brushing, beating, and scrubbing. It took most of the day, but by teatime everywhere was as clean as they could make it.

Alice even attempted the blackleading of the range, in spite of the fire's heat. 'You've got more on you than the stove,' Rosie teased, moved by the sight of the grinning face smeared along one cheek and with a black tip to its nose. Alice groaned and sat back on her heels. She pushed at a stray lock from her pinned-up hair with the back of her wrist. 'You shouldn't overdo it, you know,' Rosie went on. 'I'm sure we could've found someone to do some cleaning for us if we'd tried.'

But neither of them was at all sure that that would be the case, though they did not say so. 'No,' Alice answered firmly. 'Let's just get in and settled again. We can fend for ourselves, can't we?'

'Of course we can, my duck. Now wash your hands and face and get that dreadful apron off.' They had tied sacking about their waists to protect their skirts as they worked. 'I'm going to top up the boiler and bring the bath in. By the time you've fed greedy guts there, it'll be ready for you to have a good long soak while I try not to massacre our supper.'

She was as good as her word, and later, while a replete Thomas burped and gurgled in his bassinet, Alice undressed up in the familiar bedroom, where the lowering sun pushed its mellow fingers across the furniture and walls, the sight of which brought tender tears of remembered warmth to her eyes. The small zinc bath was placed before the glowing fire. Because of the close proximity of the other buildings along the narrow alley, the downstairs room was almost in darkness, and Rosie had drawn the curtains and lit the lamps. It all added to the feeling of cosiness and intimacy which wrapped them in its insulating security.

She had long lost her shyness at appearing naked in front of Rosie, but she was still very aware of that ambivalent sensation of pleasure and shame she experienced at the long, frankly admiring looks the older woman would give her, and the forthright comments which often accompanied them. She slipped off the dressing-gown and gingerly tested the water with a foot, before she stepped in and lowered herself with a moan of bliss into the embrace of the enveloping heat. Because of the size of the oval tub, she could not stretch her legs fully, but sat with her knees drawn partly up. 'That is so good!' she sighed, stretching her neck, flexing her tired muscles as she slowly rolled her head round. 'Bless you. You're an angel!'

'And you're a voluptuous siren!' breathed Rosie. She came to kneel beside her, and began to wash the sloping shoulders with the cloth, squeezing it to let the water trickle down the shining flesh.

Alice's face was pink, both from the rising heat and from the deeply sensual tone of her partner. 'No, I'm not. I'm positively frumpish! I'll never get my figure back.' It was a favourite plaint, not least for the comfort of hearing Rosie's strong denial of such statements.

'Rubbish! You don't want to go back to being a beanpole, do you?' Casually, she moved, and let the drops from the flannel trickle down onto the slope of the breasts. 'I've told you. You should let me paint you again. *Au naturel.* A sight to melt the snows on the Mountains of the Moon!'

'These *are* the Mountains of the Moon!' Alice replied, hefting her breasts disparagingly, and savouring Rosie's gaze. She felt that shocking physical response in the hidden recesses beneath the cloudy water.

Although she was secretly quite relieved, Alice had protested when her portrait had accompanied them on their travels, decently wrapped in brown paper while in storage, then hung on the bedroom wall of the cottage in Heslington, a constant both pleasing and disturbing reminder of the complex relationship between them.

And linking poor Tommy to them in an equally odd intimacy, for Alice never looked at it without remembering vividly his enthralled but shocked reaction to seeing it on that unforgettable day. It was unpacked now, awaiting hanging, once more resting against the wall in the little room where it had begun life, what seemed a world ago now.

Rosie's hand lay firmly on the wet shoulder, the fingers digging in to the fragility of bone structure under the smooth skin. 'Welcome home, darling,' she whispered, and bent to place a gentle kiss on the neck, behind the ear, where the black tendrils of the swept-up hair curled. Alice stirred, shivered slightly, and leaned back into the embrace, lifting her arm behind her, bent at the elbow, and nuzzled into the warm face, her lips seeking the cheek in a tender and heartfelt response.

Their resettlement in Kingstaith was, as they had anticipated, not easy at first. But the baby made a vital difference, took the vicious edge off what vindictiveness there was. The menfolk began to josh and taunt Rosie once more with their same crude humour, to which she responded as strongly as ever. The younger ones, in particular, eyed Alice with a lust that was not always surreptitious, and their sniggers and muttered asides embarrassed and hurt her, though Rosie was usually at her side to champion her, often vociferously enough to make them blush in turn and retire with poor grace from their sport.

It was the eventual acceptance of the womenfolk which crucially altered the balance. They started by acknowledging the baby, stopping to talk to him, and to admire, then, almost grudgingly at first, including Rosie and Alice in their greetings. One Sunday, Alice bravely declared her intention of going to St Peter's, the 'Fishermen's Church', though Rosie steadfastly refused to attend. 'My God doesn't live there,' she told her, with no further explanation.

Alice's courage failed when the rows of white bonnets turned with one accord, and she felt the merciless exposure to all those eyes. Her legs were jelly; she doubted if she had the strength to turn and flee, sinking down at the nearest end of one of the rearmost pews, staring down into her hands in her lap, her face ablaze. She half expected the vicar to intone a thunderous denunciation of her wickedness from the pulpit, but no such shame took place. His mind was on more general sins, and on a grander scale than hers.

Afterwards, outside on the street, the women gave her that aggressive, hard stare which seemed typical of all of them, but several nodded and muttered a greeting. She waited in the doorway, nervously determined, until the vicar came out. 'Could I have a word with you?' she asked faintly.

He nodded at the verger, who, with a hint of reluctance, moved on. 'Good morning. Nice to see you, er....'

'Miss Guthrie. Alice Guthrie. It's – I have a baby. Thomas. He's seven months. Nearly eight. I'd like him christened.' Her face burning, she forced herself to go on. 'I – he was born out of wedlock. His father – we were going to get married. He was killed. At Jutland. I—' Desperately, she struggled not to cry, and not to look, or sound, ashamed.

There was an excruciating pause. 'The sins of the fathers, eh?' the deep voice said quietly.

Alice lifted her head. Her eyes held his. 'And the mothers.'

He nodded, and smiled. 'I'm sure we can arrange it. Can I call and see you? Where are you living?'

The ceremony was performed on a weekday morning, in a church deserted save for Alice, Thomas, the vicar – and Rosie. 'I'm the godparent. Godparents,' she corrected, emphasizing the final sibilant. 'I'm all he's got. God help him!'

As they were bumping the pram over the cobbles and down the steep slope of Church Street, back to the harbour side, a tall, strong-boned girl of striking attractiveness, despite her drab outfit of coarse dark skirt and overall, approached and nodded. She spoke abruptly. 'Are ye wantin' somebody ter come in an' do for ye? I 'eard ye were, like.' Rosie nodded in turn. 'That's fine then. Ah'm seekin' a bit extra work. Ah'll call round temorrer. Right?' She bent over the pram, smiled and shook her head at the staring infant. 'By, 'e's a bonny bairn, i'nt 'e?'

Alice smiled proudly, and gazed after the retreating figure with interest. 'Looks like we're no longer pariahs, after all.' She was feeling particularly happy now that Thomas was baptised. 'Who's that? Do you know her?'

'Yes. That's one of the Wheatley girls. They live up by Chapel Garth. Handsome creature, isn't she?' She grinned, winked at Alice. 'She posed for me once. And her sister!'

'What?' Alice stared at her. 'You mean—'

'Yes! Of course! Never turned a hair, either of 'em. *The Amazons*, I called the picture. Sold it for fifteen guineas, my dear. Worth a fortune some day. As yours will be. Though you should let me revamp it a little. *The Beanpole* doesn't have the same ring to it somehow, does it?'

5

Alice paused at the beginning of the long rise of the hill which led up to Port Hilda. To her left, she could see St Hilda's grey tower showing through the tracery of the tall trees which had lost most of their leaves, in contrast with the still brilliantly green, close foliage of the yew trees which stood at either side of the high porched gate. A picture came into her mind of the family carriage pulling up on the rutted space in front of the church, and herself as a child, climbing out in her Sunday best, and waving to Tommy on his way to the chapel along the High Street. To her right, in the forecourt of the Black Swan, there was a motor van, and two cars. Vehicles like those were a common enough sight now. She remembered the excitement their appearance caused when she was little. Tommy's enthusiasm for them had rubbed off considerably on her, she recalled. When he had first gone away into the navy, she had pestered her father's driver to teach her how to drive, until Pa had warned her in no uncertain terms to stop bothering him.

She put her weight behind the white bar of the pram handle. She was already tired and a little footsore after the two-mile walk along the coast road from Kingstaith. She would have much preferred to take the much more familiar path along the clifftop, but it was no route for a perambulator. At length she got to the top of the rise and felt that tender stab of pain at the sight of the familiar row of chimney pots that marked Mine Row. Her eyes misted, her vision blurring, at the equally familiar vista in the further distance, of the chestnut trees and the taller, more imposing chimneys of Port Hilda Hall. For a second, she had an almost overwhelming urge to turn left, along the rutted, muddy lane, to go in through the stable yard, pass by the kitchen, and stand once more in the hall itself. To present herself before her mother, to fall weeping into her arms. Could she reject her?

Blinking rapidly, she went on towards the long uniform row of the workers' dwellings. She stopped briefly, quickly wiping the instep of her soft, shining boots on the backs of her black stockings. In her short, mid-calf skirt, and the tight-waisted jacket, she knew she looked schoolgirlish still, despite the carefully swept-up hair on which her little hat was pinned.

She was glad of the simpler fashions that had become popular since the start of the war, in particular of the new, more flexible corsets and the simpler undergarments, like the shorter knickers she now habitually wore. 'You don't need to truss yourself up in any of that nonsense!' Rosie had declared, when they first bought one of the foundation garments. And usually Alice didn't bother, it was true. But today she wanted to look her best.

She had written to Mrs Cousins, telling her that she would call in next Tuesday, with Thomas, and had received a carefully rounded, two-line reply in the next post, saying that they were looking forward to her visit. She had only just reached the first cottage when she saw Ginny Cousins appear on the front step, waving to her. 'Yer can leave t' pram out 'ere at t' front. It'll be all right, miss.'

Then there was a long silence, while she bent close over the perambulator, and Thomas, who had woken a few minutes before and who returned her gaze with his unblinking, clear blue eyes. When Ginny Cousins straightened, two tears hovered on her eyelids, then broke free to trickle down her cheeks. ''E's like 'is da, Miss Alice, isn't 'e?' Alice reached for her, and they embraced tightly, there in the street, weeping together, holding on to each other.

Ginny was on her own, as Alice had hoped she would be for this first awkward visit. Except that it very soon wasn't. Talking became easier and easier as they sat at the cloth-covered table in the kitchen-living room, drinking from the best china. Ginny asked for all the details of the confinement and the birth, and reminisced about her own deliveries. Finally, she said, 'Ow are ye managin', Miss Alice? Money-wise, ah mean? Ah've bin that worried.'

Alice had given up trying to get her to drop the 'miss'. She smiled reassuringly. 'Everything's fine.' She nodded at Thomas, whom Ginny was cradling. 'As you can see.' She blushed a little as she continued, 'My friend, Rosie Dwyer, has been so good – more than I could ever tell. She's quite a bit older than me – a lot, really. But—' her voice faltered, then picked up strongly, 'my own mother couldn't have done more. She's looked after me as though I was her own. She's wonderful!'

'Ah'm right glad,' Ginny said, with a simple fervour. 'We'd 'ave loved to 'elp out if things were easier.' She reached out, with a hint of shyness, and touched Alice's arm briefly. 'Ah want yer to know – if ever you are in any trouble – whatever – you'll be welcome 'ere. Our Will's a bit of a rough diamond, but 'e doesn't mean no 'arm. We'd stand by yer, miss. Yer'll keep comin', won't yer? Promise? We want ter see the bairn. 'E's part ours, after all, bless 'im!'

Alice sniffled, dabbed at her eyes again. 'Oh don't! Look! You've started me off again!' She smiled through the tears. 'That's lovely. Of course I'll keep coming, if you want me.'

When she laid Thomas back in his pram, carefully tucking the thick blankets about him, Ginny reached past her and pushed something into the tiny fingers before she could pin the little arms under the covers. It was a shiny florin. 'Oh no!' Alice exclaimed involuntarily. 'No, please! It's all right.'

Ginny looked at her, shocked as well as a little hurt. 'Nay! Fust time we've seen 'im, the little mite! We 'af ter give 'im silver, don't we? It's on'y right!'

Alice knew how much a sum of money like that must mean to them. 'Thank you,' she said, and leaned forward to hug the pleased woman tightly once more.

6

Life at Salmon Cottage resumed once again the idyllic substance it had taken on during their earliest days together, with the added bonus of the baby to cement their already indissoluble bond and in spite of the dark events of the world stage as the war moved into and then past its fourth complete year, the sombre anniversary coming three days after Alice's twentieth birthday. They had ration books now. The government had finally reluctantly adopted the scheme at the beginning of the year. Conscription had been brought in more than a year previously, while the majority of people at home seemed as fiercely patriotic and determined as ever.

Alice had gone along with Rosie to one of the new cinematograph shows which were being held regularly in the village hall at the top of the long hill near the station. It depressed her to see the triumphant newsreels, with what she suspected were their grossly exaggerated claims, and the lurid, short horror films depicting Hun atrocities. She was glad of the excuse which a mewling Thomas gave her to leave early. 'You stay,' she whispered to Rosie, who seemed entranced with the new medium.

'When is it going to end?' she asked wearily, later. It was an answer no one knew any more. No more 'over by Christmas' now. When she looked at Thomas, her heart ached with compassion for her mother as she imagined how she must feel to suffer the loss of her first born, to lie worrying each night over the safety of her second son. At those times, Alice longed to go to her, wished fervently that she could let her know she understood. She wrote a very brief note to both her parents informing them that she was back at Salmon Cottage. She said nothing else, did not ask again if she might visit them. There was no reply.

A storm cloud of an altogether closer, more personal nature than that of the world conflict was gathering, one with tragic consequences for the happiness of the little home and the close-knit triangle. It had begun slowly, almost unnoticeably, a while ago, like so many tragedies. A fleeting wince of discomfort, flickering over Rosie's ruddy features, eventually an irritable, 'God! My gut! I don't know what I've done. Pulled something, I expect. Unless it's this blasted rationing! Goodness only knows what they're passing off as meat these days! I'm getting old, that's my trouble. Your Rosie's getting past it, sweetheart.'

'Nonsense! You're strong as an ox. You'll see me out, I'll bet!'

The pains did not go away, but kept recurring, no matter what she ate. One day, Alice returned early from her walk because of a sudden heavy shower, to hear the sound of retching from behind the closet door in the yard. She was startled, and dismayed, at the drawn look on Rosie's face when she emerged. 'How long has this been going on?' she asked severely. Rosie mumbled vaguely, and dismissively. 'Now listen!' Alice rejoined firmly. 'If it's not better by the morning, you're going to Dr Freeman's. All right?'

'Bully!' Rosie smiled, struggling to hide the vicious torment in her abdomen.

It was a week before Rosie finally gave in. 'Look, I'll go, all right? But I'll go on my own. I'd be embarrassed with you yapping away in my ear. I'm a big girl now. Yes. I promise I'll tell you exactly what he says. Cross my heart and hope to die!'

One look at her face, the failure of those usually steady grey eyes to hold hers for more than a second, gave Alice a scary, sinking feeling that Rosie was not telling her the truth. 'Listen,' her friend said, with a hearty levity in her tone, 'can you hold the fort for a while here? Seems I've got a bit of a gyppy tum. The doc feels I could do with some treatment. Probably at the superior establishment where young Master Tom popped out into the world. They may need to cut a bit out of me.'

'Oh, Rosie!'

'Don't be daft! I'll be right as rain in a few weeks. You'll see. I'll be back in no time. Have to be, otherwise I'll be worried sick over my darling little duck not taking care of herself.'

Dr Freeman was hostile at first when Alice made her appointment to see him, and questioned him about Rosie. 'If she's chosen not to confide in you, then that's up to her. I have to respect confidentiality, you know.'

'She doesn't want to frighten me!' Alice burst out frantically. 'And I'm going off my head with worry. We – she's the closest person to me in the whole world! I thought you knew that! She's all I've got!' He stared at her in grave silence. 'Is it serious? Please – tell me!' She began to cry.

His voice was as quietly modulated as ever when he finally spoke. 'There's a growth. It's malignant. They'll have a look, but I suspect there's little they can do. I'm sorry.'

The two of them kept up the fiction. Rosie's eyes glittered, her chin lifted challengingly before she stepped into the private car she had hired to take her to the hospital. 'I'll write and let you know if you need to visit. Or when they say I can come back. Chin up, eh?' She grabbed fiercely at the weeping girl, kissed her savagely, and flung herself into the interior of the vehicle. 'Toodle pip! And stop blubbing for God's sake! Don't start planning the wake yet!'

12 JUNE, 1927

1

'Don't stay too long, Mr Turner. She's very tired. She'd had a bad time of it, I'm afraid. She'll be all right, and the baby's fine, but it was a difficult birth.' The sister smiled at him. Alf nodded distractedly. He found it hard to focus his spinning thoughts, conscious mainly of the trembling weakness of flooding relief at the words 'she'll be all right'. This nurse seemed all right, too. Quite kind and concerned. Yesterday – was it only last night? It seemed a lifetime ago – Maggie had whispered when he saw her in the ward that the other women said she was a 'right bitch'. 'They say she slapped a poor girl the other day,' she had told him, her big eyes fixed on him solemnly. 'Just 'cos she was making too much noise. I bet she's never had to go through it herself!'

'Why is she – like that?' he asked the nurse, nodding through the open double doors into the small side ward. Her feet were still raised, held in the stirrups. He could see the pale slenderness of the ankles, the slim curve of calf and the backs of her lifted thighs, disappearing – thank God – into the snowy folds of the sheeting draped and bunched to hide her helpless body. A sheet rose tent-like over her knees at the front.

'We had to do an episiotomy,' the sister said, saw the flare of alarm in his troubled gaze, and smiled again, with reassurance. 'It's just a small incision. In the perineal tissue. To help the delivery. We didn't want her to tear herself. We'll leave her like that just a bit longer. Only a few minutes.'

They approached the bed. She looked small, shrunken, her black hair spread lankly over the pillow, her face yellow. Her eyes closed, the lids very dark. Alf felt tears prick his eyes. He was swamped by a massive guilt. He swallowed hard. 'Maggie!' he croaked.

'She's a bit woozy. We had to give her an anaesthetic.' The voice rose to its professional briskness. 'Come on, Mrs Turner. Wake up, dear. Your hubby's here. You said you wanted him. Come on.' She reached out, shook the thin hand hard, and the exhausted face frowned, stirred, the mouth curling like a child about to cry.

'No,' Alf said hoarsely. 'It's all right. Leave her—'

'Wake up, dear. Maggie! Look who's here.'

She drifted back to the pain, whimpering as she felt its sharp bite once again, flinching, trying to hold herself back from it. She heard the faint voices. Maggie? What were they saying? 'Alice,' she muttered wearily. 'Alice Guthrie. Rosie – where's Rosie? Has she seen him? Rosie, isn't he just beautiful?'

Alf turned away, the muttered words hitting him like a blow. He wanted to hide his face from the nurse, from everyone, afraid that the tears welling up would show. He glanced at the crib, at the plentiful dark hair, which was almost all that he could see of his new-born daughter. My first child, he thought wondrously. Ours.

Again, he tried to stifle the hurt he felt at Maggie's unconscious mutterings, and the secret sadness he always felt at his exclusion from her earlier, former life. It was hard that, right now, at just about the proudest and happiest moment he had known, she should have been carried so far back, and far away, from him. Back to ten-year-old Tom's birth. Back to the time when she had not even been 'Maggie'. And back to the time of that strange, legendary figure of Rosie, of whom he had become at times more secretly and ashamedly jealous than of the poor dead Tommy who had fathered her first child.

Perhaps it was because she had been much more reluctant, or far less able, to talk about that relationship than about the pathetic little tale of childhood sweethearts and budding love which had been stamped out so cruelly before it had a chance to grow. Yet it was a love which would, in any case, have had enormous difficulties in surviving, even if the young man had lived. Perhaps that was why he could never feel really jealous of Tommy, why he felt an innate sympathy with him, for, had Alf himself met the seventeen-year-old girl who lived at Port Hilda Hall, he, too, would have been considered totally unsuitable and unworthy of her. If she had still been Alice Margaret Guthrie, he knew well enough he would have stood little chance of winning her.

He knew far more about the dead sailor lad; she had talked far more easily and readily about their doomed, youthful love. Rosie's story was altogether different, gave Maggie a different, deeper pain to talk of it, which she had done only gradually, in bits and pieces, with a hesitancy that made it seem as though it were being torn from her, bit by bloody bit, though he had never pressed her. It was almost as if, he thought, she could not fully understand herself the depth of feeling, of intimacy, the two women had shared.

His awkward. embarrassment with it, his uncomfortableness, shame even, stemmed from a private sense of shock which in itself disturbed him. Part of his mind, the debased, prurient part, sniffed around it like a dog at a scent. Did he suspect an illicit sexual liaison between the two women? He shied away from such speculation, but certainly the intense way in which Maggie struggled to describe or explain their feelings hinted at something of that nature.

That portrait she had painted of Maggie – the 'beanpole', Maggie chucklingly called it – was definitely charged with sexuality, beyond any doubt. However much Maggie might scoff, it was a highly rousing picture of a young girl leaving adolescence. The small, tilted breasts, the delicate shoulders, the tones of the slender, revealed flesh, the nakedness emphasized by the white fold of cloth at the loins. A nakedness of spirit, too. The artist had captured powerfully the sensuality, as well as the innocence, and, in doing so, declared the sensuality which which she viewed her subject.

The portrait hung in the privacy of their bedroom. Maggie was quite easy and comfortable with it, joked about it, but he could never get used to it. He always felt as though he were about to blush every time it caught his eye. And that made him feel even more guilty at his own unexpressed thoughts about the relationship.

He succeeded for the most part in not thinking about it. He could not help but consider a physical affair between women a shockingly perverted phenomenon. He did not want to believe Maggie capable of such a thing. It was only at times of their own, after sex intimacy, in the low, exploratory tones of confession, as she lay in his arms in the dark of the bedroom, that she had talked of it, and not often. But she had mentioned the comfort she had found, the physical comfort, and relief, in Rosie's arms, and in the kisses they had shared, while he lay silently, disturbed by his thoughts, not wanting her to go on.

However much it hurt him, he had to acknowledge that the women had shared a passion, a passion that, in the deepest recesses of his sensitivity, he grieved that he and Maggie would not share. For him, it was there. His heart, as well as his body, blazed with it. It was the most profound, the deepest sensation he would feel. But that inner, most vital spark that lit the flame was not present in her. It had been there, he guessed, in the girl that had loved the sailor lad. It tormented him to think it might have been there for the plain, almost middle-aged woman who had shared her life in that brief, traumatic time ten years ago.

In his most selfish moments, he tried to look on Rosie Dwyer almost as a perverse seducer, a substitute male lecher, who had seized on a young, innocent girl at a most vulnerable period, taken advantage of her need for comfort, and support. That didn't work for long, though. He might not understand it, but he knew that such a simplistic and one-sided view of the relationship was far short of the truth.

All that he knew now, as he looked at the dark, tufted little head of his new daughter, was that he loved the sprawled, defenceless figure in the bed there, who had let him into her life. And all he wanted was the chance to take care of both of them. Maggie had known enough of pain and loss in her young life, and, if it was up to him, he would protect her from such blows for the rest of his days.

2

Alice disliked the sharp, disinfectant smell that permeated hospitals. Not just the wards. It floated down corridors, seemed to penetrate everywhere. Not that unpleasant in itself it harboured all the associations with pain and sickness and tears she found so distressing. She remembered the euphoric relief the day Rosie had come to collect her and little Thomas. The nine days she had spent in the nursing home after the birth had seemed longer than any other period she had known in her life. Worse even than that interminable week leading up to those small child Christmases back at Port Hilda Hall.

'Thank goodness I'm never going to have to go through *that* again!' she declared dramatically, shuddering as she gazed down at the papoose-like bundle of the baby before she stepped into the waiting taxi, Rosie's hand on her elbow.

'Don't speak too soon!' Rosie chided lightly. 'Who knows what will happen?'

Alice looked at her archly, the brown eyes sparkling with laughter. She lowered her voice to a husky whisper so that the driver would not hear. 'Why? You're not going to get me pregnant, are you?'

Now that smell was back, strongly, assailing her nostrils once again, and overlaid with a sickly, mystical aroma which Alice shied away from with horror, afraid to acknowledge it as death. She was shocked at the changes she saw in the strong face, was helpless to hide her emotion. Rosie's countenance was grey, and so scored with lines, deep folds where the flesh had fallen from it, the parchment neck above the bedgown a series of obscene, horizontal ringlets. The grey eyes were blurred with drugs, but rimmed and shadowed with pain. They filled, the tears spilled over, rolled freely down the gauntness, matching her own weeping, while they stared at each other mutely, and Alice, appalled, thought that this was the first time Rosie had allowed her to see her cry so openly.

She bent over her, let their tears mingle, while the sickly odour of ether and perfume, and that dreaded, unknown smell which was not quite cancelled out, wafted up from the bed. The hand that lifted gently, caressed Alice's cheek in that beloved, brief gesture, was a ruin. The long, capable fingers were prominently knuckled, the bones and tendons thrust themselves on her sight with their awful message of decay.

Rosie cleared her throat noisily, her voice, when it came, hoarser than usual, and laboured. 'Sorry about the blubbing. Not at my best. Never am when I'm sick. Can't deal with it.' Her brow furrowed. 'Where's the little one?'

'They found someone to look after him. He's downstairs. They won't let him on the ward. I'll pop down presently and see he's all right.'

'I would've liked – I bet he's a handful now, eh? Now that he's walking properly?'

'He's into everything. I take him down to the beach most mornings. He loves it. And the beck.' Alice paused, drew in a deep breath, forced herself to meet Rosie's look.

The wearied, ruined face lit up with a smile. 'Go on. Tell me all about it. I love hearing about it. What about the cottage? Is Sally still coming?'

When Alice saw the matron later that day, she had to fight against the tide of grief waiting to swamp her. 'Why isn't she in a room of her own?' she asked first.

'She insisted she preferred some company,' the matron answered equably. 'And of course it *is* considerably cheaper. She *did* say she didn't want to incur any unnecessary expense.' The matron paused, went on in a more deliberately delicate tone. 'We will move her in any case. Soon. It'll be better – for everyone.'

'There's nothing? I mean – any hope....' The tears came again, choking her, and she pushed her handkerchief over her mouth.

'I know you've seen the difference already in the time she's been here,' the matron said kindly. 'It's never long, with this type of illness. Once the disease has spread, attacked the lining of the stomach—'

'She kept putting me off!' Alice cried bitterly. 'Telling me they were going to operate. That I should wait to visit—'

'She didn't want to distress you, my dear. The surgery was merely exploratory, to confirm the prognosis. She won't last long, she's perfectly aware of that. And we'll ease her suffering as much as possible.'

'She can come home!' Alice wept. 'If there's nothing—'

The matron's voice was soothing. 'That wouldn't be wise. The difficulties of looking after such a patient. Constant nursing, supervising of the medication. Really, in the circumstances. You with the little boy.' Again, there was a slight, delicate pause. 'As a matter of fact, Miss Dwyer insists that she wishes to stay here. Please accept her wishes. She's doing it for you. Allow her that.'

Next day, Alice brought Thomas to the doors at the end of the ward. He stood there, staring interestedly around, holding firmly to Alice's hand. Rosie was propped up high on her pillows and lifted her wasted arm in a cheerful wave. 'There's Auntie Rosie,' Alice managed. 'Wave to her.' She raised his chubby hand, waggled it, turned away.

When she came back later, alone, she was startled at the brilliance of Rosie's eyes. Piercingly bright, and black, they held her remorselessly. The face was flushed, looked animated, in spite of the lines of her ordeal. She was breathing with quick lightness. 'We've got to talk, my duck,' she said, with all her old, no-nonsense, gruff authority. She caught hold of Alice's hand, held on to it. 'And you can just shut up for the moment and listen, while I'm *compos mentis*. Right?

'I've been in touch with my solicitor, and he's getting in touch with your family's chappies. What are they called? That young feller that's keen on you? The one your sister wanted to marry you off to. Surtees! That's right. Don't worry. They'll still handle your business even if they think you're a scarlet hussy. Never known a legal wallah to turn down the chance of making money. There shouldn't be any opposition from my family. My folks are dead. Apart from a few aunts and uncles and the odd cousin, there's only a brother. He's a stiff-necked old sod, but he knows what I want. I've already been in touch with him, too.

'So, old girl! You're my sole heir. Or heiress, rather! Salmon Cottage is mine, by the way.' Alice gaped at her, through the tears which glistened on her face, and Rosie chuckled, squeezed her hand playfully. 'I was going to surprise you. Give it to young Thomas on his second birthday or something. No! Shut up! You can have your turn in a minute. Don't stop me now! I know I was renting it but I thought what the heck! Anyway, it's yours now. Not that it's worth very much, but it's a roof over your and the infant's heads, for the moment. Until you move on to something better.'

She held up her hand, constraining Alice to further silence. 'And there should be enough money to keep you and the little one for quite a while, if you continue to live in the penurious lifestyle we have grown accustomed to.' Her breathing was becoming more and more laboured, her features reflecting the distress she was feeling, but she grinned again from the pillow. 'And there are of course my priceless canvases. Some day, my girl, they will enable you to live the life of Riley, I swear.

'There! That's about it!' She gasped, sighed with satisfaction, sinking back a little, with an air of exhaustion. The grip on Alice's hand had weakened a little, the brown head shook against the whiteness. 'You'll be all right, darling girl, never fear! And no more of this dreadful blubbing, eh? It isn't good for us. Just one more thing. Something I'd like you to do for me, my sweet. Last request and all that. Kiss me Hardy etcetera.' Her voice was a whisper now, her eyes pleading, awash with her tears. 'Bugger off back to Salmon Cottage, there's a good girl. Go back to life there, with little Tom. Leave me to shuffle off in peace.'

It was one of the few requests Alice could not obey. She *did* go back to Kingstaith, but made the long journey to the nursing home twice more, the second time when Rosie had lapsed into unconsciousness and the doctors were convinced that she could not last another twenty-four hours. She sat with the moaning, muttering figure, wasted now to a pitiable skeleton of her former robust frame. When she left, after a long vigil, she met a tall, broad man in expensive clothes whom she recognized immediately as Rosie's brother.

Foolishly, she was unprepared, shocked at the look of vehement loathing he directed at her, and the disgust which thickened his speech when he forced himself to address her. 'Rosie will be buried in the family plot,' he said baldly. 'At her request, I might add. I trust you will have the common decency not to cause us any embarrassment at such a distressing time. I'd be obliged if you'd keep well clear, Miss Guthrie. I don't think we will ever need to meet again.'

There was a final note from Rosie, which she had obviously written with great difficulty a few days previously.

My Darling Girl
  Don't fight over my remains, will you? I have a mind to be laid
at rest back home after all. I hope you'll understand. Really a sop
to the family, I suppose. Anyway, it won't be me there. I'll be in
Salmon Cottage, and wherever else you choose to go. I'll be in my
pictures, and in your heart. I've loved you so much, my sweet. The
best, the purest love, always. God bless,
  Rosie

Alice mourned in private, though she was deeply touched by expressions of sympathy from many of the Kingstaith folk. On the day of the funeral, which took place far, far away in the south of England, Alice wrapped up Thomas and herself, and braved a blustery and bitter November wind to climb up the steep, broken path leading out of the village on the southern side, and up on to the cliffs she had known so well since childhood. The wind was off the land, so the grey waves were not too high, though their tops were foam flecked all the same. A few hundred yards out from shore, a rolling wall of mist blocked off all further vision.

She moved along the narrow, familiar path, Thomas yelping with delight as his sturdy rubber boots stamped through the mud and puddles, lifting his little face to the rain fret which clung to their skins. Down below, she could see the narrow margin of shore were she and Tommy had first come upon Rosie, and those naked boys. Alice remembered again the guilt of the thrill she had felt at seeing their pale, slim grace, the shocking, beautiful, budding promise of their sex before she had turned hotly away.

She walked on until she was almost at Port Hilda and, looking up the gentle slope of the bare fields, she could see the chimneys of the hall, rising disembodied through the billowing rain and mist. It was here, the same day, that Tommy had suddenly pulled her to him and kissed her properly, for the first time, on the lips. She looked again at the dark fingers thrusting up from the pointed roofs. How long now since she had set eyes on her parents, her family? Two years and more. She was twenty now. She felt old, almost. And very much alone.

A stab of guilt caught her at the impatient tug of Thomas's hand in hers. She blinked back the tears, brushed swiftly at her wet face with determination. How could she even think such a thing? She looked down at the swathed little head. 'Come on. Let's go home,' she said, and turned back the way she had come.

She saw something lying against the blue front door, and, when she got up to it, she saw that it was an evergreen garland, shining with silvery raindrops. There was a small card, with a carefully printed message: *In memory of Rosie.*

She had only just got their outdoor things off and was thawing out in front of the fire, trying not to look at the clock and think what was happening in that distant place, when she heard a commotion, then a rapid banging at the door. Sally Wheatley was there, and a couple of other married women. They were all gabbling and crying, clutched at her hands when she opened to them. 'It's over, miss! It's over! At last! The've signed an armistice! The've stopped fightin'! The war's over!'

3

The fisherfolk families took her under their sturdy wings. The gossip and scurrilous rumours, the stigma of Thomas's illegitimacy, all died with Rosie's death. Alice never lacked for visitors, or for invitations to visit. Sally Wheatley married, like her sister, Sophia, but there was a succession of young, willing helpers to take over the cleaning and washing for a shilling or two a week. 'Yer need someone ter live in wi' yer,' the women kept insisting, against Alice's consistent, laughing denials.

'I can manage quite well, thanks,' she told them. 'I like it fine being on my own. I couldn't do with another body in the house.' They found it hard to grasp that someone of her background and upbringing could be so independent and self-contained. Their anger turned now against her family, with whom, in the beginning, they had sided so righteously.

'Disgustin', the way they've left a young lass like that ter fend fer 'erself. All alone like that!' They added with vehement satisfaction, 'Any road, the reckon the mine's droppin' off now that the war's over. Stuff's goin' up by rail ter Redcar. The's not 'alf the boats usin' Port 'ilda nowadays.'

Alice became a regular visitor to the Cousins, walking one way and riding back the one stop on the train, or catching one of the new motor coaches operating along the coast road. She still felt ill at ease with Will Cousins, who had little to say when they met, which was not often, for she tried to time her visits during the weekdays, when he was likely either to be at work or down in the Mucky Duck in the village. The tiny cottage at Mine Row, which had always seemed such a vibrant, crowded place during the days of her childhood when she used to call for Tommy, was quiet now, the children all up and away. Louise was married, living somewhere near Leeds, and Dora was there, too, having stayed at the end of the war to find work in one of the mills.

Alice was deeply touched at the way that Ginny Cousins kept a small photograph of the portrait of Alice and her babe in arms, which Rosie had insisted should be taken at Mr Sutcliffe's studio in Skinner Street in Whitby, beside the pictures on the mantelshelf of Tommy's older brother, Bert, and his wife and their children. ''E's a bonny bairn,' Ginny declared. 'And 'e's a grandson, when all's said an' done.'

Alice would have been wounded had she known of the sometimes bitter arguments Ginny's action caused in the cottage, and of the venom with which Bert's wife upbraided him in private. 'Why's she keep a picture of that little bastard next ter the bairns?'

At the end of one of these visits, Alice was leaving Mine Row, and passing the end of the lane which led to the hall, when she saw a woman's shape, in dark outdoor coat, waving to her. With a jolt, she recognized Evie Swain, her mother's maid, gesturing as she came over the rutted track towards her. 'Miss Alice! Miss Alice! Yer mam – Mrs Guthrie asked me – to try and catch you. Would you – come along?' She gestured behind her, in the direction of the house. 'She'd like to see you. To talk.'

'Is everything all right?' Alice's heart was thumping. Thomas was tugging at her hand, anxious to be off down the hill, and a ride on the coach.

'Far as I know, miss,' Evie answered, rather stiffly. 'She just wants to talk, that's all. There's nobody there. Only Mrs Guthrie.' There was an awkward silence between them as they walked along the lane, the centre of which was raised, covered with grass. Two deep channels, caused by the passage of vehicles, ran either side of this raised portion. 'He's a fine looking boy, miss,' Evie said shyly.

'Thank you.' Evie led her off to the high iron gates of the main entrance on the worn stone pillars. She swung one open, stood to let Alice pass. Their feet crunched over the small stones of the wide, circular drive, to the shallow steps up to the front porch. Her mother appeared at the top of the steps, erect and trim, her hands clasped theatrically at her midriff. Her waist was still thin, her hair dark, though she seemed somehow smaller to Alice.

'It's good of you to come,' Mrs Guthrie murmured quietly, with a curious formality.

Alice stepped forward, and put her hands lightly on her mother's elbows, pushed her face forward and kissed the proffered cheek equally lightly and fleetingly. 'It's good to be asked,' she answered, quietly also.

'Bring us some tea, Evie,' Mrs Guthrie said, leading Alice into the front sitting-room. Thomas was silent for the moment, clinging to his mother, gazing in awed, round-eyed wonder at the wide dimensions of the room, the solid furniture, pictures on the walls, the ornately carved ceiling, the huge bay of the windows. 'And this is little Tommy, is it?' Mrs Guthrie said, bending forward slightly to him, her voice betraying an unsteadiness.

'Thomas,' corrected Alice firmly.

Her mother looked up at her, flushing a little, began to murmur an apology. Suddenly, her face crumpled. Only then Alice noted how old and worn she looked, as she gave a muffled sob, and all at once reached frantically for her daughter. They fell together, their frames shaking as they sobbed. Not to be outdone, Thomas, too, started to whimper in uncertainty. 'You – you silly, silly girl!' Margaret Guthrie wept, clasping Alice to her, pressing her face into her neck.

'You haven't waited three years to tell me that?' Alice managed, through her tears, and her mother shook her head, hugged her all the tighter, refusing to let go of her, while Thomas pulled at her skirts in increasing alarm.

'No, no! Of course not! I've been so worried – all this time. Wanting to see you again. Afraid—'

They had pulled apart, and were dabbing with their small handkerchiefs, and Mrs Guthrie was trying without success to win a smile from the little boy, when Evie brought in the tray and laid it on a low side table. 'Thank you, Evie.' For a shocked instant, Alice thought the maid was going to remain there, part of the reunion, for there was a distinct pause before Mrs Guthrie said, with a hint of apology in her manner, 'Right. That'll be all, Evie.'

'I'm sorry about Alex,' Alice blurted clumsily when they were alone, and saw her mother turn red. She gave a nod.

'I know. We – it was your father. He's still – he can't forgive you. I – I – it was wrong, Alice, what you did! But I – couldn't – I had to see you. He doesn't know.'

'Will you tell him?' Her mother made a small, helpless gesture, and Alice felt a deep compassion for her. 'He'll probably get to know anyway.' Again, her mother shrugged. 'Never mind.' Thomas was sitting on the carpet, crumbling a biscuit. 'It's a nice day,' Alice continued. 'Shall we take a walk in the garden? It'll be good for Thomas. He's not used to sitting still.'

'How old is he now? Must be three....' The look of embarrassment returned as Mrs Guthrie's voice faded, and Alice could almost hear her thoughts. Born only three weeks before the official grandson, Alex. Olga had two children now. There was a girl, Vera, born fourteen months ago. Not that the family had informed her of the arrival of her niece, but her visits to Tommy's ma ensured that she was up to date on all such events.

It startled Alice to take stock, and to realize that she had been living alone, except for Thomas, in Salmon Cottage for over a year and a half. She had been happy enough. Looking after her son had taken up most of her energy and time. It was in the evenings, particularly in the long, wind-rattling darkness of winter nights, which began with the lighting of the lamps before Thomas's tea time, that loneliness sneaked upon her, occasionally, when she sat before the banked fire, Thomas safely tucked asleep above, and the wind roaring in the chimney. She would contemplate the empty chair opposite, and the tears would start, the pain of grief sharp, for, despite that promise in her last, badly scrawled note, it was not Rosie's presence but her absence that clawed at Alice's heart.

Then came a disturbing guilt, at mourning for her friend like that, when Tommy's death, Tommy, her one true lover, had been so much more accepted, and allotted a tender place which did not tear with such jagged, snaggled edges at her memory. I didn't live with you, Tommy, she told him penitently. We didn't live together, ever. We went to bed, upstairs, in a furious passion I can scarcely comprehend or recall now, it was all so unique and unknown to us. But we never spent a single night together. Rosie's arms are the only arms that I can remember holding me in pure comfort, and love, night after night, caring and protecting. And I watched her die, Tommy. I was there.

There were other nights, many, when she stretched her bare feet to the warmth, and felt a sensuous pleasure and contentment at being alone, and thought of the bond which held her to the sleeping infant, wrapped them together like a safe, insulating blanket. She worried vaguely sometimes about the future. When she saw and heard the roughness of the village boys, and girls, charging about the sands, or the hard on which the boats were drawn up under the towering cliffs, she was ashamed at her sudden anxiety about what would happen to Thomas. Already, his infant speech was comically peppered with the broad dialect and accent, exotically mixed with the more rounded and refined accent of her own speech.

How would he grow up? Where would he be educated? At the school up the bank? What else? They had ample means for this modest life, but money for education? More than once she scolded herself, promising that she would do something, make an appointment with Mr Surtees or his partner. Even Philip, whom she had, thank goodness, met only once, and that briefly, at the office when she made one of her rare visits there. But she must find out, exactly, where she and Thomas stood, as far as their financial future was concerned. Otherwise, he would be another 'raggy-arsed' village lad. She blushed ashamedly at the crudely descriptive epithet. Just like his dad, came the even more painful thought, to make her blush all the more with shame.

It was during the summer of 1920 that an idea began to form in her mind, which refused to let go and which recurred with growing excitement as the year drew to its close. It was engendered by an article she read one week in the *Whitby Gazette*, predicting in glowing terms the emergence of Whitby as one of the premier east coast tourist resorts, and the need to cater for the increasingly varied types of summer visitor. The writer argued that, since the war, more and more of the 'less elevated sections of society' recognized the benefits of an annual holiday, and that, apart from the established hotels up on the West Cliff, there was a dearth of suitable accommodation.

An ideal opportunity for resourceful females, many of whom are now, alas, tragically alone after the recent terrible conflict, to earn a modest but secure living and assure themselves of independence. At the end of the article were several advertisements for boarding-houses: 'Sea views. Private sitting-room. Hot and cold baths. Near the golf links, tennis courts. Excellent cuisine.' The claims jumped out at her, her heart fluttered with a fearful excitement.

She had continued to call in at the hall during her visits to Port Hilda, generally when her mother was alone. Olga carefully avoided meeting her. Her father was always out, though her mother told her he was now aware of her visits, of which he disapproved, but did not forbid. 'He has a lot of worries,' Mrs Guthrie said defensively. 'The mine's dreadfully run down, you know. He's had to pay a lot of men off.' She gave a refined little sniff and added, 'I expect Tommy's mother has told you,' and Alice nodded. 'He doesn't think we'll keep going much longer. He's been trying to sell out but it's hopeless. And he gets no help from the Powers. Luke's uncle can't even be bothered to attend board meetings.

'But Luke's worth his weight in gold!' Mrs Guthrie said warmly. 'Your father doesn't know what he'd do without him!'

Alice was ashamed of the mean resentment she felt at the mention of her brother-in-law, whom she scarcely knew. He had taken Alex's place with a vengeance, especially since Bertie had gone off down south as soon as he came out of the navy in 1919, showing his usual disregard of the family business or their wishes, and now ran some kind of transport company with two of his ex-service colleagues.

Her mother was hardly able to conceal her horror when Alice waxed enthusiastic about her scheme to purchase and run a boarding-house, which did not put Alice off at all. Some days later, she sat in the solicitor's office in Baxtergate, with nervous determination. 'Best bib and tucker,' she grinned at Sally, before she set out, umbrella in hand, for the station at Bank Top. The girl had commented on how smart Alice looked. 'A proper lady,' she said emphatically, and Alice was pleased at the compliment, though she saw there might be a back-handed element about it. I wonder how I normally look then? she asked herself, with a wry inner grin. Coward-like, she sneaked away while Thomas was distracted by the wily girl, and hoped he would be all right until she got back.

She was blushingly confused now when Philip appeared in the small reception area and ushered her into an office, looking almost as ill at ease as she felt. He was fleshier, but more handsome than she remembered him. He had seen a brief period of action on the Western Front, as an artillery officer, in 1917, in the battle of which Sassoon wrote, starkly, 'I died in hell (They called it Passchendaele).' But then he had the fortune to get a job on the staff, for which he was to feel eternally grateful and guilty, and saw out the war safely.

Now he murmured apologetically, 'Good to see you, Alice,' and waved her to a seat, while she thought, with grim humour, you could've fooled me! 'Pa thought, as we're old chums, it might be a good idea if I looked after you.' His hands twitched over a buff-coloured file, and she felt sympathy for him. Like her brother, Alex, he had never been much good at standing up to 'the old man'. However, he knew his job, and, after half an hour, he told her, with some confidence, 'With the money we should raise on Salmon Cottage, and the other bits and bobs, we should manage to find a suitable property. Bagdale, or somewhere round there. Splendid old houses. Ideal for what you want.'

Fate lent another kind hand. Not much more than a week later she received a letter from Dora Cousins, asking if she could come out to Kingstaith and visit, as she had a week's holiday from the mill. Alice wrote back immediately, insisting that she come and stay overnight, or until she got 'fed up'. When the girl stood smiling shyly on descending from the train, Alice was taken aback for a second, seeing the beloved features which, sometimes, memory had mercifully blurred somewhat, transposed into a gentle and beautiful feminine setting. She hugged her tightly, unable to keep back the tears entirely. 'It's lovely to see you,' she whispered, and it was true.

They talked non-stop, all through tea, and Thomas's evening ablutions, performed with cosy informality before the fire. 'You're going to sleep in your own bed tonight,' Alice told him proudly. 'He usually sleeps in with me,' she explained to the visitor, who at once demurred.

'Look, ah can manage on the sofa. Or a shake-me-down, anywhere. Honest, miss—' She laughed, shook her black hair ingenuously. 'Sorry! Ah mean Alice.'

'Nonsense! It'll do this little mister good. He's getting far too big to be sleeping with his mam. Besides, we're going to be talking half the night anyway. It's not often I get the chance for some real grown-up conversation.'

Alice was not far short of the mark in her estimation. They lay together, a little shyly at first, though the limited and primitive facilities of the cottage had already blunted their shyness, and decreed an element of intimacy. In any case, both girls had grown up sharing beds with siblings as a matter of course. Soon, they were snuggling, heads touching on the pillow, as they whispered their recent histories, and shared fond memories.

'Yer'll meet someone one day,' Dora prophesied. 'A nice man who'll take care of yer.' Dora felt the shake of the head close to hers, and sighed, then gave a smothered little giggle. 'Ah'm still waitin' meself, ah must admit.' She stirred, enjoyed the feel of Alice's arm about her waist, her warm body fitting around hers. 'Ah dunno,' she murmured. 'Ah'm fed up with me job over at Leeds. The lasses there.' She shuddered fastidiously. 'Ah think ah'm going to look for something nearer home, maybe. Ah wouldn't mind goin' back into service.'

Alice felt that quickening heartbeat of excitement once more. She squeezed the pliant body next to her, pulling her even closer. Her nose brushed against the soft wisps of hair. 'How would you like to

come and work for me?' she asked, her voice bubbling with delight,
and a rising hope.

4

Dora found it very difficult at first to remember the new name, but
Maggie kept on at her, with laughing but remorseless persistence.
'Uh-huh! It's Maggie, not Alice! I've told you! A penny in the jar
every time you forget!' Eventually, Dora did not forget, the new
name stuck. It had begun in a half-joking way, when they first went
excitedly together to look at 13 Prospect Mount, and realized, even
more excitedly, that the big old house was just what they were
looking for, and was also just within their price range. 'A new life,
and a new name to go with it. I've never liked Alice, anyway! I've
got to turn respectable, and Mrs Maggie Guthrie sounds much
more your typical landlady, don't you think?'

Others found it hard to readjust also, except for her own mother,
who refused to make the effort. 'You'll always be Alice to us,' Mrs
Guthrie senior insisted, and Alice soon gave up arguing. When the
first boxed advertisements appeared in the Press, her mother said
with assumed indignation, 'I hope to goodness people don't think
I've descended to taking in lodgers!'

'There are worse ways of making a living,' her daughter retorted
drily. 'And it's a white lie, after all, calling myself missus. In fact,
it's a highly respectable trade. That's why I've done it.'

Apart from her mother, and Ginny Cousins, there were very few
regular callers who had known her before she metamorphosed into
Maggie. The villagers of Kingstaith rarely ventured the eleven
miles down the coast which separated them from Whitby, besides
which, although Alice had been born and raised a mere two miles
away, and had lived with them for almost five years, in a
community where, if grandparents had been born beyond the
boundaries of the village you were still considered an incomer, she
had never been looked on as anything other than a bird of passage,
and a pretty exotic one at that!

As for sister Olga, she made it plain that she wished to have no contact with her, even though they now lived in the same town, less than three miles apart. Their first accidental meeting took place outside Botham's bakery, in Skinner Street, where Maggie had been to place an order for the cakes and pies she planned to serve as part of the 'Yorkshire High Tea' which seemed to be *de rigeur* in the town's guest-houses.

Maggie smiled cautiously, prepared to wave the olive branch readily enough, but Olga's freezing look was eloquent. 'I've got nothing to say to you,' she announced bluntly. 'I saw your vulgar little notice in the paper. P'raps you'll do well at looking after lodgers. Mama told me all about it. I gather you've wheedled your way back in with her. I must say I was surprised to hear you'd had the cheek to get Philip Surtees running around after you. I just hope his fiancée doesn't get to hear of it. Didn't you know he's engaged? Or doesn't that bother you?'

Maggie had stood there, blinking, cheeks glowing as she faced this briefly hissing tirade. Now, she recovered. Her voice was low, but throbbed with her anger. 'You bitch! You supercilious bitch! I've a good mind to box your ears for you!'

'You really *have* acquired the common touch, haven't you?' Olga sneered, but she moved back on the jostling pavement nevertheless, and looked to make her escape. 'I suppose we'll bump into one another occasionally like this. Can't be helped. But I'd rather you didn't acknowledge me, if you don't mind!'

Maggie was seething still when she got back to her new home and told Dora the tale. 'I would have done, too!' she fumed, as they sat at the kitchen table. 'If she'd stayed another second I'd have smacked her face for her!'

'She's right. Yer've been too long among them fishwives!' Dora giggled, and they both dissolved into laughter.

It was harder than either of them had imagined, building up a business and a reputation, but they worked with huge enthusiasm from dawn until well after dusk, until, gradually, the same summer faces kept appearing, while they also had both casual and regular 'business gentlemen', in sufficient numbers to keep them going throughout the year.

When Alf Turner first came, in his sober suit and grey trilby, the girls assumed he was a 'traveller' in some area of commerce, and Dora was more than a little put out when she discovered that one of the items in his washing was a pair of workmen's overalls. 'He must take them out with him and change at work,' she surmised, almost indignantly, as though he had been practising a deceit on them.

'You're a snob!' Maggie laughed teasingly, and Dora pulled a disapproving face.

'Well, it's not good for us, is it, if somebody sees him comin' in in a pair of mucky overalls on a night? Ah'm going to ask him what it is he does exactly. We ought ter know.'

'No, you can't! The poor man'll die of shock! He's so shy. He blushes every time we say good morning!'

But even his inhibiting shyness was not proof against Maggie's winning, easy friendliness. She didn't rush things, but soon she was able to tell an intrigued Dora, 'He's some sort of engineer. To do with electrics. You know that new equipment they've had put in at the Empire? He's been working on that.' The town was still very proud of its first purpose-built cinema in Station Square.

They expected that their latest 'business' guest would be moving off after a few weeks, so Maggie was quietly pleased when he told her, glowing pinkly above his dazzling collar as he often did at the beginning of their conversations, 'Ah've got some work coming up in Saltburn. If yer don't mind me keeping me motor bike out the back in the yard, ah'd like ter stay on here, and travel.' He grew even shinier and redder, but forced himself on. 'Ah've felt that – settled here. It's been such a pleasure – the best lodgings ah've had.'

'That's grand, Mr Turner!' she said quickly. 'I'm very pleased to hear it. And we'll be delighted to have you.' She smiled at him, her eyes dancing mischievously. 'Tell you what: when Mr Evans moves out on Thursday, you can have his room, if you like. It's much bigger, and you can actually see the harbour.'

'I think he's keen on you, if you ask me!' Dora concluded that night, and Maggie blushed as she gave her a vigorous shove. 'Don't talk daft!'

When romance *did* rear its head, it was Dora who was its first victim, by which time Alf Turner was their most regular guest, practically an institution, having been with them a year and a half. Goggled, helmeted, and trench-coated, he braved the elements on his Norton as far afield as Scarborough down the coast, and Pickering, inland over the moors road, as more and more communities awoke to the pleasures of 'electric theatres' and the magic of the cinema screen.

The young man who captured Dora's heart, and her hand, was no stranger. She began referring more and more to Len Gough, who was a native of their own Port Hilda, and a nephew of old Sam, who had been head gardener at the hall. At first, she saw him once a week, when she visited her folks, but soon he began making the journey into Whitby, to take her out for the evening, or to sit with her in the kitchen when Maggie had retired to the room upstairs which she had made into her sitting/bedroom.

Maggie was not really surprised when, late one night, Dora came up to her room, clearly both excited and apprehensive. 'D'yer fancy a cuppa?' she asked, as a preliminary, and Maggie nodded.

'You've got something to tell me,' Maggie declared presently, smiling at the clearly disturbed figure.

'Ask, more like!' Dora blurted. She blushed deeply. 'It's about me and Len. He's asked me – ter get engaged. He wants us ter wed. Not till the end of the year!' she added quickly and apologetically.

Maggie rose from her armchair and moved to Dora, who was sitting across from her in front of the hearth. 'Congratulations! That's wonderful news!' They hugged and kissed, and shed simultaneous tears, through which they laughed and clung together. 'What are we blubbing for? Listen! You grab him as soon as you can! Don't let him get away! I couldn't be happier for you, my dear!'

'Ah'll still want ter work with yer. As ah say, it won't be till near Christmas. And even then, ah can come and work, mebbe four days a week or something.'

'We'll see,' Maggie answered. 'First things first, eh?' She grinned again. 'Romance is in the air this year, it seems like!' The papers were still full of the wedding of the Prince of Wales's younger brother to the beautiful Lady Elizabeth Bowes-Lyon, which had taken place two weeks before, in April.

'Yer'll 'af ter see what you can do yerself,' Dora teased. 'With our Mr Turner,' and Maggie pinked as they both exploded into a fit of giggles, still clutching at each other.

'1923. It's not even a leap year, so I can't pop the question myself!' Maggie laughed. 'Can you just imagine? Poor Alf would run a mile!'

'Don't you believe it! The poor chap's dotty about you!'

5

Though there was little to substantiate Dora's claim concerning Alf Turner's feelings for Maggie when she first made it, two years later, by which time Dora was a wife and the mother of a six-month-old girl, Clarissa, it was an accurate assessment of his emotion towards his young landlady. In fact, of course, he had been smitten long before. Normally undemonstrative, and modest to the point of diffidence about his own appeal, he had harboured a secret but sweetly cherished affection for Maggie from his early days at Prospect Mount.

He was no romancer, and he kept his increasing devotion decently to himself. He was happy enough being able to see her nearly every day, to exchange a few blushing words with her, and, gradually, as his stay lengthened into what seemed a kind of permanency, to have the chance to be of service for the umpteen jobs of repair and renovation the old property required. 'It's so nice to have a man about the house,' Maggie said, with unoriginal but sincere appreciation. She would have been surprised, not to say startled, had she known the emotional turbulence such praise aroused in the steady breast of her favourite lodger.

It was many months before he felt truly at ease when Maggie invited him into her private room for a drink, or for supper with her and Thomas, for whom Alf, being a handyman, became something of a hero, fixing up their first magical crystal set, and, even more wonderfully, firing up and getting to run smoothly the model steam locomotive which Maggie had, rather ambitiously, bought her son for his eighth birthday.

Eventually, in spite of his shyness, Alf began to look on such moments as treasured, and to talk a little more freely about his personal life. His family – father a railwayman, dead early, of drink, when Alf was still only ten; the widowed mother who had died when Alf was twenty-two, just at the outbreak of war. He joined up immediately after the funeral, and was put in the Army Ordnance Corps, completing his training just in time to be shipped out to the Gallipoli Peninsula, to take part in the second phase landing at Suvla Bay, in August 1915.

He was part of the chaos and confusion of the beachhead, where, because of the incompetence of the generals and the rawness of recruits fresh off the troopships, the British and their allies became bogged down yet again. Weeks of nightmare stalemate followed, from which Alf was rescued by an attack of dysentery which almost killed him, but eventually got him back to Blighty and out of uniform.

Alf did not tell her much of his suffering, but, ten years on, the horrors and the sickness of those few months were as vivid as anything in his life. Lonely, not easily given to talking in intimate terms about his feelings, he was himself shaken by the depth of his love for the lovely young woman. He grew afraid to speak, assuming she would either be horrified or grotesquely amused to learn such a thing. But finally, he was driven to it, compelled by the very force of the emotion he could no longer suppress after enduring it for the better part of the four years he had been at Prospect Mount.

Somehow, agonized, sweating and beacon red, he stammered out his love, and his proposal of marriage, was stunned, then perplexed, by the storm of her tears he had unleashed. 'It's wonderful,' she sobbed, and put her hands trustingly on his forearm as she bravely faced him, her frame shaking with her grief. 'I'm deeply honoured. You're a wonderful man, but – I haven't been honest with you. And I'm going to hurt – and shock you – now. I'm not a widow. I've – never been married. Tom's father – we weren't – when he was killed. I wasn't even eighteen—'

'Nay, lass, what's that got to do with anything? Yer daft 'ap'orth, come here!' And, for the first time ever, he put his arms tightly around her, and pulled her into him. Their mouths closed on a long and giddy kiss. When she had recovered, and shyly agreed to marry him, and they had kissed and cuddled again, still quite decorously, on the sofa, Alf told her, 'You've nothing to be ashamed of, ever. You've done a grand job with Tom.' There was the briefest pause, before he added, 'His dad would be right proud of him. As I am.' She wept again, clinging fiercely to him, savouring the strength and warm protectiveness of his arms about her, and the secret, pulsing desire hidden deep within her which his male heat and power aroused.

14 NOVEMBER, 1941

1

Helena looked very young, and very frightened, her eyes huge as she gazed at Maggie from the pillows piled up behind her to keep her upright. 'Just pop your feet under the blankets again. Keep them warm. The taxi will be here soon, love.'

'What if it's a false alarm?' Helena asked, her face twisted with anxiety. 'The pain's stopped now. Except for the backache.'

'Best place for you is the hospital. If it *is* a false alarm, they can always send us home again. But I don't think it is. Remember, you're talking to an old expert here. Four of them, I've had, so I know what I'm on about.'

Listen to you, you cheery old fraud, Maggie thought. Trying to kid this poor lass that it was nothing to be scared of. 'This time tomorrow you'll have a bonny bouncing boy in your arms and you'll be feeling on top of the world' – and all the time she was remembering every stabbing agony of the twins' birth, and every torturous nightmare of the weeks that followed. The mercifully rapid death of the first poor mite, Ginny, after only a week, the cruel heartache of hope dashed to despair, that went on and on, for the long three months while Valerie fought to start her life before she gave up the hopeless struggle.

Ten years ago, and she couldn't recall it without that choking tightening of the throat, the ache in her breast, and the vivid picture of that tiny, delicate coffin resting on top of the chest of drawers in this very bedroom. The translucent skin of that

peacefully still little form, the delicate darkness of the fragile
eyelids. Suddenly, another, much earlier picture swam clearly into
her mind. Thomas cradled in her arms, a week old, as she bent to
get into a taxi, and the words she had uttered so confidently.
'Thank goodness I won't have to go through *that* again.' She had
gone through 'that' twice more, with Vicky and the twins. No more
fears now, though, she and Alf made certain there would be no
mistakes.

It was funny, though. Since Alf's war work took him away for a
week or more at a time, they were having sex far more regularly
than they had during the past few years. Getting to be a habit, she
joked grimly to herself, with that habitual feeling of shame and
guilt which came whenever she thought about sexual matters in
their marriage. She could not help feeling that she had never
fulfilled his secret hopes, or perhaps expectations, as far as sex was
concerned.

They had married quietly, waiting until the end of the season in
1925. Dora had been her Matron of Honour, her husband, Len,
acting as Best Man, because Alf insisted there was no one he wanted
who was closer to him. There weren't even any of his relatives at the
ceremony. 'No problems with in-laws, anyway,' Dora had quipped.
Not that there had been many from Maggie's side either. Her
mother had come alone, which did not surprise Maggie at all,
though the invitation had been to both parents. Mrs Guthrie made
the excuse that her husband was too tied up with the affairs
involved in winding down the mine. They were selling off land and
properties, had already disposed of Port Hilda Hall and bought a
more modest house on the Hampshire coast.

'I'm putting some money aside for you and the boy,' her mother
told her, blushing a little, but speaking over Maggie's rising
protests. 'No, this is *my* money. It came from Aunt Vera, a lot of it,
and it's what I want. And there's some available for you now, if you
need it. Mr Surtees knows all about it. Talk to him. Call it our
wedding present to you, if you like.'

She was offhand but polite to Alf, whom she had met several
times, for she had been a regular visitor to Prospect Mount over the
past four years. Clearly, she was not very impressed with her

daughter's choice of husband, but probably thought beggars couldn't be choosers, Maggie surmised.

The wedding was in November. Maggie had arranged for Dora to take over the supervision of the boarding-house for a week while they honeymooned at a hotel on the shores of Lake Windermere. The rain rattled against the windows of their room, and the lake, no more than fifty yards away, was invisible through the white mist. 'We can't even get out for a walk,' Alf smiled nervously. 'Early night, eh?' And turned beet red, while Maggie giggled like a schoolgirl, and apologized.

'I'm sorry, Alf,' she said simply, when they were alone in their room again. She unbuttoned her blouse, went up to him, blushing but brave. 'I'm nervous. I'm not very experienced at this. We only – it was only the one time. I – I feel like this is the first time for me.'

Alf was even redder. His eyes had an almost trapped look as he struggled to hold her gaze. 'Ah know – it's – it *is* – first time – fer me!'

As far as the pain and embarrassment went, she was right. It *was* like the first time. But the trouble was, it wasn't the first time. Secretly hurt that Alf fled to the bathroom along the corridor while she undressed and slipped on the new satin nightdress, she climbed, shivering, under the bedclothes. Alf got in beside her, pyjama clad, and moved awkwardly to embrace her. Then memory came cruelly flooding back, and comparison, and she began to relive Tommy's loving, their passion, hating herself yet helpless to stop it, feeling soiled and shameful while Alf clung and kissed smotheringly, scrabbled frantically, even tearing the lace edging from the hem of her nightie, thrusting himself on her, forcing himself into her, afraid, and desperate himself, and out of control.

'Ah'm sorry,' he whispered, afterwards, choking back the tears, lying there stiffly at her side, afraid even to touch her.

'No, no!' she sobbed, suddenly rolling over to cling fiercely to him. 'It was fine. Fine! It just hurt – that's all. I told you – I've never really—' And she held on to him, weeping, until his tenderness seeped through her anguish, his arms and body warmed her, and she sank into the comfort of the security he brought.

But the past seemed morbidly reluctant to let her go, she felt, for, on the third day of their stay, while they were late breakfasting in the deserted dining-room, the proprietor came up, disposed to chat, and lugubriously delighted with a bona fide disaster to pass on. 'Isn't it terrible about that submarine?' And brought them the morning papers, which proclaimed the loss of the M-1 and all sixty-eight of the crew in the Channel. To Maggie, this news of a naval tragedy was like a private portent, a comment on her own action in marrying. It was days before she could shake off the feeling, though she strove valiantly, and, she hoped, successfully, to hide it from Alf.

More guilt feelings troubled her when she began to counterfeit a physical satisfaction she was far from experiencing in their love-making, though she could easily justify this to herself as her duty towards the man who clearly loved her. As she did him. His tenderness, his concern for her, were apparent in his every look, every gesture, and she savoured it, revelled in it. What she felt, or didn't feel, in bed, was not all that important, she kept telling herself. That was something wrong with her, not Alf, and she would die rather than let him be hurt by it. They never talked about it, in any case. His hasty, embarrassed, 'Was it all right?' was as far as they got, and her hasty, embarrassed, 'Yes, lovely', seemed to do the trick.

As she looked at the wary, fearful young face before her now, and the beautiful, vulnerable brown eyes fixed with such desperate trust on her, Maggie felt that engulfing love, and tenderness, which made her whole body ache with the desire to clasp the girl tightly to her. She acknowledged that its power was both sexual and emotional, that sweetly confusing blend she had known years ago, when she had needed the strength and reliance which Rosie had brought to her. There was a hint of shame there, which she had never been able to reconcile quite, though far stronger was the feeling almost akin to pride that this was a most precious sensation, a closeness she should, and would, treasure always.

Did Helena sense it? Did it even matter if she didn't? Perhaps it was something that existed on a subconscious level, too, Maggie thought, for, certainly at the time, she had never formulated it like this when she was with Rosie. Enough that it was there, and she knew it now.

She had insisted that, as the time drew near, Helena move down
and share her bed with her. Helena's protests had been lacking in
conviction. She derived a great measure of comfort from having
Maggie near, even from the touch of her gently curled around her,
the gentle hand rubbing the swollen drum of her belly, sharing the
thrill of the beats and the vigorous kicks of the life sealed in her.
'It's a boy all right!' Maggie predicted, as had a number of other
women when they saw how big Helena was. 'Are you going to call
him Ernest?'

Helena looked a little guilty. She blushed. 'I never really liked
the name,' she admitted, ashamed. 'Ernie. It isn't – he didn't like
it, either,' she added, as a kind of excuse.

Maggie smiled. 'You're right. You've got to think about it. The
poor bairn's got to live with it all his life. Unless you're like me!
And decide to change it for yourself.'

Helena hadn't realized. When Philip Surtees came to call, back
in June, to discuss the legal implications of Helena's pregnancy, she
had been bewildered at the awkwardness of the first minutes, the
look that had passed between Maggie and the solicitor. 'Alice,' he
said, taking her hand, and she had corrected him firmly, blushing a
little.

'Maggie. Don't forget. It's Maggie now.'

Several nights later, Helena and Maggie had sat talking long after
Vicky had gone up to bed. There was a confessional intimacy about
the lateness of the hour, the cosy, insulated atmosphere of the
kitchen. Maggie told her history to Helena, in every detail, while
the younger girl listened spellbound, with an increasing sense of
wonder. 'So you see, love,' Maggie said, her voice trembling a little,
'there's so much we share. That I feel for you. It's like it's all
happening all over again. Why I feel so—' She shrugged as though
it was hopeless to try to explain. 'So close.' She reached for
Helena's hand, clasped it, and held it to her tear-damp cheek.

'Oh, Maggie!' With a low cry, Helena rose. They both stood, and
embraced. They kissed, their mouths softly together for a long
time.

'Sleep with me tonight,' Maggie whispered, her eyes shining with
her tears.

'I'm restless as anything these days,' Helena answered, patting the discernible bulge of her stomach. 'I'll keep you awake all night.'

'I don't mind. I'd like it, in fact. I don't think I'm going to get much sleep anyway. Even though they *do* say confession is good for the soul.'

For the first time, Helena had looked at the framed portrait hung discreetly on the wall. 'Gosh! It's wonderful!'

Maggie chuckled softly, came and stood beside Helena in front of the painting, and put her hand on her shoulder. 'Poor Alf. He can't really get used to the idea of his wife stuck up there naked for all to see.' She snorted and clapped a hand to her mouth. 'Oh God! I didn't mean – that sounds bad, doesn't it? I don't exactly have a parade passing through my bedroom, honestly!'

Not long after they were settled, with the lamp out, Maggie gave a gasp, and sat up, scrabbling for the switch on the bedside table. 'What's wrong?' Helena asked, startled. She saw that Maggie was quivering with suppressed laughter, her dark eyes wide. 'What is it?'

'What was Ernie's surname? Wheatley, wasn't it?'

'Yes, but—'

'I've just remembered! Oh my God! What's his mother's name? Her first name, I mean!'

Helena's face puckered in puzzlement. 'Er – I'm not sure. I can't—'

'Not Sally, is it?'

'No. No. Something like that, though. Why?'

Maggie had seized her hand, was staring at her, her expression a mixture of shock and mischief, like a child faced with the delightful outrage of a rude word. 'Wheatley. Sally's sister. God, what was her name?' She screwed up her face again in an effort to recall. 'Sophia! That was it! Sophia!'

'Yes. I think that's Ernie's mother's name,' Helena said, agog with impatience herself now. 'Why? What on earth...?'

Maggie gave a gasp of shock again. She nodded at the wall. 'There's a picture of her! And her sister! Like that! I remember Rosie telling me. Both of them together! *The Amazons*, she called it. She sold it – to someone down south. It's probably hanging in some stately home now! Or a museum somewhere!'

'No! It can't be – it's—' Helplessly, Helena began to shake with laughter, in which Maggie joined, until, tears streaming with hysteria, they clung together, and bit at the sheet to keep their mirth from exploding around the house.

There was no laughter now, though, in Helena's face, only the worry and clenched anticipation of the unknown pain to come. 'Thank goodness for these siren suits, eh?' Maggie said, in an effort to distract her. She gestured at the bulky top and elasticated, baggy trousers she had pulled over her jumper, and the bloomers and thick woollen stockings. Helena was wearing one, too, over her night things. She had had to push the elastic waistband down to crotch level almost at the front to accommodate the taut thrust of her belly. They had used some of the precious coupons to buy them, for even clothing had been brought into the rationing scheme a few months ago.

Maggie tried to stop herself from going over to the window and squinting through the heavy blackout curtains. 'Maybe you'd better get up, get your shoes on. Taxi'll be here—'

Helena gave a wail, and stared at her in horror, before she scrambled frantically out of bed, flinging the covers aside. 'Oh God!'

Maggie darted forward, panic stricken. 'What is it?'

Helena began to sob, clawed at the loose-fitting pants, dragging them down, hauling up her thick nightdress. 'I've wet myself!' Weeping helplessly, she squatted, pulling down the cotton knickers, tugging at the thick pads wedged in them. She was hampered by her bulk, sank clumsily, knees bent, crying for her clumsiness and her lost dignity, on to the chamber pot she had dragged from under the bed.

'Never mind, never mind. Here, give me that!' Maggie crooned, kneeling, and cradling her dark head, arms over her shoulders. 'It's all right. That's the waters. That's good.'

'The bed!' Helena blubbered, her face red, cheeks shining, staring up at her, a picture of despair so child-like Maggie couldn't help smiling, then laughing softly.

'It's all right. Look! Nothing! Just sit there. Everything's all right.'

'I can't move!' They began to laugh and cry at the same time, holding on to each other, and in the distance they heard the door bell ring.

2

Maggie couldn't shake off her secret, guilty picture of God, or maybe, even, a whole bunch of Them, exercising a malicious pleasure in interweaving the skeins of human life, drawing together significant features, to impose on the helplessly ant-like mortals awareness of the divine malevolence which controlled them. She thought of the central pivot joining her life to that of the girl she had come so quickly to cherish, each a reflection of the other's tragedy. The embarrassed young sailor who had stood on the doorstep with the shy, pretty lass less than a year ago could have been a reincarnation of Tommy himself. The very sight of him, of them, standing there together, had stirred her deeply.

The tragedy of the loss, with the life he had left her quickening inside, made a mockery of the twenty-five years which lay between their shared experience. The unexpressed, perhaps in its fullest depths unexplored, closeness, love, they also shared, was also part of that pattern. She had been vouchsafed to take on the role which Rosie had played in the bond between them, and how glad she was to be given that blessed chance. But sombre, darker links hovered close at hand about them.

She remembered now a similar feeling of sadness sixteen years before, at the time of her marriage to Alf. And to the very day, too. The coincidences, or ironies, went on and on. Just a week ago, they had 'celebrated' their sixteenth anniversary, though that was hardly the word with Alf sixty miles away. She remembered the honeymoon morning at that Lake District hotel, the news the proprietor had brought with the morning papers of the loss of the submarine. And now, again, with Helena's baby only a few days old, the wireless bulletins, and the newspapers, reluctantly told of another sea disaster – the loss of the aircraft carrier *Ark Royal*, in the Mediterranean, sunk by torpedo, and on the very day when

Helena had given birth.

She hoped that Helena might not have heard, or seen a paper, but she knew she had, as soon as she entered the polished ward of the Cottage Hospital. Helena's face was red, almost healthily glowing, but her eyes were puffed and sore-looking and she could see she had been crying. 'It's awful, isn't it?' she said, not waiting even until they had greeted each other.

Maggie bent over and kissed her on the cheek, then pulled her chair in close to the side of the bed. 'Yes,' she answered, almost abruptly. 'I suppose it must be true this time or they would never have announced it.' The *Ark*, as she had become affectionately known, had been sunk several times, according to German propaganda. 'Lord Haw-Haw'll have a field day with it. Now.' She glanced around her. 'Where's my bonny bairn?'

'They just took them out about half an hour ago. After feeding time.' Helena glanced down automatically at her breasts, decently concealed beneath the nightgown and the embroidered, ribbon-decorated bed jacket which Maggie and Alf had bought for the big event. She looked troubled. 'They don't know – they may have to start giving her bottles. She was – a bit restless this morning. Mind you, Sister Benson said it was my fault for getting all upset. One of the orderlies had heard the news. She told us when she came on.' Helena knew almost all the staff, and was treated as a privileged patient because of her work here.

Maggie grinned, shook her head, determined to take Helena's mind off the gloom. 'I still can't get over you doing the dirty on us and going and having a girl. And so big, too! A reet Yorkshire lass. That's probably why she's guzzling so much. She'll eat us out of house and home.' She grunted. 'That'll make two of them. What with our Vicky.'

Helena reached out and held on to Maggie's hand on the blue and white counterpane. She blushed, her mouth quivered, and her voice shook with the encroaching tears. 'I just want to say – I can't ever thank you – I don't know what I'd've done – without you.' She shook her neatly combed black hair, unable to hold back the crying any longer. She gulped, her chest heaved.

'For God's sake!' Maggie could almost hear Rosie in her assumed

gravelly tones. 'I've told you, girl! It's the best thing that's
happened for me since I had Vicky! I'm thrilled to bits, believe me!
It's me should be thanking you.'

The shoulders shook, the weeping redoubled, and Maggie lifted
herself from the chair, bent close and hugged her tightly. 'Don't be
daft! You're starting me off now! Besides, they'll all be looking at
us. They'll think we're one of those – funny couples! You know!'

She released her, and sat back, while Helena fought to control
her fit of crying, and wiped at her eyes with her handkerchief. She
managed a tremulous smile as she worked. 'What? With me just
had a baby? And you with two? Some lesbians we are!'

'Listen, don't you forget. My Tom's twenty-five in January. And
you're what? Just turned nineteen! So I'm more than old enough to
be your mum!'

There was an instant of painful awkwardness. Maggie felt yet
again the powerful stab of compassion at the timidly appealing look
flashed at her from the brown eyes. 'I phoned your folks,' she went
on carefully. 'Yesterday morning. I told you'd had a baby
girl, that you were both well. I spoke to your mother.'

'Did she – say anything?'

'Just that she was glad – that you were all right. And the baby,'
Maggie lied, remembering the cold, clipped 'Thank you', followed
by the click of the receiver. 'I expect they'll be getting in touch.
Listen,' she blundered on, too hastily, yet wanting to save her from
further distress, 'have you thought of a name for her yet?'

'Ernestina, of course,' Helena replied at once, gazing
straight-faced at Maggie, who strove to hide her shock and nodded.

'Oh. Yes. Very nice. Very grand—'

In spite of her still grief-marked face, the teardrops which clung
to her lashes, Helena grinned with childish mischief. 'D'you
honestly think I'd inflict that on her?' And they laughed, holding
hands, while Maggie acted out her indignant protests.

'You devil! You really had me fooled then!'

It was almost dark, and the nurses were pulling the floor-length
blackout curtains together over the taped windows when the bell
rang for the end of visiting. Helena winced as she sat up, reaching
for Maggie to exchange a final kiss. 'They say I might be able to

come out on Saturday,' she said anxiously. 'That tear's still a bit sore, but it's healing up. Oh God! I hope I can come out!'

'Where are we now? Monday? Well, you be a good girl and do as you're told. If it's not the weekend, it'll be early next week. The room's all ready.'

'Look! I've told you! I'll be fine up in my own room, honestly! There's no need—'

Maggie had insisted she and the baby should move into Tom's room, which was down two floors, on the same level as the other family rooms. 'Now shut up!' Maggie declared sternly. 'After Alf spent his entire time off doing walls and ceiling! Just for a few weeks. Till you're fighting fit again.'

Helena watched Maggie's slim figure retreating clickingly down the ward with the other visitors. She felt herself choke up again, her eyes prickling. No! She couldn't get all weepy again! She'd done nothing but cry all day. She had to keep calm. Sister Benson had warned her all this emotional turbulence could affect her milk. But really, when she thought about Maggie, and how wonderful she was, her whole body seemed to ache with the sweetness of the love she felt for her. There were times, especially lately, when she was disturbed at the knowledge of how much the older woman meant to her. How she had virtually replaced her mother. And more, she blushingly admitted, for she could never have found the comfort which Maggie had brought, that stirring, warm love which the touch of those tender hands, the gentle kisses, gave her. Like – like a lover! she thought hotly, glowing with shame, recalling Maggie's joking words earlier, her own remark. Was she, after all, one of 'those funny women'? Maggie would be horrified if she knew these deep and devious thoughts. Or would she? Helena wondered, shivering slightly at the memory of their shared embraces, the intimacy of their gently enfolded bodies.

One thing: guiltily, she determined that she would make fewer demands on Maggie's attention, and her time. She was a married woman. She had a husband – a truly good man. And Vicky, too. Her thoughts drifted on, thinking of that long ago first love, of the son who now was far away, fighting again, in another war. She knew how worried Maggie was for him. She of all people could appreciate how her friend must feel. For a second, Helena experienced a rush of fierce gratitude that her baby was a girl, then reflected sombrely that that was no guarantee of safety. Her birth came on the very anniversary of the raid on Coventry, when hundreds had lost their lives.

Guilt dogged her still, as she let her mind dwell on Thomas. A smile tugged at her mouth at remembering Maggie's telling her about the name, and how she had been determined to prevent him being dubbed Tommy, like his dad. Tommy. Ernie. Yes, there were so many things that seemed to draw them together. Blushing more, Helena tried to recapture Tom's physical features, from the photographs she had seen but took little real note of. The latest, a thin, dark-haired young man, bare-headed, in army pullover and dusty slacks and boots, sitting on the side of a tank, or some such martial vehicle, the bare desert scrub all around them. A group of them, all grinning at the camera, lean, tanned. Young warriors.

Her fingers curled, her body tightened with disgust at the war. Why didn't they all just say to hell with it? Come home and take up their lives again. All that death. Ordinary people. Young men with futures, with life and love ahead of them. Slaughtered, slaughtering, in thousands. The pain of Ernie's loss assailed her, like a weight, seizing her chest, squeezing her heart, petrifying it with the desolation.

A small flurry at the doors of the now brightly lit ward broke in on her thoughts. Sister Benson came down the polished floor swiftly, and Helena blinked in surprise as, behind her, she saw her sister Elspeth, and a yard behind her, looking sheepishly furtive, the mop head of her brother, Kit.

'They can only have ten minutes,' Sister Benson announced disapprovingly. 'I've told them visiting's over until tonight. But they've just come from school. They can see the baby on the way out.'

The tears came again, in which Elspeth joined. Oddly enough, her school uniform, once she had pulled off the broad-brimmed hat, made her look more grown up, with her bosom thrusting out blouse and tie, and cardigan, while her legs, generously on view in the black lisle stockings beneath the short skirt, were the long and shapely limbs of a young woman. In contrast, Kit looked very young, and scrawny, red wrists poking lumpily beneath his blazer cuffs, grey-socked legs stick-like under the grey flannel shorts. He was still beet red, his blush showing no signs of dying as he bent and stabbed swiftly at Helena's tear-smudged cheek.

Elspeth finally settled in the hard chair. Helena patted the bed, and Kit parked one buttock gingerly on the very edge, as though he feared to inflict mortal danger. 'Well! What a lovely surprise! I didn't think—'

'We don't care!' Elspeth asserted. 'It was our idea. We heard – yesterday. So we made up our mind we'd come, after school. And here we are.'

'Mum and Dad don't know?'

'No. It doesn't matter. We wanted to see you. I'm sixteen now.' Elspeth glanced down, blushed. She lifted her gaze, met Helena's eyes. 'I'm just sorry we – we haven't been to see you. Aren't we?' The question was directed fiercely at Kit, as though it was somehow his fault, and she punched his red knee. He simply nodded.

'I want to come and see you regularly. If that's all right. I'll tell Mam and Dad. It's not fair—'

'Don't get yourself into any trouble. I know what it's like. It'll be nice though, just now and then.' She swallowed hard. Her face lit up. 'Maggie. My landlady – at Prospect Mount – she's been marvellous. And her husband,' she added quickly. 'They treat me – like I'm one of the family.'

'That's good.' They talked about the village, and Helena asked Elspeth about her plans.

'Well, I've started my Higher now,' her sister said, an apologetic tone in her voice. 'I did quite well at School Cert. Got Matric.'

'That's wonderful!' Helena exclaimed, and squeezed her hand. 'You must stick in. It'll be so important to have good qualifications. After the war—' With a jolt, she realized it was the first time she had thought much beyond the birth of her baby.

A nurse came along. 'Sorry. Sister says—'

They kissed again, hurriedly promised to be in touch, and were ushered out of the ward. Sister Benson passed them, coming along to make sure they were leaving, fussing around the bed, and Helena said gratefully, 'Thanks, Sister. It was good of you—'

There was a squeak of shoes on the linoleum as Elspeth came skittering back down the ward, her face aglow. 'Sorry! Just had to tell you! She's gorgeous! A perfect little angel!'

'Right now. Fine,' Sister Benson said dismissively, failing to suppress a smile at her enthusiasm.

'Right! That's it! Thanks, Beth.' Helena beamed up at them. 'That's what we'll call her! Angela!'

3

'This is absolute nonsense!' Maggie breathed, her nostrils pinched, her dark eyes flashing with belligerence. Her hand jerked contemptuously towards the sheet of paper lying on the kitchen table, the official, buff envelope in which it had come half hidden beneath it. 'They know you've got a child! It's a disgrace!'

Helena was not really surprised. She had half expected it, ever since her twentieth birthday in September over a month ago. 'Register for war service!' Maggie was declaiming, in full flight. 'We'll give 'em war service!' Helena shifted uncomfortably, thinking of the other act of registration she had carried out just before the end of last year, her hot-faced shame at the undisguised condemnation and contempt in the look of the Registrar as he recorded the facts of Angela's parentage. 'Illegitimate.' 'Unmarried.' 'Father's occupation. Sailor.' Each word, each phrase, driven with the thud of a nail into her sensitivity.

'They count me as single,' she said now, almost as if she were apologizing for them, and Maggie snorted again. 'Well, I am, aren't I?'

'What's that got to do with anything? There's loads in the same boat as you, with bairns to look after and their husbands away – or worse,' Maggie added grimly. 'I'll come along with you to the Board. If necessary, we'll get Philip Surtees to write to them.'

Helena said tentatively, 'They might let me do something part-time, that doesn't keep me away.'

'You've got a daughter to bring up!' Maggie answered, with the same righteous indignation.

Helena didn't say anything. In a way, she was half hoping she would be made to go out to work, for she felt it would be a chance for her to start earning something, giving back a little of all that she had taken over the past year and more. It was no use saying anything to Maggie. She knew the fierce rebuttal she would get if she did. Maggie had refused even to discuss the question of money when Helena and the baby came home from the hospital. And 'home' was just the word Maggie used. 'Where else would you go?' Maggie had said, with that look, implying that she was wrong in the head to think otherwise. 'And don't talk about money. We're *in loco parentis*, if you know what that means. Oh! You do, eh?' She pretended to look annoyed. 'Clever clogs! I thought I was the only one round here who knew Latin. Well then! No more, you hear?'

At Christmas, Angela was the focus of attention, which added to Helena's feelings of guilt, as well as heartfelt gratitude. Feeding bottles and nappies appeared to have taken over the kitchen. The terrifying looking apparatus which served as gas mask, in which the baby was to be cocooned and zipped in tightly while air was pumped through the thick trunk, stood discreetly behind the door.

When Helena tried yet again to express her appreciation of all they had done for her, the inevitable tears threatening once more, Alf, who had managed to wangle the luxury of both Christmas Day and Boxing Day off, forestalled her, with his embarrassed surge of heartiness. 'Nay, lass, yer one of the family now, whether ye like it or not. And we've got summat to celebrate now, all right. Just a matter of time now. Adolph's 'ad it.' He shook his head. 'Done us a favour, have the Japs.' The attack on the American base at Pearl Harbour had occurred just under three weeks ago, bringing America into conflict against Japan, and then, two weeks ago to the day, had come the formality of Germany and Italy's declaration of war on the USA. 'Mind, the've took their time. Just like the last lot.'

Maggie's determinedly festive mood was all the braver, Helena knew, because inside she was sick with worry for her son. Although letters were infrequent, and heavily censored, Maggie was all too aware that, attached as he was to the 7th Armoured Division, soon to be glorified as the Desert Rats, he would be in the thick of the fighting which had intensified with November, and the first signs of success against General Rommel. Indeed, in the same week that America's entry into the war was announced, came the news that the allied forces had succeeded in relieving the garrison at Tobruk.

Maggie's voice trembled a little when she nodded towards the photo during their Christmas Day meal, and proposed a toast to his health and safety. 'He won't be in the front line, love,' Alf said with well-intentioned clumsiness. 'He's too brainy for that.' He turned to Helena in explanation. 'He's in my old mob,' he said proudly. 'The RAOC. He'll be on the repairin' of vehicles and that.' He turned back to Maggie, injecting the same bluff assurance into his tone. 'We'll be hearin' from him, soon, never fear. Just think! It'll be blazin' hot out there right now!'

After the holiday, Helena had wanted to move back up to her room on the top floor, but Maggie had remained adamant. 'It's too cold for the baby,' she insisted. 'Besides, you don't want to be trailing up and down those stairs all the time. It doesn't make sense.' And Helena had given in, gracefully enough. There was no pretence of any separate existence now. They ate and lived together.

'I'll have to go back to work,' Helena argued, when Angela was four months old. 'I can't go on like this, living off you and Alf. It's not fair.' She struggled on, over Maggie's mounting protests, 'You can't keep two extra mouths. Not with things like this.'

'Do you think that's all you are? An extra mouth to feed?' Maggie said, with a quiet intensity that made Helena blush.

'No, but you know what I mean. I want to—'

'Listen. You work like the devil round the house, don't you? I've only got Doris coming in now, you know. I'd be paying someone a heck of a lot to do what you do. We manage pretty well between us, don't we?' Her mouth opened, and she nodded slowly, in a parody of dawning comprehension. 'Ah! I see what this is all about! You want wages, don't you? I wondered how long I'd be able to get away with it. I was just saying to Alf last week—'

'Shut up!' Helena stepped forward, grabbed her wrists, shook them in frustration. Her voice dropped to a whisper. 'My God, Maggie! I love you!' She kissed her quickly, on the lips.

'What's all this? You two going soppy?' Vicky grinned at them, dropped her bag down on the table. 'Where's little un? Still asleep?'

'I was just trying to persuade your mam to let me go out to work.' Helena laughed, moved away, twin spots of red highlighted on her cheeks.

'Fat chance!' Vicky grunted. 'She's got us where she wants us. Not even wage slaves! Just slaves!'

'See?' Maggie smiled triumphantly. 'Now who's going to start on the spuds? Constable Burns is on late shift so he'll be wanting supper early. I'll pop up and see if Angel's awake yet.'

Helena went into the larder to fill the basin from the bag of potatoes standing on the floor beneath the wide shelves. She filled a saucepan with water, then began the task of peeling. 'Vicky,' she said, with shy hesitation, 'you don't mind – me being here, do you? I mean, being around – like family, all the time?'

The fourteen year old pinked a little. 'No, course not. It's smashing having little Angela around. Mam gets a big kick out of her, you know.' There was a slight pause. 'She was really cut up about the twins. I was too young. Can't really remember, but I know she was. New lease of life for her, this.' She laughed. 'She loves having people to boss around. Haven't you noticed?'

When Helena's call-up papers came, Maggie's reaction was not unexpected. Helena herself was ambivalent in her outlook. She secretly treasured the constant proximity to Maggie, knowing she was rarely more than a room or two away. She worked as hard as she could about the house, though in truth Maggie's own efficient management and energy made the household chores less than arduous. There was always time enough and more for Angela. Every afternoon, unless the weather was atrocious, the two women would put the hood of the pram up, button and scarve themselves against blustery winds or slanting rain, and head off down the hill towards the harbour and along past the swing bridge.

'I remember the official opening,' Maggie told her one day. 'Pa was in the VIP party. I was only about ten. They had some grand lady to cut the ribbon. Then we all went charging across. There was hordes of people everywhere.'

'Gosh!' Helena grinned, manoeuvring the pram over the high

kerb at the bottom of Flowergate. 'I keep forgetting how ancient you are!'

The clerk at the Ministry of Labour offices was so rudely offhand on the day of her appointment that Helena was relieved initially that she had managed to persuade Maggie to allow her to attend alone. But when she was passed through to an inner sanctum, the official in charge was a Mrs Goodall, who was a friend of Philip Surtees, and had, in her capacity as a member of the Education Committee, met Helena's father on a number of occasions. She was only slightly less embarrassed than Helena as they faced each other. 'Let's see. How old's the little one? Just coming up a year? I'm sure some form of part-time work will be quite in order. You say you worked at the hospital? That would be excellent, if they can take you back there.'

They could. The day Helena started, the church bells pealed out from St Mary's, on the cliff across the estuary, next to the ruins of the abbey, and from the other churches, terrifying the few souls who did not keep up with the war news; for a couple of years before, people had been listening with dread for that very sound, which would herald an invasion.

'Christ! Ah didn't know you wuz *that* important!' quipped Eva, one of the auxiliary nurses who had been working there during Helena's previous period of employment. But the bell ringing was to celebrate the recent significant victory out in the desert, against the Desert Fox, at El Alamein.

A few evenings later, Helena eased off her shoes, and waggled her stockinged toes luxuriously. She stretched out her legs before her, smiled gratefully when Vicky put the freshly poured tea in front of her. It was quarter past ten, and she had just got in, face glowing, after a late shift and a hazardous trip through the freezing fog of a pitch black-night. 'Thank the Lord that's over!' she yawned.

She chatted easily to Vicky, until Maggie said, 'Come on, lady! It's late! School tomorrow. Off you go!'

Helena was aware at once of Maggie's tenseness. 'Everything all right? How's Angela been?'

'She was a bit restless. Took some settling down. The poor

bairn's beginning to think she's got two mums. She notices now, you know. She'll be a year old in two weeks.'

Helena blinked at her in dismay. She felt her cheeks grow warm. It was so uncharacteristic of Maggie to speak sharply, or critically, like that. 'I know. These late turns are a nuisance. But I have to do my share,' she returned defensively.

'It doesn't make a lot of difference,' Maggie said, in the same tone. 'On the early shifts you're missing when she wakes up. That's just as bad.'

The atmosphere crackled with the sudden unease. 'I'm sorry, Maggie,' Helena said quietly. 'I don't – I have to do it. It's not that I like leaving her.'

'Still. Gets you out, doesn't it? A bit of pocket money.'

Helena opened her mouth, shut it again. She blinked more rapidly, felt tears pricking behind her eyes. She felt bruised, and tender, as though she had been struck. Don't be ridiculous, she told herself, but she could feel her throat closing, her breath catching. Maggie's just in a bad mood. An off day. 'I'd better get off to bed,' Helena muttered, pushing herself to her feet.

'Don't you want anything? A sandwich? Biscuit?'

'No, I'm fine, thanks. That tea did the trick. I'll see you in—'

'No! Wait! I'm sorry, love! I didn't mean it!'

Helena stared at her, saw the anxious face, the eloquent eyes, their luminous appeal. A wave of contrition swept over her, and fierce anger at her insensitivity. You selfish little bitch. Everyone going on and on about the Libyan campaign, the marvellous victory. And poor Maggie. Torn with her fears for her son. 'Have you heard anything?' she asked now, afraid. Maggie shook her head.

An instant later, they were hugging each other, pressing together, arms clinging, both crying, and kissing, and longing only to share the closeness which had become so natural to them. 'He'll be all right, I know he will,' whispered Helena, her lips against Maggie's ear, feeling the curls of hair tickling her mouth and chin. The thin frame shook against her.

They held each other while Maggie's weeping quietened, and she was at last able to reach for a handkerchief. She wiped her cheeks then blew her nose vigorously. When she had restored herself to order, she gave a sheepish little smile, reached out for Helena's hand and held on to it, placing it at her breast. 'My darling girl,' she murmured softly. 'What would I do without you? Promise you won't get sick of your crotchety old Maggie? Please?'

A hasty airmail letter in the distinctive Forces' colour arrived just before the birthday party. Tom was well, on the move, along with the rest of the triumphant Eighth Army, so there was a double celebration. Pride of place went to the delicate sponge cake which Maggie had sacrificed precious eggs for, refusing to make do with the yellow powder in the stars and stripes packet. There was a heightened air of hope and festivity all around, the air was still ringing with Mr Churchill's stirring rhetoric, which concluded that the desert victory was 'the end of the beginning'.

The North African battles came home to them on a much more personal level, when Vicky came in at eight o'clock one night, after the first house of the Coliseum, practically hysterical with excitement. 'Tom! Tom!' she almost screamed, while Maggie and Helena gaped in alarm. 'He's there! On the news! I saw him!'

'What? What? No! You can't have! You've made a mistake!'

But it was no mistake. Maggie and Helena went down, with Angela, the following afternoon. Blushing and stammering with embarrassment, Maggie spoke to the manager, and they were ushered in to the rear stalls. There was a brief review of the desert campaign, a few scenes of a darkness lit by booming flashes, then, suddenly, a group of laughing, uniformed figures gathered round a NAAFI van which was dispensing tea, and there he was, grinning widely at the camera, open neck, dark hair blowing in a tuft at his forehead, holding up his tin mug. 'Oh God!' Maggie wept, and clutched convulsively at Helena's arm.

The manager came down afterwards, looking for them. 'Listen,' he said, 'we've got the reel for a week. Come down any time. And don't you pay, mind. Complimentary. Make the most of it, eh, luv?'

4

Elspeth gradually became known to Maggie and her family, for she called when she could, and often accompanied Helena on her trips out with Angela. 'Mam knows I see you,' Elspeth confessed. 'Not Dad, though.' She looked with troubled eyes at her sister. 'You know what he's like.' She sounded ashamed, as, indeed, she was. 'I ought to just tell him and to heck with it. But there'd be an almighty row.' She shrugged hopelessly. 'He'd only tell me I mustn't see you again. And Mam would get it in the neck, as well, for not letting on.' She paused, her voice even more hesitant. 'You know, I think Mam would really, at the bottom of her heart, like to see you. And Angela. But—' The shoulders heaved again. 'You know how things are at home.'

'It's all right. Really. I'm just glad we can still see one another. Anyway, you'll be leaving this summer, won't you?'

Elspeth nodded, her face lighting up. 'Yes. I've applied to Durham.'

'University?'

'No!' She looked askance at Helena. 'I'm not *that* much of a swot, for goodness sake! No. Teacher training. I'm really quite keen,' she added apologetically.

'That's marvellous!' Helena enthused. 'It's a good job. And you'll be good at it. I know you will.'

There were times, as the war moved into its fourth summer, when Helena was tempted to take the train through to Kilbeck and simply turn up on the doorstep of the cottage on Kilbeck Side with little Angela in her arms. Her mother would not, face to face, turn her away. And yet, sickeningly, Helena could imagine just such a rejection taking place, though she was ashamed even in her imagination to be able to allot such unfeelingness to her. No, it wouldn't be unfeelingness. Her mother would suffer, of course she would. But, however much it hurt, she might well act out of a sense of loyalty – of love? – to the man she had chosen to honour and obey all these years.

There was little doubt concerning her father in Helena's mind. If her mother *did* find the courage to forgive, it would be in the certainty of facing her husband's wrath at such a betrayal. There would be no forgiveness on his part, she was sure. If she were to approach him literally on her knees, begging abjectly for a reconciliation, it would be only on his terms, and she knew how eternally harsh they would be.

She tried as hard as she could to recollect just one tender scene with her father during all her childhood and growing up, and could think of none. It appalled her now to think how frightened she had been of his coldness. 'God bless Mummy and Daddy,' she had prayed every night, and, as she got older, tried to convince herself that it was respect for him she held.

But her most vivid memory was of an incident when she was eleven. She had taken Elspeth down to the village for some fête, both of them in their best organdie frocks, hair beribboned, white ankle socks, gleaming, buckled patent shoes. A group of village kids, farm workers' children mostly, had been playing on the muddy bank of the river, beside the stepping stones. They had been friendly enough in the main, and gradually Helena had joined in their skylarking, flinging handfuls of gritty sand, heaving stones into the shallow water, until the sisters' finery was liberally spattered with dirt. Then Elspeth had slipped on one of the flat, wet stones and gone headlong into the stream, to rise, drenched and wailing, to the huge amusement of the onlookers.

Helena had run with her up the long hill, piggy-backing her part of the way, arriving breathless and tearful herself at home. Her father had been there to receive them. She could almost feel the sting now across the tops of her thighs, the cruel bite of his fingers clamped on her skinny upper arm as she skipped and yelped in a vain dance of agony to escape the cracking blows. The bruises were dark smudges on the white skin of her arm for days, and the red outline of his hand was branded on the tops of her legs, over and over. Worst of all – and the memory of it made her hotly uncomfortable and ashamed even today – was the red-faced emotion, the animated shine of those eyes as he struck again and again at her flesh.

If she had not had Maggie – and Alf, she always had to assure
herself with hasty propriety – she might have yielded to her
temptation to try and force a reconciliation with her parents. But
really, she had never felt this close to anyone. Her life was full. At
times, she would be pulled up short, smitten with painful guilt at
the realization of how her grief at Ernie's death had been assuaged.
I won't ever get over you, my darling, she would whisper in her
mind penitentially.

Inevitably, though, the wound was healing. The war news was
better as the second anniversary of his death crept round. The
Germans were driven out of Tunisia. Maggie's Tom had come
safely through the campaign, and his mother began to allow herself
to think that he might be home again soon. Then the papers were
full of a daring RAF raid, carried out with some new kind of bomb,
which had smashed the dams in the German industrial heartland
and would thus cripple their war production. 'It's not *if* now,' Alf
asserted cheerfully, 'it's *when.*'

In one of their beloved kitchen confessionals one night, Maggie
raised again the subject of Ernie's parents. At first, Helena had put
off getting in touch with them, saying, to Maggie and herself, that
she would get round to letting them know 'one of these days'. But
the more she thought about it, and remembered the closed
atmosphere, the hard faces of the women, the way she had been
made to feel alien, the more reluctant she was to make a move. In
particular, she recalled with genuine revulsion the way Reg, Ernie's
older brother, had held and pawed her, his hot breath and wet kiss
forced upon her.

'They've made no effort to get in touch with me,' Helena
countered now. 'They knew I was in Whitby. They could have got
in touch easily.' She halted, blushed a little. 'I remember his
brother – even at the time. Just when it happened.' She shuddered
slightly. 'He was horrible. He came with me to the station. Tried to
– you know. Get hold of me. Asked if we could meet. In secret.
And he was married!'

Maggie smiled fondly. 'It's a wicked world, my sweet.' Helena
laughed, reddened more. 'I know, they're a funny lot out there,'
Maggie went on. 'Believe me. I lived there for four years or so,

remember.' She smiled again, leaning towards Helena, holding her gaze in that intimate way they shared. 'It was the women that scared me more than the men! They were so hard-faced. And big, too! As strong as the fellows and twice as tough!'

She collected their cups and saucers and carried them over to the sink. 'Oh well. Bed time, I guess. You can have a lie in tomorrow. Send Angela in to me. I'll give her her breakfast.'

Helena laughed. 'Try keeping her out. It was hilarious the other day. She nearly had a fit when she saw Alf in with you. She came racing out, shouting, "Man! Man!" She was horrified!'

'Didn't do Alf much good either!' Maggie retorted drily. 'Good job we're too old for any malarky, eh?'

'That'll be the day!' Helena quipped, and Maggie came up behind her and gave the back of her head a vigorous shove.

'Less of that, cheeky!' She gave a mock groan, and put her hands to the small of her back. 'I'll be forty-five this August. Too old even to be caught by this new Act.' The government had a few weeks ago introduced a Bill making it compulsory for British women between the ages of eighteen and forty-five to do part-time work.

'They don't know what they're missing.' Helena stood, waited for Maggie, who put out the light. They made their way quietly along the dimness of the hall and up the first wide flight of stairs. 'You know, I should move back up to the flat,' Helena murmured outside Maggie's door. 'If Thomas comes home he'll—'

'Let's not jump any guns.' Maggie smiled. 'You won't know what's hit you then, my girl. He's a bit of a lady's man is young Tom!'

'Probably got a steady girlfriend by now,' Helena answered lightly. 'Good-looking chap like him.'

'What? An Arab lady, all veils and bangles? I hope not! No. I think I'd rather put up with you than that!'

'Charming!'

'How'd you fancy me as a mother-in-law, eh? That'd strike terror into you, I bet!'

They kissed and separated, with whispered 'good nights'. The thought lingered intriguingly in both their minds as they settled to sleep.

5

'Hello. Derek Pringle. I wrote – Mrs Turner?'

Helena stared at the man standing there with the large blue suitcase. In spite of the mildness of the April day, he was wearing a soft grey trilby, the brim turned down, and a tightly belted mackintosh. 'Oh yes!' She gave a nervous laugh, reddening a little. She stepped aside, ushering him into the porch. 'No, no. I'm not Mrs Turner. You're the new lodger, yes? I'm Helena Barr. I live here, too. Mrs Turner won't be long. I'll show you up to your room. This way. Bit of a hike. Second floor.'

She led him up, then opened the door and stood aside to let him enter first. 'Here we are. Bit small, I'm afraid, but I hope it'll suit you. Three weeks, wasn't it?'

'Yes, that's right. I've got a bit of leave. Sea air and all that.' His laugh was nervous, too. He had taken his hat off. He looked very young, his brown hair cut short, his face thin almost to the point of gauntness.

'Where are you from, Mr Pringle?'

'Well, I work up at Wilton. At ICI. This is sick leave, really—'

Helena could feel herself growing redder. 'No!' she answered quickly. 'I didn't mean – I meant, your accent. It's not – you're not from this part of the country.'

'Oh – no, that's right. I'm from Godalming. Surrey. Near London. That's where my folks are. But I've been working up here, oh, over two years now.'

'Sorry. Please don't think – I wasn't being nosy, honestly. Well. You get settled in.' She gestured awkwardly towards the small chest of drawers, the narrow single wardrobe. 'Pop down when you're ready. Mrs Turner'll be back soon. There'll be a cup of tea in about half an hour.'

'What do you think of our new lodger, then?' Maggie asked that night when Helena had got in from her late shift. 'Seems a nice young chap, doesn't he?'

'Not a Jerry spy then?' Helena asked teasingly. 'In spite of his funny accent.'

'Doesn't he talk lovely?' Maggie sighed. 'I could listen all day. Apparently, he's been quite ill, from what I can gather. He's already been off work a couple of weeks. Been at home, but his folks both work in London. He needs some peace and quiet, building up a bit.' She lowered her voice dramatically. 'He's got quite a hush-hush job. Some sort of boffin. War work.' She tapped the side of her nose significantly.

'You seem to have found out quite a lot already. You should've been a spy yourself. "Thees ees Fumf speaking!" ' She imitated the guttural tones of the catchphrase from *Itma*.

Almost a week passed, and she had scarcely seen the latest guest, except to nod to a couple of times. It was her day off, and the first day of May was bright with the promise of an early summer. She was clipping the reins on to a struggling Angela when he appeared, coming down the stairs behind her. 'Going out? Do you mind if I walk along with you?'

'No, of course not. I'm just going up to Skinner Street. Then I thought I'd take her nibs for a walk along the West Cliff. Down to the spa. We might even venture down on the beach if you're a good girl, eh?'

They were shy with each other at first, and awkward. Helena was slow to realize that he wanted to remain with her, that he had possibly waited until he could catch her leaving the house. 'I didn't realize you were married,' he said. He nodded at Angela, whose meandering steps were dictating their leisurely pace. 'Your husband – is he in the Forces?'

'Didn't Mrs Turner tell you? He's dead.'

'Oh! I'm – I'm so sorry.' He stood there, stricken, his eyes wide, looking so hurt that Helena felt at once penitently ashamed of her abruptness. She was also touched by the concern and pain so clearly revealed.

'That's all right. I'm – it was three years ago. He was on the *Hood*.'

He gave an involuntary murmur of sympathy, busied himself staring around for a while as they walked up the slope. All at once, she stopped, pulling Angela up short, and faced him, gazing at him very directly. 'I'm not married. He was my boyfriend. We were engaged. Going to get married. But he was killed.' She turned away again, walked on, and he stepped forward hastily, to keep abreast of her. He said nothing.

Helena felt much better after her sudden outburst of shocking truth. It ought to have made things even more painfully difficult, and, for the first brief minutes after she had told him, she wished he would have the sense to make his quick excuses and leave her alone, but he didn't. Instead, he made no comment, just began to chat, easily, and inconsequentially, displaying a quirky sense of humour at once appealing, so that she was soon laughing quietly. Things were never a strain after that. Later, she marvelled how swiftly she had felt a sense of rapport, how quickly she enjoyed being with him. He found out what shifts she was working, began to be around when she was off. He even walked across to meet her from work one afternoon.

He told her about his illness. 'I got a touch of pneumonia, it was pretty bad for a while. Run down really. We were working all hours in the lab. Turned out I wasn't as fit at I thought. Still, a couple of weeks of this'll put me right as rain!' They couldn't keep the war from their conversation, however much Helena tried. 'The place is swarming with Yanks down south,' he said. 'They must start this second front any day.'

'You must be doing really important work,' she said admiringly. Her expression changed to comic dismay. 'Gosh! I'm not trying to pry or anything. Careless talk and all that!'

He laughed. 'I'm not into any state secrets. Anyway, I'd much rather talk about you. Far more interesting.'

'Not really.' Her voice softened, grew very slightly unsteady. 'Apart from my lurid past, of course. A fallen woman and so on. Even my parents disowned me. There's only Maggie – and Alf.'

'I can't believe that.' She felt herself hotly blushing at the serious tone. 'You being a fallen woman, I mean. You could never be that.'

He plucked up courage to ask her out to the pictures. She knew it was no easy matter for him to do it, and was both touched and amused at his shy gallantry. She was also shocked at the realization that she was flattered and wanted to go with him.

'Derek Pringle's asked me to go to the pictures with him. Can you look after Angela tomorrow night? I thought we could go to the second house. I can give her supper, get her bathed and everything before I go.'

She knew at once that Maggie did not really approve, though she agreed readily enough to the request. The next morning, while she was feeding her daughter, she said tentatively, 'Do you think I shouldn't go?'

Maggie's face was pink as she answered forcefully, 'Don't be daft! Do you good! It's only a bit of company, isn't it? You're only young once.'

Afterwards, as they walked back the short distance through the blackout, he linked her arm respectfully. They climbed the steps up to the front door and held the torch while Helena was fumbling in her bag for the key. She felt the light pressure of his hand on her elbow. 'Thanks, Helena. I can't tell you – I've really enjoyed it.' She saw the dark shape of him loom towards her, and she turned her head neatly, accepted his kiss on her cheek.

'So have I!' she declared brightly.

Maggie was still up, reading in the kitchen. 'Hello. Was it good? Kettle's on.'

The three of them chatted while they sipped their tea. Derek showed no inclination to leave them, until, finally, Maggie yawned unmistakably, and said, 'Come on, young Helena! You've got to be up and out by six, and it's after eleven now. Up you go! I'll clear these. You go and get your beauty sleep. Not that she needs it, eh, Derek?' She looked at him quizzically, and he rose in embarrassment, glad to make his exit.

6

'What's this then?' Vicky gave a yelp of delighted laughter, as Helena squealed softly in alarm, instinctively crossing her arms over her chest.

'Keep still, for goodness sake!' grumbled Maggie. 'We don't want this stuff everywhere.' She held up her hands, the fingers deeply stained, the wad of cotton wool a flattened, dark-brown mess. 'And make sure you wash all this muck off before you get into bed tonight, otherwise we'll never get the sheets clean.'

'Hurry up!' whined Helena. She glanced down at the grinning Vicky. 'I didn't know who you were.' She was standing self-consciously on the kitchen table, her bare feet on a pile of spread newspapers. She was dressed in brassiere and knickers only, and her legs, from upper thighs down, were a deep tan colour from the lotion which Maggie had smeared over the skin.

'You'll have to do her feet,' Vicky observed critically. 'At least the tops. It'll look weird if you don't.'

'Where's that pencil?' Maggie muttered, in a flustered voice. She picked up the black eye-liner, and Helena flinched at its touch on the back of her leg. 'Keep still, girl! Otherwise it'll look like the hind leg of a donkey! Oh, I can't draw a straight line!'

'Just do it quick,' Vicky advised. 'Straight down. That's it. That looks OK.'

'I've told you. Don't use those American expressions,' Maggie reprimanded, and Vicky pulled a face.

The youngster was staring with admiring envy at Helena, who stepped down gratefully on to the chair and then on to the floor. She twisted round, squinting down to see the backs of her legs, with the imitation stocking seams running down. 'Thanks, Maggie. That's perfect.'

'Just pray it doesn't rain while you're out,' Maggie said.

'Well,' Vicky murmured wickedly, 'if you'd only find yourself a Yankee boyfriend instead of some poor old British sap, you could have the real thing instead of having to paint your pins like this.'

'No thank you! Have you seen the way they go on? They think we're all – well, they don't show any respect at all for English girls! And Derek is not a sap, if you don't mind!'

Vicky chuckled unrepentantly, then went on tauntingly, 'I see you've got your best frillies on then! You look like Jane! Still. I'm sure they'll be appreciated.' She smirked, and, blushing furiously, Helena reached for the discarded dressing-gown and drew it quickly around her.

'There. It'll be dry now.'

'You watch your tongue, young lady!' Maggie snapped, sounding genuinely annoyed.

'I meant the dancing, that's all!' Vicky exclaimed with righteous indignation. 'You know. With this new Yank stuff. The Jitterbug. They can see everything you've got the way they chuck you about.'

'You're getting far too wise for your years, my girl!' Maggie warned. She turned to Helena, her tone hardly less critical. 'You'd better get some clothes on. Derek'll be here soon.'

Maggie rattled the crocks with unnecessary force as she washed them at the sink, and breathed deeply, ordering herself to calm down. She admonished herself with painful honesty. You're getting steamed up, old girl, because Derek Pringle's coming through again. And because Helen's as fidgety as a schoolgirl at the thought of seeing him. You old green-eyed monster!

After his initial stay, Helena had been so quiet Maggie knew immediately that she had formed a feeling deeper than mere friendship for the boy. She had not been able to help noticing the letters that started coming regularly, letters that she assumed were answered just as regularly. She was not surprised, therefore, when a letter came for her, in the same hand. It was Derek, stating that he had a free weekend, and asking if he could book in.

It was a momentous time for everyone, and should have scaled down the significance of their private lives, for at one o'clock on 6 June came the announcement that the long expected second front had at last begun with the allied landings in Normandy. Maggie was glad, but she felt bitter, too. That was doubtless where all the new blood would go to feed the war machine, while she was left to worry and pray every night for her Tom, who, far from coming home to England after the victory in North Africa, became embroiled in the Sicilian and then the Italian invasions.

There had been bitter fighting, she knew, though, only two days before the Normandy landings, had come the news of Rome's capture, the same day she received a hasty, cheerful note from Tom, complaining of too much sun, and passionately grateful signorinas. She was doubly ashamed of her resentment against Derek now, for she recognized how unjust it was. She was angry because he was safe, and paying court to Helena, while Tom was still far away, and in danger, and it was four long years since she had seen him.

Helena was young, and lovely. And lonely, of course. Derek was a good boy, she was sure. How could she feel so mean spirited about them? She tried to make up for it, greeting him warmly, enthusing with them, urging them to enjoy themselves, all the time her mind a disturbing whirl of conflicting emotions. Was she jealous of him for his youthful attraction, for his obvious feeling for Helena? Or was she jealous of her, of her interest towards him?

Not long after they had left for the Saturday night dance at the spa pavilion, Alf arrived, weary, and glad to be home after another week away in the west. She told him of Derek's visit, the young couple's outing. 'That's nice, eh?' he said, smiling at her. 'He's a nice lad. Do her good to get out a bit.' He nodded conspiratorially. 'Ah reckon he's keen on her, don't you?'

She glanced over at the photo of Tom, squatting there, grinning away beside his tank in the foreign heat. 'Yes, I think you're right.'

They were still out when she and Alf went up to bed. Maggie could feel his eyes on her as she undressed, and when he reached for her in the still chilly bed, she put her hand on his wrist. 'D'you mind just cuddling me? My tummy – I'm feeling a bit upset tonight.' She smiled wryly, although she suddenly felt more like weeping at her subterfuge. 'I'm an old woman now, you know. I think I may be getting past it.'

'Nay, lass. It's me. I'm a randy old goat, aren't ah? Ought ter know better. Trouble is, you still look like you did when ah first saw you.'

She turned over, easily, letting him press into her as he fitted himself to her curving back, and she felt far worse when she felt his throbbing excitement against her cushioning flesh.

Alf woke suddenly from his dream of being lost, and late, supposed to meet Maggie somewhere and a series of endless frustrations preventing him. It was a dream he had had before. He awoke agitated, and relieved to be out of it. 'Maggie?' The bed was wide and empty, her side cold, the blankets turned down slightly. The house was silent, apart from the usual soughing of the wind, the blackness of the room impenetrable. He wanted to reach across and switch on the bedside lamp, but something stopped him.

It must be some time in the early hours, he was sure. He guessed at once where she would be. He thought of their coming to bed, remembered his earlier arousal, felt it stir faintly again, and lay there, his arm outstretched to the cold emptiness of her place, overwhelmed by a deep and tender sadness.

He was right. Maggie had lain torturously awake, listening in the dark. She heard them come in, the soft, distant click of the kitchen door. She couldn't sleep. A long, long time later, she heard the faint creak of the stairs, sensed rather than heard the careful footfalls along the landing to Helena's room. It wasn't long before she heard him ascending the narrower flight of stairs to his room on the second floor.

And a long time after that, unable to help herself, she slipped with breathless care out of bed, feeling her way in the blackness, easing open the door, creeping along the thin strip of carpeting on the landing. Lamplight showed beneath Helena's door. She tapped softly and went in.

A book was open on the counterpane but she didn't look as if she had been reading. She looked a little startled, then guilty, at Maggie's appearance. 'Sorry,' she whispered. 'Did we wake you? We were as quiet as mice when we came in. We've been in ages.'

'I know. I couldn't sleep.' Maggie tiptoed over to the cot in the far corner, looked down at the sleeping infant. Helena watched from the bed. She could see the dark shape of Maggie's body through the cotton nightgown, in the soft lamplight.

'You must be frozen. Get in.' She held the blankets back and Maggie obeyed at once. 'Gosh! You are!' Helena shuffled at the touch of her icy limbs, then moved to hold her, give her her warmth. 'You're worried, aren't you? About me? And Derek?'

'No,' Maggie answered, far too quickly, blushing. 'It's just – I worry that you – you know what you're doing?'

Helena faced her bravely, despite her embarrassment. 'I like him, Maggie. A lot. I haven't – slept with him!'

Maggie's face burned. 'I never said – it's just – there are ways. The clinic. I went – years ago. After the twins. You can be safe.'

'I told you! I haven't sle— had sex. Not properly! It isn't that. Though' – she forced herself on – 'he *does* excite me – that way. But it isn't that! Not just sex. I know about – there are ways I can –

bring relief. For myself.' She was propped up on her elbow, and her black hair swung as she shook her head vigorously. Her voice caught, on the edge of tears. 'It isn't that! I don't know yet—'

She sounded so uncertain, helpless. Maggie felt the ache of her love for her. 'I just don't want you – to make a mistake again.'

Helena jerked, her hands reached out, grabbed at Maggie's wrists, held them in a convulsive grip. Her young face blazed with her intensity. 'I didn't make a mistake! *You*, of all people, should know!' Her voice quivered with passion. 'We didn't make a mistake! Did we?'

They cried softly together, wriggling down in the cocoon of the narrow bed, arms enfolding each other. Helena felt Maggie's bent knee, and her thigh, slip between hers, and she moved accommodatingly, and they clung and pressed even closer, their warm flesh mingling, transmitting their warmth. Their lips and mouths were together, moved against each other as they spoke. 'I'll always love *you*, Maggie. Nothing can change that. Any of this.' She moved expressively, felt the corresponding echo of her love.

'I know. I know, my darling girl!' Maggie sighed.